Jonathan Trigell was born in Welwyn Garden City in 1974. In 2002 he completed an MA in creative writing at Manchester University.

His first novel, *Boy A*, won the prestigious John Llewellyn Rhys Prize for best work in the Commonwealth by an author under thirty-five, and also the Waverton Award, for best first novel of 2004. It has now been made into a film by Channel 4.

His second novel, *Cham*, has also been published by Serpent's Tail.

Praise for Boy A

'A compelling narrative, a beautifully structured piece of writing, and a thought-provoking novel of ideas' Sarah Waters, Chair of the John Llewellyn Rhys Prize Judges

'A fine and moving debut novel…Harrowing at times, this compulsively readable novel is more optimistic than it sounds…a rare treat' *Independent*

'A thought-provoking commentary on human nature…A gripping and disturbing read, *Boy A* is a carefully cultivated work that challenges readers while also being entirely gripping' *Good Book Guide*

'The book bristles with issues of personal responsibility, social justice and the reformative value of prison life. It would give reading groups much to ponder over' *New Books Mag*

'This debut by Trigell is ultra-stylish and just dark enough, dealing with a difficult subject without plastering on the rose-tint. *Boy A* deserves recognition as a formidable and engrossing read' *BookMunch*

'This modern day immorality tale about the attempted rehabilitation of a child implicated in murder…[is] delivered with a horrific sense of foreboding' *Arena*

Dad and Mum

Acknowledgements:
Anna Davis
Suzannah Dunn
David O'Malley
Pete Ayrton
Elena Lappin
The whole team at Serpent's Tail

Jonathan Trigell

A complete catalogue record for this book can
be obtained from the British Library on request

The right of Jonathan Trigell to be identified as the author
of this work has been asserted by him in accordance with
the Copyright, Designs and Patents Act 1988

First published in 2004 by Serpent's Tail
Published in this edition in 2007 by Serpent's Tail,
an imprint of Profile Books Ltd
3A Exmouth House
Pine Street
London EC1R 0JH
website: www.serpentstail.com

ISBN 978 1 84668 662 7

Designed and typeset at Neuadd Bwll, Llanwrtyd Wells

Printed in the United States

10   9   8   7   6   5   4   3   2   1

Boy A

Contents

A is for Apple.
A Bad Apple.

He's seen noses broken over less: the fag butts on the pavement have been carelessly tossed, five drags left in them.

Jack's his name. He chose it himself. Few people choose their own names. He's seen a lot try, adopting hard or suave AKAs, but those snide-nicks never stick. Jack picked his name from a book, *The Big Book of Boys' Names*, a good place to start. Normal but cool, that's why he likes it. Jack of all trades, Jack of hearts, Jack the lad, Jack in the box, car Jack, union Jack, bowling Jack, lumber Jack, steeple Jack, Cracker Jack. Always the childish pursues him: denied his own childhood, denier of another. Also Jack the Ripper, he didn't spot that until later.

Beside him walks Terry. As they've walked together a thousand times, though always before in corridors; never in the splendour of this new unroofed world. Even with Terry there, Jack's nervous. For all the promise of the sun and the baby-blue sky, he's cold. Terry smiles at him and he can see the excitement there; he tries to look calm and happy. Maybe this is Terry's moment, not his. Terry's spent fifteen years working for this, waiting to see Jack striding down a sunny street.

Terry knew Jack when he wasn't called that. Terry knows his birth name, the name he shed. Now lying like a sloughed snakeskin, in a file, in a cabinet, in a vinyl-tiled office in Solihull. Terry met Jack when he was called simply *A*, a letter for his name. Child *A*, a court name, to distinguish from a second child, *B*. Friend, accomplice, instigator, nemesis perhaps to Jack; now dead, no matter. Found hanged in cell, suicide presumed. 'Good Riddance', said the *Sun*, and a nation cheered. Jack felt nothing but a numbness when he heard the news. He alone now knew what had happened that day, and that even he knew less with each week that passed. But he also felt a fear that his cover was blown, and considered a spell with the fraggles, seeking sanctuary with the sick.

Jack's feet feel light in the box-fresh, bright white trainers that Terry gave him to wear. They cushion and bounce him, lift him up. Terry says that his son wears them, that they're the height of fashion. Jack's seen the new lads coming in with them for a while now, but he's still pleased with them. They've set the seal on his day. New and radiant and airy, that's how it feels; there's so much space around him. He could run in any direction in his new Nikes and nothing would stop him. He knows he could outrun Terry easily. Terry's old enough to be his dad. He looks at him: the soft smoke curls in his grey sideburns, gentle eyes, brown like his Sierra. Jack used to wish he was his dad, used to think that none of it would have happened if he had been. He could never outrun Terry, because he'd stop when called. Jack could never let Terry down.

'How're you feeling, son?' Terry asks. 'What do you think of the wide world?'

'I dunno.' He always feels childish around Terry. A chance to let down barriers and bravado. 'It's big.'

He realizes 'wide world' is not just an expression. Streets are broad, houses high, horizons unimaginably vast, even corner shops are commodious. Big dens of pop and videos, fags and beer. The trees are greener close up, the walls are redder, the windows more see-through. He wants to tell Terry all of this, and more. He wants to tell him how great wheely bins are, how every house should have a name like the one back there did, how telephone wires drape like bunting. He wants to shake Terry's hand with thanks and hug him with excitement and have Terry hold him tight to quell the fear.

But he only says: 'It's big.'

They pass a skip painted dazzling sunflower-yellow. Jack remembers skips as full of shit and bricks, but this one's empty except for a cocoa armchair. He wonders if only Stonelee skips were full of shit; but the flies wafting above the chair must believe it's on its way.

It was Terry who suggested they walk the last few terraced streets to Jack's new home. Their driver is waiting outside, in a biro-blue Camry, with a stick-on taxi sign. The letters of its number plate spell 'PAX'. Jack thinks this is a good omen, like they used to say when they were kids. Before 'the incident', as his assigned psychologist called it. Pax meant you made up, that the past was forgotten, a truce and amnesty declared, begin afresh.

The Camry is the third car that Jack and Terry have been in today, weaving a false trail, even though apparently unfollowed. The press knows that he's being released; even the liberal papers called for a working committee. The *Sun* said 'Tell The Public Where He's Going And Let Them Sort Him Out'. Terry says they're just being sensationalist, that most people believe he's served his time. Terry reminds him that they haven't got a photo taken since puberty. That he's a special case, not going on the offenders' register, untraceable. Even Jack didn't know where he was going until an hour ago.

'It's a city,' is all Terry would let on. 'Plenty of new faces around, specially with all the students, no one'll notice you, and no one'd think to look anyway.'

Terry explained there may have been better situations

than this one, more controlled environments for Jack to move into. But they went for anonymity, and for speed. If Jack had stayed in prison while extended plans and preparations went on, there might have been a change of heart, a change of Home Secretary. He could easily have ended up inside for another ten years.

The car is outside tan-bricked number 10. Two suitcases in its boot contain a manufactured life. The life belonging to Jack Burridge. Jack Burridge has just finished the last of several short stints for taking and driving away. His Uncle Terry has found him a room and a job. Jack Burridge has no connection to the fuss in the papers. Jack Burridge feels like a caterpillar, about to embark upon a second life, a phase he didn't know, didn't even dare hope, existed.

The driver is a policeman, special protection squad. He's a professional; if he's disgusted his thoughts don't show. He nods granite-faced to Terry, who leads Jack up to the door with a broad-leafed hand on his back. Jack feels like his legs will collapse but for the strength pouring into him from those fingers. Terry is his parole contact, his only true friend, and now his uncle. He might just as well be God. Once, as a boy, though he can't now remember it, Jack thought that he might be. Terry's hand is the hand of redemption certainly, the hand that reached out to save a drowning child, the hand that raps three times on a door that's painted a garish granny-smith green.

'Hiya,' says Terry with artificial exuberance to the woman that opens the door. 'This is my nephew, Jack. Jack, this is Mrs Whalley.' He pronounces it like 'Wall'.

She says, 'Kelly,' as she shakes Jack's hand, her own a little too slim for her fullish form. Legacy perhaps of a slighter youth. Not that she's old, somewhere in a make-up blur of thirties, two to five. Her eyes, blue themselves, are shadowed in a brighter tone, so that the blue inside them looks like green. They flick unconsciously to Jack's crotch as she asks them in.

'You must excuse the mess,' she says, though none is in evidence. 'I'm working nights this week, I've only just got up, really.'

The lounge they sit in is small but seemly: pink walls, pine polished floor, framed pictures of parents and holidays; and a large print of a famously obscure couple kissing in Paris.

'Cup of tea, Jack?' Kelly asks.

He looks hesitant.

'Lovely,' Terry answers for them both.

Kelly gets busy in an interconnected kitchen while Jack and Terry get the cases from the car. The policeman-taxi drives away. Two more are watching from the windows of a guesthouse over the road. Terry will also stay there tonight. Just in case. Though Jack has a panic button, state of the art, disguised as a pager, that goes straight through to Terry at any time. Cuts to the protection squad if Terry doesn't take it. He should never be out of reach of safety.

Kelly knows none of this, only that she has a new lodger. She probably thinks he looks young for the twenty-two she's been told, though really he is two years older. His skin is doughish pale, and she'd be right if she thinks there's a kind of awe and innocence in the way he looks around him.

She moves her uniform from the back of the sofa to let Terry sit down. It is a sensible nurse navy, not the short curvy white worn by strippers and schoolboy fantasies.

'Thank you,' says Jack, as he takes the tea from her. Not a trace of the broad accent of his youth remains. Long years spent trying to fit in at Brentwood then Feltham have removed every taint. He sounds more rough South East than anything. Jack Burridge comes from Luton.

The tea is too sweet, which makes it extravagant somehow, and Jack savours it.

'Which hospital do you work at?' asks Terry.

Kelly's reply vaguely washes over Jack's ears, but he watches her face: round, kind, wilful, helpful.

Then she asks him a question, something about the weather or the journey. It takes a moment for the words to achieve significance in a mind still reeling in new sensation. Sensing his stumbling, she redirects it to Terry.

A cat slides easily through the kitchen flap, and saunters into the room, while the three of them are still engaged in this two-way conversation. It's a slate-grey tabby which, with narrowed eyes, selects Jack for its favours: rubbing against his leg, before settling on his lap to cajole a tickle. Its bones feel frail like chicken, but the fur is warm and soft, and it purrs pleasure.

'There, I knew you were all right, Jack,' his new landlady winks. 'He's a good judge of character, is Marble. Aren't you, Marble?'

She gets up to give the cat's back a quick tousle, and Jack can smell her hair. Vigorous, green-meadowed Alberto Balsam adverts.

'Marble, this is Jack. He's our new lodger.'

She addresses the cat as if it's a child, not a baby, but one that starts to be a companion.

The small-talk continues, though it's not small for Jack. Terry nods a smile with anything that Jack utters. He chose Manchester, he found the house and Kelly; and against any and all the doubters, he is sure that this boy, his boy, will make good. The fact that Mrs Whalley, whom he likes, so clearly likes Jack, confirms to him that he is right to like them both.

Even Terry can need reminding that it's OK to like Jack.

Kelly shows them around her home with enjoyable pride. She gives operating instructions on the washing machine and dishwasher, and the other white wonders of the kitchen. Jack is impressed with his room. Terry had deliberately talked it down so he would be. It's a box-room, small, with a low sloping roof, but recently decorated. The wardrobe and desk share a flat-pack freshness that the allan-key on the window sill confirms. Clean newness seems to reverberate. The exception is a slightly battered portable telly, which sits on the desk's corner, so that it's watchable from in bed.

'It'll not get ITV for some reason, Jack,' Kelly says, 'but there's nothing but rot on that channel anyway. Try not to have it on too loud if I'm on nights. House rules here are just common sense and courtesy. I can see that you've plenty of both, so I'm sure there'll not be any bother.'

After another cup of tea Kelly confides that she has promised to eat with a friend before they both start work. The daylight has already dimmed through the lace curtains. She comes back down the stairs wearing her uniform, and with it an equally functional black cardigan. She offers to let Terry stay the night, and when he refuses, begs a promise to come back soon. She shouts final friendly commands as she leaves the doorway.

'I've left a key in the pot on the kitchen table, but it's the spare I usually leave with the neighbour, so I'll have to get one cut as soon as I can. I'll not be back till the morning, so make yourselves at home. There's plenty of videos if there's nothing on the box, and any amount of fast food places at the end of the road. You'll have seen them as you came. But if you just want a sandwich or something then help yourself to the fridge. There's not much in there, I'm afraid. Anyway, I'll see you tomorrow, Jack. Bye Terry, see you soon.'

And the door slams to a still house.

'She can't half talk, heh?'

'She's nice, Terry. Thank you.'

'Ah, c'mon.' Terry must have noticed the tear in Jack's eye.

But it's quickly blinked away. Terry probably wishes he hadn't seen it, hadn't said anything. Though it doesn't matter and he's seen far worse.

Later they kick back in the spiced-fat comfort of a doner kebab. Chilli sauce burning into cans of apple Tango, almost too slippery to hold. Jack has never had a kebab, which one of his cellmates professed to miss more than his family. The Styrofoam box reminds him of something. He stares at it, pooled juices already congealing into waxy solid. It is McDonalds, only they used to come in these boxes. McDonalds was the stuff of childhood treats, another good omen. Jack is a great believer in omens. The mundanity of prison focuses the mind, tuning recognition of pattern and difference. A black grain in puffed rice at breakfast can mean a bad day, seven matchsticks left a good one. Primitive societies set great store by these things. Prison is primitive.

Together they study the Sunday night football round-up. Terry tests on players and form. Jack Burridge supports Luton Town of course: 'Luton Airport who are you?', 'The Hatters, the Hatters and we're all fucking nutters'. The odds of finding a fellow fan up here are remote, but he must demonstrate a knowledge of his team. Actually Jack has never had any real interest in football, but he can talk a good game. He's shared a cell with a Celtic Casual, a Chelsea Headhunter and a middle-aged Notts County trainspotter called Trevor who was doing five months for getting his thirteen-year-old girlfriend pregnant.

When Terry leaves, Jack prowls the house, tentatively opening drawers and doors. He feels the weight of the pans, and touches the contents of the fridge, reading sauce bottles like books. He takes the dry blast of the airing cupboard on his face. The deep hall rug between bare toes, with its well-worn trough connecting the lounge and the front door. Eventually, when he has sniffed and stroked his way to some intimacy with this dark and strange new house, he curls foetal beneath the duvet in his small box-room. And despite the unfamiliarity of everything around him, Jack feels safe, because he knows he is the apple of his uncle's eye.

It is under Terry's careful gaze that the events of the next two weeks will unfold. An orientation time for Jack. An opportunity to adjust before he starts his job. A fortnight only, to try and lose the bewilderment with which he looks at this world.

They will visit parks, restaurants, pubs, an art museum, an airport. Jack will open a bank account, fills in forms, make his name more real with each one. He is going to stand in a crowd at a Saturday morning market, shaking with fear at first, immobile while strangers' faces file around him. They will walk on a moor, where the silence is absolute, no noise but the sound of their own feet brushing the bracken. They will ride there in Terry's car, which Jack has only ever watched from afar. Has never before felt the vinyl seats under his fingertips. Heard the radio on its one working speaker. They are going to laugh when, in town one day, a rottweiler bangs its face against a van window, desperate to get at a cat. They will buy the *Big Issue*, from a guy who says he was ready to give up until Terry came along. And Jack will say that he knows how this feels.

Each day for fifteen, Terry is going to pick Jack up at 7:30 am, the time he will soon be picked up for work, and show him another alien angle on life. And every night Jack is going to close his eyes and not believe this is happening to him.

Every hour, whether with Terry or alone, he will practise his story. Learn his legend. Focus on the things he needs to do to make himself a little less a fish on the riverbank, a little more the man a different boy might have become.

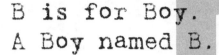

B is for Boy.
A Boy named B.

Child *B* was exactly the kind of boy that your mother told you not to play with. Probably his mother would have too, had she been there. Had she given a fuck. He had shoulder-length hair that fell naturally into tight scouse curls, and even at nine a faint bum-fluff moustache on his upper lip. He looked like a juvenile, scanky, Bobby Ball. But he was too thick to be funny. Stupid not through lack of native wit but from a determined resolution to remain ignorant. Ignorance was his armour. He walked with a swagger, advertising a readiness to fight that was ridiculous for his size. Legs spread wide, feet splayed outwards, fists balled. A strut adopted from his older brother. A brother known around town as a man not to be messed with. Who none the less messed with *B*.

He was a loner, child *B*. Not like some, because of natural inclination. He was a loner because he carried an aura, something beyond even his walk and his constant spitting. Something that kept other children at bay like wolfsbane or garlic might ward off monsters. Children can be monsters too. We know that now. But once children were just children.

★

Child *A*, before he even knew *B*, knew more than most what poisons might be concealed inside angelic frames. Of course he was to see, in glorious Technicolor, the depths to which a child could fall. But he'd already had inklings. He had experienced first-hand some of the cruel possibilities. Growing up in a run-down mining town, where the pits were everywhere.

Once *A* had walked home with one shoe. Ripped junior Y-fronts stuffed into the pocket of the trousers that he'd managed to rescue. His other shoe was still thickly lodged in a tree; impervious to sticks and stones and names and all the other things that *A* felt so deeply. He trudged with a sock sodden from the pavement, and a lopsided swaying like the plastic boy on the Barnados boxes would walk, his legs imprisoned in torturous iron callipers.

It was long dark when he made it home, shivering from the tear-cloaking drizzle. Aching from rabbit punches and dead legs and hours of futile efforts to rescue his shoe. His mother hugged him before she started shouting.

'We've been worried near enough to death. Where the bloody hell have you been?'

He'd rehearsed the story in his mind. He couldn't tell them the truth. Some bitter shame locked it in him. He knew with cockeyed childish intuition that they wouldn't understand, couldn't comprehend the depths of his anguish. He firmly believed that his tormentors would increase his suffering if he went to adults. Maybe they would have.

'I was playing football with my friends,' the word made him wince. 'The ball got caught in a tree and we all threw our shoes to get it down. But mine got stuck, and that's where I've been, trying to get it down.'

His mother stroked his hair, and this kindness was almost more than his body could take. His lip began to waver, but he caught his father's eye and managed to check it.

'Come on,' his dad said. 'Let's go and get the bloody thing

before it really starts pissing it down.' He broke off to get his keys. But in that instant of eye contact, when he had been about to cry, A had seen his father's disgust.

They both sat in silence with their shame, as they drove to the field by A's school. Water pooled with the cement dust in the back of the battered pick-up, a ladder looming over the windscreen. A felt like a condemned witch when he climbed it, a broom in hand, and a big hangman's bough above him. The rungs were treacherous, slippery even in his dry trainers. Lightning flashed like a cheap horror gimmick. And A knew, what his father forgot or ignored, that up a wet ladder under a tall sycamore was a harmful place. A route that belonged to the storm. His dad held the ladder steady, as if in a half-hearted suicide pact. And A worried, more even than death, that his father would see the ripped pants still bulging in his trouser pocket.

It went on for months like this. Years, in child time. A small boy being bullied by a group of such diversity and size that he seemed to have no moments of freedom. No respite save at home, where he tried desperately to hide his engrossing unhappiness. He lay awake much of most nights, plagued with anxiety. Sometimes he fell asleep in class.

His teacher, Mrs Johnston, née Grey, disillusioned and going through divorce, thought him lazy like his left eye. She noticed that he always seemed to be dirty, and looked like he'd been fighting. Other children told on him, even some of her nicest girls. There could be no smoke without fire. Besides, he had the same startling blue irises as her filthy, philandering fuck of a husband. Though she neglected to mention this last point at the trial.

After a while A ceased even to protest while he was punished for imagined misdemeanours. He bore all with a stoical silence. Soon he just stopped going to school.

The alternative was dull, but painless. Wandering the streets of an old coal town. Mostly *A* could stay out of the way of the few other primary kids that bunked. Stonelee was a hard hilly culture, cold and mindless, mineless. Under-employed or unemployed, the positions available. *A*'s father, an occasional demolition foreman, was firmly middle class. The Eveready battery factory floundered and failed. Other punier attempts at rejuvenation died outright, or lived briefly like the summer stingers on the slag heaps. Even the pound shop struggled. Tumbleweed Kwik Save crisp packets blew down the empty market street. Alternate Thursdays the fruit and veg stall still came. The butcher, famed for his pork sandwiches, was closed by E. coli. When *A* read this in the *Northern Echo* he thought E. coli was a bailiff. Bailiffs flourished.

'How d'you get five hundred cows in a shed?' said a boy that *A* vaguely recognized.

From his seat on the gravestone, *A* looked at him. He was from the year below, rough. His eyes were staring, burning. *A*, not sure if it was a trap, spun around, poised to flee. But curiosity kept his buttocks on the cold, grey slab.

'How d'you get five hundred cows in a shed?' the boy asked again. His voice was deep, though of course unbroken. *A* wondered if he was putting it on.

'I don't know. How?' *A* said slowly, earnestly, hopefully. He wanted this to be a real joke, not a trick or an excuse to punch him.

'Put up a Bingo sign.' The boy laughed, much more than the joke merited. *A* laughed as well, as hard as he could.

The boy kicked at a stone cross with the flat of his foot. It rocked slightly in its foundation hole. He kicked it again but it moved the same little way and no more. Looking around, as if for some new way to impress, the boy saw a brown glass bottle, left by the churchyard's night-time clientele. He picked it up, and *A* knew that he would smash it; but the boy wished to demonstrate an abandon far beyond that. He sailed the bottle grenade-like, through the trees and over the church wall, towards an unseen road. Before it had even landed A felt the attraction of this abandon, the exhilaration that it could offer him. He could just hear the pop of the bottle as it exploded, then the brakes of a car and a crunch, and more broken glass. Then came horns and slamming doors. But they were already running.

The boy ran like he walked: fists balled, arms nearly straight in his ripped green bomber. He led A onwards, inwards, through the church's doorway, left open for the poor and the needy.

It was cool in the church, an escape from the closeness outside. A remembered the big brass sanctuary knocker on Durham Cathedral, with its devilish eyeless face. Churches had always been a place of safety for criminals. Not that he was a criminal, but he was beginning to feel the appeal of crime.

Like Stonelee, the church was old and ill kept. Hanging steel lamps showed paint flaking off the walls like dead skin. A mural of Mary prayed handless, where the cement had fallen. The two boys, breathless and silent, walked around, looking for somewhere to hide. Stepping over the names of benefactors and bishops, almost erased by the shoes of centuries. They took a seat in a small side chapel, joining a plaster saint. His eyes were half-closed, like he was sleepy or stoned, and he held a coil of rosaries long enough to tie someone up.

They grinned at each other with excitement when they heard the people come in. The footsteps sounded gruff and out of place in the emptiness. But the noises soon faded, leaving them undiscovered in their private chapel. A's newest and only friend, a boy named B, stole a hymn book, while they sat waiting for the feeling that it was safe to leave. A gazed at the roof, painted a passionate blue with golden stars, looking somehow more real than the sky outside had been. It was supported by pillars, thick as God's thighs, and near their tops more anonymous saints stared down. Most bore the means of their martyrdom, some ghoulishly held their own heads.

They shared the remains of the day. Outlaws, confirmed in petty shoplifts and pointless vandalism. Acts that nonetheless bonded them, blended them. Separation from the world brought them to each other. People who saw them, while they walked homewards, would swear they were a pair. They fitted together those two boys, with letters where their names should be. *A* and *B,* united by their difference, intrinsically linked, like pen and paper, salt and pepper, accident and emergency.

But events flowed on, as steady and dirty as the Stonelee Byrne, and at the end of the road stood three figures. *A* recognized them as boys from his class, junior demons.

A had become used to long cuts: double-backs and dirt-tracks. Somehow *B*'s abandon had lured him into unaccustomed bravery.

'Let's go this way,' he said, trying to pull his friend down a side-street.

But *B* didn't recognize the urgency in his voice. 'Naw, it's much longer.' He offered *A* an Opal Fruit instead.

And then it was too late anyway. The three boys had spotted them, and were already sidling forwards.

'Haven't seen you in school recently,' one of them said.

A felt the hopelessness building inside him. These false pleasantries would slide into an attack. Sudden or slow, the pain was inevitable. All the worse because he had enjoyed the day. Now *B* would despise him, or even join in against him.

'Anyone would think you've been avoiding us. Aren't we your friends any more?'

'No look, he's got a new friend, haven't you, you little shit.'

'What's your friend called, spastic, or can't he afford a name?' The inquisitors laughed with childish brutality.

A would have run for it, but already his classmates had penned them in. Trapping them against the wall of a house.

B looked at these older boys. His neck stretched out like a weasel's as he stared slowly into each of their faces. Maybe then they suspected they had picked the wrong kid.

'All right, you, just piss off,' said one. 'It's him we want.'

There were none of the preliminaries that usually marked fights in the under-tens freestyle event. No pushing or grabbing or wrestling. *B* punched the speaker hard in the face. A proper punch with his weight behind it. Like his brother taught and used. The boy crumpled, and as he did *B* hit him again on the back of the head. The second boy started to raise his arm to thump, but before his blow was prepared, *B* had smacked him too. In the eye and then the throat and then the eye again. The boy shrieked like a baby and stumbled away backwards. The third one had already run off. *B* kicked the boy who was on the floor. Lashing at him, showering him with blows. *A* joined him, savouring his abandon, feeling its shelter. The boy on the floor sobbed and begged them to stop.

Eventually they did.

None of the passing cars did.

A was happier that night. His mum commented on it. For once he slept well. And when he woke it was with nervous excitement, at the prospect of meeting up with *B* again.

When *B* went to bed, he retrieved the stolen hymn book. He tried to read it, but most of the words frustrated him. He was barely beyond his abc. Could just write his own name, and recognize a few common expressions. 'Dog' was one of the first words he had learned, and in that book he found its opposite. Not cat but God.

That night *B* went through the hymn book, scribbling out God and painstakingly writing his own name above each reference. *B* did not believe in God. His brother had told him that God did not exist, one night while *B* had pleaded for His help. And that He did not help seemed to prove his brother's case. Perhaps, though, there remained a trace belief, or else who was he offending with his tightly gripped black Berrol? Maybe *B* too felt the heart-pounding exuberance. The power of his own abandon. Some fraction of the thrill of that fiery first rebel. Or maybe he was just trying to dare God into showing Himself.

C is for Coast.
Can You See the Sea?

Time passes for Jack with shrinking soap and growing confidence. A month has gone by since his freedom arrived. In the seamless sameness of prison schedules, days lagged and loitered. But now every hour is different; disorder is all about him. Though he seeks comfort in some small routines, these just form a raft in the sea that surrounds. He loves this sea, embraces its impossibility, opens his lungs to swallow it as it swallows him.

There's a quality, a sort of paleness, in these mornings, that Jack has quickly come to adore. Like today, he often gets up at six to have the short walk to the paper shop to himself. The thin damp air seems to welcome him to the day. He fondles the chunky pound coins in his pocket, as comforting as his testicles. This is the last he need spend of his 'pies', his prison wages. Tomorrow he will get his first fortnight's pay: a wage in pounds, instead of pence.

The paper-shop man is sorting stacks of dailies while he daydreams. He smiles a grizzled grin at Jack, his new regular, and passes him the *Star*. Not the *Sun*, never the *Sun*. Despite its promise to be implant free, Jack cannot forgive the *Sun*, whose coupon campaign to extend his sentence was such an unqualified success. He swaps one of the nuggets from his pocket for the paper and his change, and leaves the man to his thoughts.

Jack waves his thanks to the lone car that lets him pass on the zebra crossing. Amazed at how much a part of society that small action makes him feel. He notices a curious clean patch on the car's boot, where something in the shape of a fish obviously used to stick. He wonders what it was, and whether the owner knows he's lost it.

Over breakfast of toast and tea Jack reads his *Star.* There is no mention of him in it today. During the last few weeks the debate has still continued sporadically. He hopes that maybe it's finished now, and turns to page three. Her blond framed face is slightly pointed, foxly. Slim thighs, ribcage delicately lined where she breathed in to conceal her tiny female belly, just at the instant of shutter closure. Her breasts are art: formed by a man's hands for the viewing pleasure of other men. Soft planets, golden and impossibly high, and no less perfect for all this. Jack feels his virginity acutely.

Breakfast is the only part of the routine where disorder can intrude: the times when Kelly is there. Though he likes her, Jack prefers it when he eats alone, and he can prepare himself for his day. Afterwards he washes and shaves. The razor issued with his new identity is becoming blunt, and with a seminal consumer urge he resolves not to get a replacement blade, but an entirely new razor.

Brands bubble in his head as he walks to the meet: Wilkinson Sword, a bit too military; Gillette – the best a man can get; Sensor; Mach 3; I liked it so much I bought the company; Bremington; Reminton. He was allowed TV in the early years. In the home, which wasn't a home, but began to seem so compared to the prisons.

He waits by the forecourt of the garage. He's tense in the open, where so many eyes are upon him, where someone might recognize him. But it's getting easier. Jack sees a lot of garages. The job that Terry got him is with a distribution firm, delivering supplies. Servicing service stations.

Chris pulls in to pick Jack up, and coasts to a stop. As always, he's in the white Mercedes van that work lets him take home. Jack is a driver's mate. In theory he map-reads, but since Chris knows his job inside out, mostly Jack just listens to Chris and the radio until they unload.

'Morning, Dodger.' Chris calls everyone by pet names; he thinks it's endearing. To many people, Jack among them, it is. Some hate it. Everything depends on the name.

'How's it going?' Jack replies. 'What've we got today?'

'Cages.'

'Cages?'

'Yeah, cages for outside the shops. For drink multi-packs and charcoal and stuff, so they can lock them up at night. Not everyone's as honest as you, Dodger.' Chris laughs, gives a slap to the air above the back of Jack's head. Jack told him about the car-stealing antics of Burridge. Chris decided that he moved up here to escape bad influences down South, and Jack didn't dispel the story. Chris had probably never seen anyone so nervous on their first day at work. He seems to be strongly considering taking Jack under his wing. Making him a proper mate, not just for drivers.

The cages are at the depot, caged themselves behind mesh-fence and thick brick walls. They load them together.

'Got to sign them out with the White Whale before we go, Dodger.'

Jack nods, examines his hands. Imprints of the thin steel still sit in the plastic memory of his fingers. He gets blisters some days. Not painful, just a bulbous sliver of unnecessary skin. Better a fistful of blisters than enforced idleness.

'Hi, Michelle.' Chris doesn't usually call the White Whale by her name, though she knows she's called it, and that there's no spite. She's certainly not a whale anyway, someone generous about proportions would call her generously proportioned. She *is* very fair, hair almost white-blond, skin pale too, but exquisitely smooth. Probably her best feature, that skin, taut for someone of her bulk. Chris said her last boyfriend was a doorman, with gang connections. He hit her once and she left him, never went back despite threats and promises. He'd been inside too, Strangeways. She has strange ways herself, seems to have a thing for crims. She likes Jack anyway; even he sees through her charade of flirting for fun.

'Oh, Jack,' she says, as he signs the form. 'I could dive into those eyes.'

'Not with an arse like that you couldn't,' says Chris. He laughs, Jack does too, a little awkwardly. Michelle gives Chris a Paddington Bear hard stare, but her eyes still sparkle.

She smiles broadly when she looks at Jack's again. But he flicks his gaze away to his feet. She dizzies him. Jack's not exactly well versed in flirting. There were long years when the only women he saw were a few prison teachers. Some didn't bother to contain their loathing.

'So when are you going to take me out for a drink, Jack?' She's joking but she means it too.

Jack is stumped, stunned; he feels his worldly ignorance around his neck like the corpse of an albatross. Its huge wingspan is knocking over the furniture. He's not ready for this yet.

'Tell you what, why don't we all go out?' Chris says. 'Tomorrow night, pay-day. Get the whole crew. You can ask everyone today, Michelle. Give you something to do, cos you do bugger-all else.'

She throws a rubber at him, which somehow stamps the deal.

'Saved you there, mate,' Chris says as he starts the van. 'She's a man-eater, that one. Did I tell you why I call her the White Whale?'

'I thought it was because she's kind of big and white.' Big and fantastic and beautiful and pale like the snow that I haven't felt in fifteen years, Jack thinks. But he knows Chris would laugh at him if he let on that he liked her.

'Nah, it suits her, but that's not why. It was after the Christmas party, which by the way is held in January because it's cheaper. A few of us went back to this lass Claire's, one of the secretaries. Anyway we're all pretty leathered, talking crap. It was during that Harold Shipman case. It was obvious he was going down, and somehow we got on to this thing, sort of a game, where everyone had to say what they'd miss most if they got banged up. Shame you weren't there, hey, Dodger. We could have had the expert view. Anyway, so it comes round to Michelle, and she can't think for ages. I thought it would be her car, she loves that car. But everyone's ragging her and she says,' Chris puts on a comical high voice, '"I don't know … maybe dick." And Claire, who's a bit "nice but dim", thought she said "*Moby* Dick", and goes off on one about does she mean the film or the book, cos she's sure you're allowed books in prison. Hence the White Whale – maybe dick.' Chris laughs. He's got a gravelly laugh, like a dirty old man, though he's only a couple of years older than Jack. Jack feigns a chuckle and stares out of the side window, so he doesn't have to keep it up.

The array of colours still startles him, but the world out there is starting to resemble real life. Some regular routes even look familiar. The road-signs help. Jack used to make road-signs.

Chris is listening to the radio now. The *Mystery Years* has started, and he's intent on guessing the date of the tunes. He's not bad at it; most mornings he'll get two out of three spot on. He says he just remembers the events happening in his life when the songs were playing, and works it out. It's all about the feeling of era. Jack can't do this: his recent years are blurred into one long painful stretch. The radio helped the days pass, but it couldn't mark them.

His thoughts turn to Michelle, to what Chris said: that

she's a man-eater. It must be true; Chris messes about, but
he's not malicious. There isn't a dark bone in his body. It isn't
that Jack is expecting a vestal virgin, and the knowledge that
she's been around does not even make him like her any less;
but it takes her further from him, makes his ignorance more
consequential.

'Hey, you know what I was saying about prison, before.
See if you recognize this fellow. He might look familiar.'
Chris tosses over his paper from behind the dash. 'It's that
child murderer they released, they've done a photofit.'

The words tear into Jack. The enormity hits his stomach
like a black hole. Irresistible gravity sucking dry every part
of him. His words are swallowed utterly; parched lips try to
mouth something, some kind of apology to Chris for lying
to him.

He reaches for the paper. Chris is whistling, probably
going to drive him straight to the town centre, throw him
out to be lynched. Jack's ears start to buzz, some sort of
panic shut-down system. His neck won't move; it's gone
rigid. He can just turn his eyes to the page, but it's
mechanical, as if there's a switch he's moving. Like the
eagle-eye action man, with a lever running through his
drained, brain-dry head.

He reads the red top title, the *News of the World*. Then the
headline 'Kid Killer Photo Exclusive'. His vision's gone so
blurry now that the photo doesn't look like him. He can't
seem to focus. It doesn't look like him. He's aware that he
hasn't taken a breath for some time. It doesn't look like him.
The first lung-full is deep, as if he breaches a surface. It really
doesn't look like him. He gulps another. It isn't him. He
feels a sudden joy. The picture's of someone else, someone
he doesn't know, hasn't met. He grins relief. There's been a
mix-up. But no. There is something just barely familiar.

The caption reads: 'This is a computer-generated image
of the man the government doesn't want you to see. Using

the latest techniques our scientists have aged the face we dubbed the "Evilest Boy in Britain" to show what he looks like now. Geriatric judges and the limply liberal Home Secretary might think he's no further danger. The *News of the World* says parents have a right to know who's living down their street.'

The latest ageing techniques have failed. Maybe the scientists are professors of paper sales. The face they have created is twisted, mocking, leering. Perhaps they were working from a photograph that had itself been doctored to suggest darkness. But maybe it's down to Jack, to his nature or lack of nurture, his genes or his environment. As a boy his features were squashed, scrunched in a slightly dwarfish way. Age has been kind to Jack, though life hasn't. His features remained the same, but the spaces between them grew until they fitted. His hair that was silage brown somehow spun itself to gold. His wide splayed long front teeth were lost, somewhere on the journey from then to now, and replaced with neat false perfection. His eyes remain as blue as dolphins, but the left that had a tendency to dive alone now swims steady with its brother. He is not perhaps truly handsome, but he is something approaching it. He is no longer ugly. He is certainly not the man in the photofit.

Jack hands the paper back.

'Don't know him. Sorry.'

'So what did you miss most when you were inside, Jack?'

'I don't know. There's too much. Not doner kebabs.'

Jack waves from the drop-off, as Chris roars off home, the first and final forecourt of both their days. He's going to the pub with Terry tonight, he needs to, it's been eventful at work. He's not sure whether he can face going out with everyone tomorrow. He needs to talk to Terry. Terry will know what to do.

There's a pawnbroker's on his way back to number 10.

Normally he passes on the other side, but tonight something makes Jack cross over and look in its grilled display window. It's like a poor man's treasure chest in there, waiting for some poverty-stricken pirate to rake his fingers through it all. Looted gold and silver are bundled, seemingly haphazardly, together: necklaces and earrings, some set with vaguely precious stones; mountains of cutlery; assorted wedding and engagement rings, for those not bothered about omens; gold chains of varied girth; a row of 80s watches, bracelet straps stretched out like baby reptiles trying to warm in the sun; a thick braid of mixed medallions, Saint Christophers and crucifixes mingling with Lincoln imps and anchors; a tray of sovereign rings; and in the middle of everything sits a Toby Jug, grinning smugly among the debris of debt, fashion and failure.

Jack is about to turn away, when something catches his eye. Up in one corner of the purple plush, which is so scarred and faded as to make its name a joke, is a razor. It's a cut-throat, the real deal. The blade lies open, at right angles to the grip, like the carpenters' squares in the prison workshop. The handle is a light wood, with brass bands holding it in place. It must be old, Jack thinks. They don't make them any more, do they? But it looks new. The blade reflects the fly-coated strip-light above it. It shimmers; more samurai than Sweeny Todd. A tiny tag on a string says £15. Jack is not accustomed to need possessions, but he knows that he needs this. If it is still there tomorrow, when his wages come through, he will buy it.

He showers before he meets Terry; dust and diesel swirl away, with hairs and dead skin. Some tiny particles of Jack will meet the English Channel in a few days. They were going to go to Blackpool that summer. The summer of the incident. It would have been his first real holiday. Jack has never even been swimming, but he knows he would love

the sea. He doesn't spend long in the shower, though. Jack
still feels vulnerable in showers.

'Consistency is king,' Terry says. 'Look at Travelodge, or even
better – McDonalds. What you get may be firmly mediocre,
but you know what You're getting. You're allowed to
anticipate, and anticipation is half the pleasure. Most people
my age hate these Firkin pubs.' He chuckles at his
inadvertent wordplay, although the walls and staff T-shirts
are filled with variations on the theme. 'Me, I love them.'

The pub they are in is called the Figment and Firkin. The
'figment' in question is presumably one of the imagination,
because supposedly a lot of writers used to drink there. Jack
wonders if Stonelee has a Fight and Firkin, or maybe a
Fuckall and Firkin.

Jack is rapidly acquiring a taste for lager. Once or twice a
week Terry and he have been going out for a meal and a few
drinks somewhere. Just a pizza, or a pub like this. Terry
hasn't got rich on government wages. Especially with the
divorce, and several house moves, and putting his son
through university. Jack smiles inwardly. Next week he's
going to pay for everything. Just the start of making up for
the years that Terry's given him.

'What're you having, then?' says Terry.

They both decide on lasagne, and Terry goes to the bar to
order. Jack sips his beer and watches the room. There are
two blokes and a girl playing pool in the corner. She's pretty,
with an unselfconscious confidence: laughing loudly when
she misses a shot, chattering happily to her two escorts. She
divides her attention so evenly that Jack can't decide which
one she's seeing, or whether it's neither or both.

Terry is carrying another two pints when he returns.

'It'll save getting up again in a minute,' he says. Terry
seems to like going out with Jack: treating him to meals,
buying the drinks, just sitting and talking. All the things that

he says he was never able to do with his own son. He bought Jack his first ever pint, only a few weeks ago. Terry was living in a different city when his own son started going to pubs. Down in London, near to Feltham.

'So what d'you think, Terry? Should I go or not? Tomorrow night, I mean.'

'Of course you should. It's going to be daunting but you need friends. You can't just keep hanging about with your uncle all the time. Much as he enjoys it.' Terry pats Jack's arm. 'Just try not to get too drunk. Remember most of these guys from work will have been on the booze every weekend since they were sixteen. Don't try and keep up with them. In fact get a few non-alcoholic drinks in if you can. You want to still have your wits about you.'

'Now you do sound like an uncle.'

'I worry like one, Jack. But you need to start living. You know what they say about all work and no play. The past doesn't equal the future, Jack. You're entitled to some happiness.'

'I am happy, Terry. I'm as happy as I can ever remember being.'

'And just think. You've still got sex to come yet,' Terry laughs, and then blushes slightly at his own teasing.

'I'm just going to concentrate on lasagne for the moment,' Jack says.

They part company at the end of Jack's road, where Terry grabs a black cab and Jack continues alone. A lowered, red Golf shoots along from behind him. It's going far too fast for the narrow gap between two sides of parked cars. Recklessly fast, in fact. Jack's seen the Golf a few times. Usually it's outside a house at the bottom of the street. He tuts to himself. Chris would be going mad if he was there. He hates bad drivers.

Just before his front door, Jack turns around to look back

up the road. Something makes him on edge, as if he's being watched. It feels like there's a figure staring at him from the gloom of an alleyway. He has more of a sense of it than a sighting, but the sense chills him. And maybe something skulks away into the thick darkness. Jack is unnerved for a moment; but Kelly is watching *The Blues Brothers* when he gets in, and their shared laughter makes him forget about it.

He goes to bed before her, and when he cleans his teeth he takes a few wraps of toilet roll back to his room with him. With the lights off he imagines Michelle. He thinks of all the things that he would like to do to her, with her, for her. Things that he doesn't really know how to do, but which are none the less engrossing and enticing. Jack's fantasies are unsullied by details and experiences. With quick twitches of his arm he claims her. And for an instant she's his, they're together on this desert island of belief.

Her face is fixed in his mind, even as his breathing steadies again. He wipes away the dewy cobwebs that span his fingers, and turns to sleep.

No one is asleep at Terry's house. Terry is alone in his kitchen, but he is conscious of a presence that the creaking bedroom floor gives away. The strip-light is off, but the streetlight outside the window casts just sufficient glow to see the table. One plate of steak and chips sits untouched. Blisters of cold white fat lie across the meat's clammy surface, a cairn of grey peas piled beside it. The other meal looks like it's been more toyed with than eaten. Terry can imagine his son sitting there, waiting for his return, pushing lukewarm lumps of food around. Maybe humming happy birthday to himself. No, that's just Terry's grim romanticism; Zeb's not a hummer, he's a curser.

Zeb is awake, and so must be aware that his father is home, but they remain in different rooms, neither of them willing to initiate the inevitable. It will be worse for Terry;

all the blame lies with him. How can he have allowed himself to forget the birth of his one son? The boy's only been staying with him for three days.

'Hello, Zeb,' he says, as the presence finally enters the room, 'I'm sorry. Happy birthday.' He is braced for rage, for a foot-stomping tirade, but sees in his son's eyes only weariness.

'What is it, Dad? What's the great crusade this time?'

'I'm sorry, Zeb, I just forgot. There's no crusade, it's just one of my charges. I always go out with him on a Tuesday.'

'*Charges* − causes, more like. Another little criminal fuck who's more important than your own flesh and blood.'

'Zeb, It's not like that...'

But his son has already left the room, leaving Terry looking at the spoiled meal; lingering with his guilt.

D is for Dungeon. Dark and Deep.

A started to come around with an uneasy feeling: a creeping anxiety that somehow everything wasn't going to be quite right when he was fully awake. He couldn't put his finger on who he had offended, or what he had broken; but there was a muggy certitude that he was in trouble.

Then someone slapped him.

It was almost like being born again. Brought against his will from the comfort of oblivion and then hit. Like the first time, it was an honest introduction.

'They killed him,' moaned a voice in *A*'s ear, 'they fucking murdered him.'

He couldn't open his right eye at all. With a lot of pain he produced a crack through the puffy flesh of the left one, so he could see a little of the room. It was murky grey, like a clotted nightmare. He was lying on the bottom bed of a bunk. His body ached all over.

'They put him in with that racist mother-fucker. He said he was going to do it and he did,' mouthed a huge brown jaw that blocked out everything else from *A*'s thin gash of view. 'I promised I'd look after him, I fucking promised his mum and I promised his baby-mother and he's dead. The fucker said he was going to do it and he did. They might just as well have done it themselves.'

A murmured 'Who?', lisping it slightly, not used to talking without his front teeth. His swollen lips stuck together with congealing blood each time he closed them, and made a wet sucking sound when he parted them again to breathe. He had to breathe through his mouth; his smashed nose was caked shut.

'Who? The fucking screws, that's who. The screws who put my cousin, my fucking best friend, in with that murderous, white, fucking racist. They fucking knew it would happen, the skinhead fuck said it would happen. Just six fucking hours before my spar was going to be released.'

A's throat contracted, making his breathing even more ragged.

'Shut up man, just shut up and let me think.'

The speaker punched *A* in the windpipe. He rolled on to his side, doubled up, wheezing and gasping for air. With the effort of trying to breathe, he sucked down great lumps of dried blood from his nose, making him choke. He could feel his eyes bulging. Like a rabbit, he thought. Like the rabbits my dog used to catch. His mind was drifting. He wondered if that meant he was dying. If he was a rabbit he would be dead already. Their hearts give up beating when they face certain death. They don't have to go through all this pain. God looks after the meek. God, who decided the meek should be preyed upon.

'I don't know what to do, kid,' said the predator. 'I look into your eyes and I don't think you're a bad person. I mean, no worse than the rest of us in here. I don't hate you, man. I don't have anything against you. But I told them I'd do it. I said don't put no white boy in with me because I'm gonna do the same to him. I'll fucking kill him. I told them, man, fucking yesterday; and they still put you in here. Just like he told them, and they still put my cousin in there. They killed my fucking cousin, and now they're taking the piss out of me. They're calling me a boy. I told them I'd do it.' The sleeves were ripped off his borstal–blue T-shirt. His arms were huge, not swollen like a body–builder's, naturally solid like a tree; thick with veins and dense muscle.

A was no longer a boy either; no weakling, and no coward. But this man was designed on a different scale. A Mastiff to A's Jack Russell. He might just as well have tried to break through the cell door as attack him. But he'd tried both, and he'd tried shouting for help, and he'd tried pleading. So now he didn't seem to have anything left to try, but bleeding and moaning softly.

'What's your name?' said the man. His voice was deep, cavernous, but not unkind – almost gentle. 'I don't want to kill a stranger.'

A told him, told his true name, terror replaced by a kind of numb acceptance. The gallow-walker's recognition that there is no escape. That it's all too late.

The man put his long arms around A's shoulders and sat him up on the bed. He drew their two bodies together, squeezing gently into a hug. A could feel the rasp of stubble against his cheek, and the cold salt of this sudden enemy's tears biting into the cuts around his mouth. He felt beyond tears himself: bewildered, light-headed and almost relieved.

'I'm sorry,' the man said, quietly now, like all rage was spent. 'I'm so sorry. It's not your fault. But I have to do it. You see I told them. I fucking told them. It's not for me. But I promised his mum and I promised his baby-mother. I said I'd look after him. I got him in here, and I said I'd look after him.'

He moved his arms so that his large, long-fingered hands were around A's throat. This new nearness to death provoked a fresh wave of terror. A started to thrash uncontrollably. Yelling, screaming, he tried to pull the hands away from his throat. But they were too strong.

He felt himself weakening. A door opened and bright light came washing in. Was this death? Three figures poured in with the light. A knew that they were angels or devils, but

not which. Didn't they all start off the same? The pressure
eased from around his throat. He laughed; they had come
for his tormentor, not him. They were beating the
tormentor with truncheons. Pulling him away. Guardian
angels. The devil looks after his own. He laughed again.

'Welcome to Feltham,' said one of the angels.

E is for Elephant.
White Elephant.

Jack can't get the washer–dryer to work. The dryer, anyway. The washer's washed, but the clothes are stuck in there. The door won't open and Jack's whites languish like broken teeth in a thickly salivated mouth. In fact it's still half-full of water; it hasn't even drained yet. He should have done this last night while Kelly was here.

His hand is shaking when he pushes the 'dryer' button, frustration and nerves. This is the night: his first night out ever, if you don't count with Terry; and it's all going wrong already. The button doesn't do anything, Jack didn't expect it to, he's tried it twenty times already. The machine's big round mouth is laughing at him, laughing because it knows it's got his only good shirt inside it. He wants to punch the mouth, but he's bright enough to know that it won't help. He needs that shirt. Two hours to go and it's soaking wet and imprisoned beyond his reach.

He kneels down on the cold tile of the kitchen floor and examines the controls again, hoping against logic that something obvious is suddenly going to spring out at him. But all the buttons are the same, and he's tried any that look relevant. He doesn't want to set it all off again, or he'll have to wait another forty minutes.

Then he sees it, a flap near the bottom of the machine. He pushes it and it springs open, like any self-respecting secret compartment should: as if it was just waiting to save the hero. Jack is puzzled as to why the panel should be put down there. But sure enough there's a dial-like switch to twist, with the word 'drainer' written clearly above it. He turns it in the direction of the arrow, and notices a smoky smell in the room. For the first time Jack remembers the fish fingers he was grilling. He'll just sort this out and then he can make his sandwich, thirty seconds isn't going to make any difference. He twists the knob again, and then another half turn; might as well get this drainer on maximum.

The switch comes away in his hand, leaving a hole. Jack is staring at it when the water starts pouring out on to the floor. He tries to push the switch, which he sees is really a screw-plug, back into its slot. But he fumbles, and it jumps skittishly away, into the water already flowing behind his knees. As he turns to reclaim the plug, Jack sees the flames snaking out of the grill. They lick dark venom on to the clean white of Kelly's oven. He's caught for a moment, unsure which disaster to counter first. The fire makes his choice by grasping at the wallpaper. Still holding the plug, Jack leaps to his bare feet, nearly slipping in the water. He turns off the gas and thrusts the burning grill pan into the sink. The fat spits, hissing into his hand and cheek, but the flames quickly die. Although the water is barely trickling out now, and the floor is already flooded, he screws the plug back in, as tight as it will go.

He slumps down in the pool of water, covering the washing machine's still-laughing mouth with his back, and holding his burned cheek with his burned hand.

He's used to picking himself up. Pick up, put up, shut up – never give up. If you give up they find you hanging dead from a strip of sheet, or lying in the red of your own wrists.

Never give up, never give in. But the power to be able to is important. It gives a choice to the choiceless; it makes going on a decision. Your decision. Sometimes Jack believed that the option of suicide was all that kept him alive.

B made his choice too. Made his bed-sheet and hanged from it. His final felony. It's a crime, suicide. 'Felo-de-se', Terry said, the felon of himself. Was *B* unrepentant even at the end? Did he want to feel the abandon one last time? Commit one last crime? In the olden days they used to bury suicides inside prison, so that even death was no escape.

There was a prime minister once that Jack studied in history – GCSE, HMPS. It was either Canning or Castlereagh, he can't remember, though he got a C. He's not so stupid as some people suppose him. This prime minister, sick of being suspected and despised, threatened his own life. Those who believed in his worth tried to stop him. They kept watch on him constantly. No blade to shave with. Not even allowed to sleep or bathe alone. They took away his choice entirely, and probably forced his decision by doing so. While his guard was at the toilet, he gouged open his own throat with a paper knife.

Was he a coward, this man? They call it the coward's way out. Don't call him a coward till you've weighed a paper knife in your palm. Not till you've tried the frank, blunt brink against your windpipe.

After he picks himself up, Jack shaves with his new cut-throat razor. He holds the blade inwards, stroking it with his thumb, feeling the comforting sharpness, so honed it has to be restrained. The razor wants to sever his skin. That's why it feels so good to shave with. Jack feels alive this close to the choice. He senses intensely the vertigo of possibility – the fear that he might go with the urge to slip into jugular. And, having made his decision, not dying makes him feel stronger.

He grins to himself while he mops the floor, satisfied with his discovery of the 'crease guard' button. Not knowing why this should have drained the remaining water, and set the machine to spin, but contented that it has.

His good white shirt waves a trunk-like sleeve at him, as it billows around in the heat of the dryer; the rest of his clothes sit in a damp pile on the counter. A fresh batch of fish fingers are wheezing gently in a cleaned-off oven; and there is still an hour to go.

He's meeting Chris and Steve the mechanic, for a couple of drinks before they join the others. He's pleased. He's had enough of deep-ending. If Jack had ever been swimming he would be an 'ease your way in from the shallows' type of a swimmer. He doesn't know many of the people coming out tonight, but he's chatted to Steve the mechanic a couple of times. There are four Steves where they work, so Steve the mechanic is always given his full title.

Chris and Steve the mechanic are already in there when Jack pushes open the pub's heavy, brass-handled door. Chris wolf-whistles, feigning surprise at Jack's smart dress. The white shirt was a present from Terry. It used to belong to his son, who started body-building and can't fit into it anymore. It's Ralph Lauren; Jack knew its quality right away. The Chelsea Headhunter, who shared his cell for a while, had the polo horse tattooed on to his chest at just the same spot.

Jack gets a round in. He stumbles his words and fumbles his coins, when a barman eventually picks him from the pack, long after his natural turn has elapsed.

'You should have brought a tray,' says Steve the mechanic, at the inexpert way Jack handles the three pints.

'He looks like he's got enough to carry,' laughs Chris. He smiles generously at Jack.

Chris has a fantastic smile, sort of conspiratorial – 'you and me mate,' it says, 'against the fucking world; and it doesn't matter if we lose, because there'll still be you and me'. Birds love it too. They read their own versions. Actually he's not a bad-looking bloke, Chris, but he slicks his thick black hair forwards with so much gel that it looks plastic; like a Lego man's.

The drink is doing nothing so far to calm Jack's nerves. And he's nearly finished his pint, while the other two have barely started theirs. He knows he's got to go slow. 'Alcohol preserves everything except secrets,' Terry told him. Jack's stomach is churning, and even though sat down he feels strangely off-balance. He tries to take part in the conversation, but Steve the mechanic and Chris are discussing chat-up lines. The topic makes Jack feel his difference, keeps him silent.

'I'm telling you,' says Chris, 'a chat-up line only works if the lass fancies you anyway, in which case it's irrelevant. You might as well say "fancy a shag, love?"'

'I heard they did a study that if you ask ten girls for a shag one of them would say yes,' says Steve the mechanic.

'Exactly, if they fancied you anyway. Which goes to prove that chat-up lines are pointless. Although you're probably asking mingers anyway, by the time you get to number ten.'

'But if you used a good chat-up line then maybe number two or number three would say yes.'

'In which case, how would they know it was one in ten? If the second one said yes then that would be one in two, wouldn't it? It must be the last one that says yes, or the study wouldn't make sense.' Chris grins widely, chuffed with the brilliance of his argument. 'Where did you hear of this "study" anyway? I mean, who does a study on how many women put out? It's not going to be some balding, speccy professor, is it, or else there'd be none in ten.'

'It was on the radio,' says Steve the mechanic, a bit sheepishly.

'I reckon it was on that special radio in your head,' says Chris, and messes up Steve the mechanic's spiky blond hair.

Steve the mechanic looks annoyed for a moment, but then laughs.

'Come on then, Chris,' he says, 'what's your best chat-up?'

'I just told you, I don't believe in them.' He takes a sip of his pint, and then wipes a blob of froth from his nose. 'But if I did it would be: "you must have a mirror in your knickers".'

'Because I can see myself in them,' Steve the mechanic finishes with a groan. 'What about you, Jack? What's yours?'

Words flounder about in Jack's mind: half-remembered tales of ten pences and star thieves, labels and angels. But none of them come together to form anything repeatable. He feels flustered, and hoping it doesn't show, decides to shoot somewhere near the truth.

'I haven't really used chat-up lines. I suppose I just try to seem genuine, seem interested in them.' As he speaks he trails off, feeling the ridiculousness of his words.

Steve the mechanic shakes his head in wonder. Chris sucks in air between his teeth.

'I told you, mate, didn't I?' Chris says to Steve the mechanic. 'Our Dodger's a sly one. You should have seen the way the White Whale was drooling into his pocket yesterday.'

Steve the mechanic laughs, still shaking his head. 'That's really dirty fighting, that, Jack. "Seem genuine, seem interested," that's low tactics. How's anyone supposed to compete with that?'

'Mind you,' says Chris, 'you want to stay away from that White Whale. I'm telling you, she's got Penile Dementia, she'd swallow you up.'

'We'd have to change your name from Dodger to Jonah,' Steve the mechanic chips in.

Jack says nothing, he knows that he doesn't 'want to stay away' from Michelle, he really doesn't. In fact he wants to be just as close to her as it's humanly possible to be.

He sees her in the next bar they visit. She's wearing her

ultra-blond hair in a long ponytail. When she moves it seems to curl around her neck, like an animal, like a white furred fox. Most of the people from work are meeting up here. Chris and Steve the mechanic are engulfed in an ambush of clasped hands and welcomes. Jack feels insignificant: a moon orbiting around Chris. But he is conscious of some reflected glow: a couple of people say hi, or pat him on the shoulder. Michelle doesn't notice their entrance. She and her friend Claire are talking to two slightly older men in suits. Their money stinks, from right across the room.

The drinks are starting to have an effect on Jack. A little of his nervousness is leaving him, although he still feels distinctly uneasy in the crush of so many people. When it's his round he gets himself a pint of low alcohol lager, careful to place it so the other two both take a real one.

Even though his bladder feels bloated from the beer, his stomach knots each time he glances across the sea of heads in Michelle's direction. She is still apparently unaware of his presence, but laughs explosively whenever the taller of the two men speaks. Jack needs the toilet, but he's convinced that if he lets Michelle out of his sight she will fall for this suited stranger. Maybe she already has.

Conversations ebb and flow around him. Jack feels slightly dazed, catching no more than fragments. Nodding, trying to look as if he knows what's going on.

'The shark's just a shark, right,' he hears Chris say. 'No one calls it Jaws. It doesn't call itself Jaws. The film is called *Jaws*, the shark is just a fucking shark. So how can you say "I like the bit where Jaws bites the boat"?'

Jack is aware they're talking about films. Even so the conversation strikes his slightly woozy brain as bizarre.

Jack has seen *Jaws*. Actually, he didn't think much of it. When you've grown up in a shark tank you aren't afraid of big fish. He is wary of them, but he knows where to stand, where to stroke, to avoid getting bitten.

'*Apocalypse Now*,' says someone, who may be one of the other Steves.

'*Pretty Woman*,' says a small dark-eyed girl hanging off his arm. Steve the mechanic makes gagging noises.

Jack laughs, but one eye is always on Michelle. He wishes he could just go over there and say hello, start talking to her. They've visibly divided up now. Claire is chatting to one of the men while Michelle is with the other. The tall one, the funny one. Maybe Michelle's just helping Claire out, getting rid of the mate. Maybe she's no real interest except in helping her friend. If only Jack'd been able to tell her that he liked her, or give her some sign. If only he wasn't so unnerved by everything. Jack's bladder is bursting.

There's a long queue for the gents. Both the urinals are blocked. Jack has to wait, alone among strangers. His trainers, Terry's gift, swim in half an inch of communal urine. The man behind keeps putting a hand on Jack's arm to steady himself, just sober enough to realize that if he falls in here it's all over.

'You really have got the luck of the devil, Dodger,' says Chris, when Jack gets back. 'The White Whale was just over here looking for you.'

'Oh, really. Where is she?'

'It's all right. Don't panic. You're safe for the moment, she's gone.'

'Gone?' says Jack, his teeth grinding with the strain of trying to seem relaxed.

'Yeah, a whole bunch of them have gone to the club already. Steve the mechanic insisted we had one more here first. Bloody pikey's at the bar, probably just wants to get his round in where it's cheap.'

Jack looks over to where Michelle had been, and almost lets out a whoop when he sees that the two men in suits are still stood there.

★

One of the bouncers has a scar on his cheek like an action man. But there's a brutal honesty about it that you don't see on a plastic doll; this is not some ritualized duelling badge, it reminds Jack of prison faces, it talks about back alleys and broken bottles.

He doesn't care. He is exuberant, and fast approaching drunk. Steve the mechanic, as if aware of Chris's taunts of tightness, bought them a tequila each along with their pints. Jack can still feel a faint burn in his throat, even though it took ten minutes to walk to the club.

Just for an instant, before they go in, Jack looks up at the night sky and is struck by the unreality of it all. This feels like another world, another lifetime. A cool late summer's breeze blows him the perfume of a beautiful black girl who's one place in front. He's with his friend Chris and his new friend Steve the mechanic. He has drunk tequila, and told people his favourite film; it's *The Blues Brothers*. He didn't know that until tonight. And inside this club, this wide-windowed warehouse, is the girl who maybe, just maybe, he could love. Jack is torn between bitterness, that he has been deprived of all this for so long, and feeling that this moment has made every other moment worth while.

It doesn't occur to him that maybe he doesn't deserve it.

Jack's never heard music as loud as this. The base is vibrating his stomach. It's shaking the floor, making his legs tremble. Or are they trembling anyway? His white shirt is the brightest thing around. It glows in the dark, with an eerie blue luminescence. Chris moves off straight away, twisting and winding, never taking his eyes from the bar. Jack and Steve the mechanic go after him. Following his breadcrumbs deep into the forest.

When they see Chris again, even he is struggling to get the barman's attention. Jack has never seen so many women in such a small area. These are not the same girls he has seen out before with Terry. They are not even the same as the girls that he has seen tonight. They are dressed purely for clubbing. What little they wear is designed to magnify, not to conceal. In fact the garments, all laces and lycra, are somehow more suggestive of nakedness than nakedness itself could ever be. They are closer to wrapping paper than clothing. Jack doesn't know where to look. He is torn between gazing, mesmerized, and trying to look unfazed. Every turn of his head brings into view a new species: of legs, of lips, of breasts, of hips, of eyes, of thighs.

The girl who was in front of them in the queue alights next to him. Her closeness is painful. She catches his eye, and through the confidence of the beautiful forces him to look away. She laughs, though not unkindly, and turns to talk to her friend, about things of consequence to them.

There is no sign of Michelle, but the club is filled with corners and crevices. The whole of the dance floor is sunken in the centre, like a rave in the *Blue Peter* garden. People are dancing everywhere though, not just in the middle, but by the bars and the railings, and even as they move through the crowds. Three girls flick and grind their hips beside a pillar, beguiling Jack, taking him somewhere ancient and instinctive.

'Girls that dance like they're good in bed never are,' Chris shouts in Jack's ear, seeing where he gazes.

'Chris is full of shit,' Steve the mechanic shouts in his other ear.

Jack nods, to either or both, and drinks the bottle of beer that Chris handed him. Chris says something to Steve the mechanic and dissolves into the hot crowd, immediately lost in the mingle of short-distance travel.

'Where's he gone?' Jack asks.

'He's gone to get something. It's a surprise,' Steve the mechanic tells him.

Water drips on to Jack's forehead, condensed sweat from

the ceiling. Some of the blokes on the floor have got their shirts off; they're coated in a sheen that reflects the colliding kaleidoscopes of light. Most of the dancers seem to be doing their own thing. A few around the edges dance in pairs or small groups, but those in the thick appear almost oblivious to people around them. There are no formalities, no rules; no two people are dancing the same way; except for the few who move the least, who look as though they would rather not be dancing at all. Jack knows that he would be one of these: uncertain, wary of humiliation, marking himself because of this.

Jack has never danced. Not just never in public, never at all. No school discos, no family weddings, no parties, no clubs, no front rooms, no miming in front of the bathroom mirror. Never. Jack is not even sure that he could dance as well as the few foot-lifting marginals. How could he? Where would he begin?

One cluster fascinates him. They stand half on the steps that lead down to the sunken circle. Their hands and fingers move rapidly, but out of time, too fast even for the DJ's raging BPMs. When the strobe starts the cluster's movements stop altogether, or at least it seems that way to Jack. They just appear in position. Like a series of strange still photographs. It is only when one gives a thumbs up that Jack realizes. Not dancing but signing. They are all deaf. A club within the club. Where the conversation-killing music makes their disability an advantage. Jack wonders if they can still feel the base up their spines, like he can.

Then he spots her: Michelle is down there, dancing with Claire and the small dark-eyed girl and a couple of the lads. He watches her easy movements, she isn't an amazing dancer, not like the hip grinders, but she is effortless, unencumbered. She has an unpractised grace that makes the tiny girl beside her seem almost ungainly. Maybe feeling his eyes on her, Michelle looks around to meet them; her ponytail wafts down to her shoulder like a feather boa. She smiles at him and waves him down. For a moment Jack sees himself striding down there, strutting – no, slinking – like John Travolta. He sees the crowd parting slightly to let him pass, waiting, anticipating his moves. But Jack has no moves, and the vision sinks away from him. He shakes his head at Michelle, trying to keep up his smile and mouths 'maybe later', which he doubts she gets from that distance.

Michelle keeps dancing, but facing his way. She is wearing a black dress that shows miles of her milk-gum breasts. Jack can feel his pulse in his throat.

'She wants you bad, my friend,' says Steve the mechanic. Jack had almost forgotten he was there. 'If you want to go there, then go there. Don't pay too much attention to Chris. Yeah, he'll probably rag you for a couple of days, but that's life: you know what they say about fat girls and mopeds. But that Michelle's a good lass. Brainy, too, there's more to her than meets the eye.'

Chris comes back, face split with a grin like a grapefruit, before Jack can find out what 'fat girls and mopeds' is supposed to mean.

'D'you get them?' Steve the mechanic asks.

Chris nods. 'I'm out of beer though. Come on, Dodger, your round.'

Jack heads off to the bar. This is starting to be a very expensive night. Does it always cost this much to go out? Five or six hours ago he was the richest he'd ever been in his life. Now he seems to have drunk a big chunk of that wad.

He's a little unstable on his feet as well; but despite the strangeness of everything, he's more at ease than he can ever remember being. He's spent the last seven years in a state of permanent tension, looking for clues as to who's going to kick off, screening his words for fear of being stained a nonce, watching for where to sit and when to shit and waiting to breathe. Now he feels relaxed. Maybe it's the drink, but he's suddenly sure that no one's going to rumble him. It's all going to be all right.

He has a problem finding Chris and Steve the mechanic, when he gets back to where they were. But he spots them a wave away, where they've secured a high round table. Chris leans on it with accomplished nonchalance.

'Cheers, Dodger,' he says, relieving Jack of a bottle of Bud. 'Now open your mouth and close your eyes. I've got a present for you.'

Certainly alcohol is a big player, but there's more than this, maybe it's trust in Chris. Maybe Jack's just used to obeying orders. Whatever the reason, he does what he's told. He feels a lump on his tongue, which tastes somewhere between salt and sulphur, and when he's told to swallow it, he takes a swig of Bud and it slips away.

'What was that?' Jack asks, his bleary mind aware that something peculiar just happened.

'An Elephant,' says Chris. 'A White Elephant. They're supposed to be dead good.'

'An elephant,' Jack repeats. 'I don't understand. What d'you mean, an elephant?'

'A pill, Dodger, that's what I went to get. We've just had ours. I thought Steve had told you.'

'I thought you were going to tell him,' Steve the mechanic protests. 'It was your present.'

It's evident from Jack's face that he's not happy. Chris puts his arm around him: 'Look, I'm sorry, mate, I should have said something earlier. I mean, I thought you knew. You being the bad boy, I assumed you'd be up for it.'

Jack doesn't know what to say. He can't tell them that he's on licence for life; that any minor infringement of the law could put him back inside. He can't say that he's spent seven years, longer if you count the homes, trying to stay away from drugs. That Terry told him there were people who would use any blemish on his prison record to prove he wasn't reformed. How could he explain that he's already dazed beyond belief with novelty, and battered by the alcohol, and that this night had been the best night of his life, but now it's suddenly not?

But he doesn't have to say all this because his eyes tell a tale; and Chris is drunk not stupid.

'Look, it's cool, Jack, it's no big deal. We'll be with you, we're all in the same boat, and it'll be wicked. Nothing bad's going to happen. What could happen? Losing a bit of control never killed anyone.'

'Yeah, no one dies on pills, unless they take like twenty and dance for two days and die of exhaustion,' Steve the mechanic joins in. 'Or they drink too much and drown, or not enough and overheat their brains. Or…'

Jack doesn't know Steve the mechanic well enough to tell if he's being very dry or very dense; but Chris says, 'Steve!' and raises an eyebrow, which is sufficient to shut him up.

'It'll be fine, Dodger,' Chris says. 'But we're all getting a bit old for that peer group pressure shit. If you really don't want to that's no big deal either – go to the toilet and make yourself sick. Just bring that baby right up.' Chris laughs. 'You're looking a bit worse for wear anyway, a nice chunder'll probably do you good.'

The DJ shouts, 'Scream if you want to go faster!' like they used to on the waltzers at the fairground. People do scream. There's a roar from the sunken garden; but Jack realizes that he doesn't want to go any faster. That everything is moving quite quick enough for the moment.

'I'm sorry, mate,' he says. 'I don't mean to be ungrateful, but I think I am going to go to the toilet.'

'That's cool,' says Chris. 'It's not a problem.' And he is clearly doing his best to organize his soused features into an expression of brotherly concern.

Jack was worried that he wouldn't be able to make himself

sick. As soon as he smells the toilet bowl he realizes these fears were unfounded. Before he can even get his fingers near his mouth a sudden retch brings a beer-based stew gushing into the scarcely cleaner water.

'Someone's having a good time tonight!' a stranger's voice cackles from beyond the cubicle.

Jack spits to try and remove the swinging strands of mucus from his mouth. They cling like creepers, though, and he has to use the back of his hand to wipe them away, putting a stripe across a shirt cuff at the same time. He peers into the khaki swamp at the bottom of the bowl, hunting for the elephant. He can't see anything pill-like, but the effort of interrogating the organic matter so closely brings forth another volley of vomit.

The sinks outside are coated in cups and screwed-up paper towels, but the water tastes flinty and fresh. Jack washes his hands and his face, and tries to clean off his cuff a bit. Beside him a skinny, ginger bloke is filling a plastic bottle with water. He is dripping with sweat, and chews gum with a bottom jaw that chomps sideways like a manic cow. His pupils are huge, like pebbles polished round and smooth, but with a warmth in them that makes a grin shoot across his still swaying mouth when he sees Jack looking at him.

'It's fucking heaven tonight, innit?' ginger bloke says, with a real strong southern accent. But before Jack can even start to form an answer, the man is off, already dancing as he passes through the toilet door. Just as it's about to close, he turns and shouts: 'Be lucky, mate.'

F is for Family, Fathers, Fidelity.

It was the twelfth of December, the twelfth month. *A* was twelve. The electric clock/radio by his bedside table said 12:01. *A* was waiting for it to read 12:12, he hoped there would be some sense of cosmic rightness when it did.

At 12:11 there was a knock on the door. It was Terry, *A* could tell. He hadn't known Terry long, but there was something calmer, more patient, that separated Terry's knocks from the rest of the staff. He knocked from genuine politeness, not formality.

'Come in,' *A* said, although the lock was on the other side.

Terry did. 'It's your mother,' he said. 'There's no easy way to say this.' Though he had just used the easiest, because *A* now knew the rest.

A's face froze, as it tried to catch up, as it tried to register the news. Then it crumpled, and while he considered this fresh blow, the tears came.

He had known for three months his mum was dying, but still it hadn't steeled him to the shock. Neither had the long periods without seeing her. They had only made him miss her more. So he cried. He cried for her, he cried from guilt, he cried from self-pity and he cried for the loss of his last link to love.

Terry put his arm around him. Like he meant it. Like he might be a new link.

The last time A's mum had visited him in that home she reeked of perfume. As if by application of eau de toilette she could somehow persuade the staff she'd been a good mother. Maybe she was just trying to hide the stink of death. But perfume's attraction lies in the smell of decaying fruit, and A could see she was disintegrating before his eyes.

She never wore make-up when she came to see him. It only ended in sad clown streaks. Probably she never wore it at all anymore. She didn't know anyone in the town she'd been moved to, so why bother? She seemed like she didn't even know his dad any more. She looked old, and A understood that she was old. Because although she was barely middle-aged, that word supposes another half of life to come; and his mother didn't have this. She looked as ill as she was. The skin that hung limply from her face was a sallow yellow, the colour of congealed lard on unwashed dishes. When she told him that she had ovarian cancer, A could not dismiss the feeling that he was the seat and cause of this: the original cancer that came from those ovaries.

A's father had never visited. The first time that A saw him in eighteen months was at the funeral. He looked smart, that was what struck A first. He had never seen his dad in a suit, even at the trial. He looked too smart, A thought. He looked smarter than he looked sad. And he looked a lot smarter than he looked pleased to see A.

There were not many mourners. Both A's parents were only children, and A their only child. All the grandparents were long dead. The whole family was genetically inclined to disappearing. And a lack of relations had helped his parents vanish too.

The motorcade was one car long. Two if you counted the car his mother was in; stretched out in the back of a black hearse. Three if you counted the undercover protection squad officers, who followed just in case.

Protecting who?

Terry rode with *A* and his dad, in leather luxury. *A* cried freely. His father looked out of the window. *A* wished that Terry would comfort him. But it was his dad's job, not Terry's. Even if his dad didn't want it.

A had not been into church since the day when it all began, but it brought back no memories. This new-town church was red brick and squat, tacked on to a town hall and leisure centre. The sign outside was solid and bold, freshly painted. Fresher than the decrepit-looking vicar, with his greasy grey curls and pocked cheeks.

Reverend Long shook the hands of Terry and *A*'s dad, clearly unsure which was the parent of this boy. He managed to squeeze sympathy into his smile for the adults, but *A* could see he just wanted the funeral to be over.

The three fathers followed the coffin-bearers in, and *A* followed them all. There were a few more people inside the church. Mostly from his mum's new work, *A* supposed. New work, new identity, new town, new church, new life. She had a new life now, if you believed in that stuff.

The choir sang the 'All Creatures Great and Small' song. It was like a creature itself, a many-legged, many-backed white beast. Being a school day, it was mostly made up of the retired and the half-witted, over-enthusiastic substitutes. *A* couldn't remember his mother ever having been religious; but she had enjoyed repeats of the television series about the vets. He pictured his mum and him curled side by side on the sofa. His dread of a new week at school had always spoiled Sundays, and at the same time made him savour every second. There were no Sundays left now. They were all piled into a wooden box with brass handles.

A sat between his dad and Terry on the front pew. The vicar climbed the three steps to his oak soap box, and swallowed a burp, before saying: 'Dearly beloved.'

This minister, who didn't know *A*'s mother, spoke of things about his mother that *A* didn't know. Things about her life before he was born, and since he'd been gone. Things that his dad must have told the vicar to say, things that left a space where a child should have fitted.

The Jesus behind Reverend Long's head was full of space as well. Like the church itself, it was modern and simple and probably cost a lot more than it looked like. The cross was just two planks nailed together; and the figure of Christ on it was fashioned out of a single length of barbed wire. Like the thorny crown had spread all over his body. There was something frightening about the gap between the wire ribs, and the legs dangled spastically; badly made, as if the sculptor was already bored with his creation when he got to them.

A pushed his hands into his empty trouser pockets, twisting the spiral of unravelling material that he'd discovered at his trial. It had been his security blanket, that spot in his pocket; at a time when security was all around him, and nowhere to be found. One of the papers described him as 'nonchalant and arrogant' at the end of the first week. *A*'s lawyer must have known this wasn't true, but he was afraid the boy's body language was wrong, and *A* had to keep his hands on his lap for the rest of the month in court. It didn't make much difference to the jury.

The hole was deep. Six feet is not far up, but it's a long way down. Brown water lay at the bottom, and a worm struggled to escape it. *A* wondered if the worm would be better off not fighting. Drowning was supposed to be quite pleasant, if you just let yourself go.

★

A had gone into a gasping hiccuping state, where the tears no longer came. On the whole he preferred crying. When he cried he was less able to think about the pain.

A's mother had always told him that she wanted to be cremated when she was gone. She'd said she wanted her ashes thrown from Hartlepool pier, where his father had proposed. She hadn't talked to *A* about it at all when she knew she was dying. He supposed she'd changed her mind. But he didn't like the idea of her being eaten. Of the worms tugging themselves through her.

The bearers lowered the coffin down to plug the slit in the earth. 'Nature abhors a vacuum', his mother had told him once, when she was weeding her flower-bed. *A* realized by the graveside that his mother had filled a space in him. A vacuum that even nature refused. Maybe that anyone would refuse but a mother.

It was a hard sensation for a child to frame. It was a bit like when his father had taken down the hallway mirror. *A* had always glanced in it when he went past. Not from vanity, *A* was not equipped to be vain; more from brooding curiosity, to see what it was that made him so despised. After the mirror was gone *A* continued to look there for weeks, and the space always filled him with a yearning dread. When what he wanted was evidence that he existed, there was something horrific about finding just a blank wall, with a hole where a nail had been. That's how it was when he buried his mother.

It had been frosty for days. He could still see the caterpillar tracks in the grass of the miniature JCB they'd had to use for the grave.

On the vicar's direction, *A* and his father both took a handful of the hard earth. Which scattered and bounced on the coffin lid, like a soft drum roll. But nothing happened. There was no trick, no Paul Daniels to make it not be true.

The barely reverend R M Long finished with a drone that confirmed this was just work to him. Work that was nearly done. There wasn't going to be a reception for *A*'s mother. *A* had to go back to the home with Terry. His father had to sort out some affairs.

Though he was not supposed to, Terry left the two of them alone for a few moments before they got into the car. A chance for them to speak unencumbered by the presence of strangers. Something they had not done in nearly two years.

As it turned out, they didn't have a lot to talk about. When there's so much, where do you begin? They shook hands, brittly. And *A*'s dad told his son that he loved him, and that he'd come and visit soon; as mechanical as the digger in the distance. *A* said that he loved his dad too, and that he'd look forward to it.

A lie for a lie. A truth for a truth.

A month later *A* received a letter from his father. It explained that he had been offered work abroad. Part of a government contract in the rebuilding of Kuwait. Part of a protection plan, to shield him from the hate and the hysteria. He said he had to leave immediately, wouldn't be able to visit before he went.

An eye for an eye. A tooth for a tooth.

They weren't the only family separated that winter.

Terry told himself it was nothing, at first. Ignored the fact that his wife had started to rush to pick up the phone at certain times. Times when she was in any case lurking near it. Not setting any great store by his own appearance, Terry was curiously sensitive to that of others; and on some level he was aware that she was now wearing to work clothes which had previously been reserved for occasions. But he liked to see things used, and thought that this was good, marked a change perhaps in her hoarding habits. Even when a certain pair of French knickers appeared in the spiralled

Ali–Baba basket. A pair of white silk pants that aroused him even in thought. That he had only ever known her to wear when she wanted him to see them. Even when he found them dirty for the third week running, he could still believe that nothing was wrong.

Some people would simply not have spotted the signs, but little got past Terry. Friends, of whom he had many in those days, would describe him as acute, sensitive, intelligent; he was not a man easily duped. But above anything else they would call him optimistic. He was more determinedly positive even than Oscar, his hyperactively happy Labrador. Terry could set a spin on dark facts at which unemployment statisticians would hesitate. Engrossed as he was with his new charge, and the nagging question of whether the boy might indeed be as innocent as he continued to protest, Terry was easily able to sweep aside little inconsistencies in his wife's daily routines.

He took pride in his family and in his family life. His son, Zeb, having turned fourteen, was becoming a young man, in body at least, being still slightly tantrumous in temperament. Whenever Terry looked at him he felt a warmth in his chest, a happiness that life could have allowed him to produce such a thing. A human being had grown from nothing, a whole new person from the love of him and his wife. And now the tiny creature, that he had nursed and nurtured, that had once had hands so minute they couldn't wrap around Terry's smallest finger, now his son was beginning to want his freedom. To begin the part of life that Terry had always hoped would hold a father's greatest joy: watching his son carve his own place in the world; find the things that would make him an individual; perhaps some of the qualities of Kippling's 'If' poem, that Terry had hung in the bathroom.

They ate every night as a stable nuclear unit: father, mother, son. Home-cooked, nutritionally balanced meals, prepared, Terry presumed, with love. He and Zeb never did any of the cooking, but they sometimes did the washing up. Terry believed that his place at the dinner table was to try and discuss adult themes, to build his son's sense of self, and of right and wrong. Though he could feel his wife wasn't entirely comfortable with it, he often talked about his work in the secure accommodation, and in particular about the boy, only two years younger than Zeb, who had come into his care. Sometimes he even played up his charge's positive attributes a little, to try and show Zeb the complexities of life. How nothing was ever as straightforward as it seemed. How even criminals could be victims. How even killers could be in need of love.

Only when he felt sufficient gems of wisdom had been imparted would Terry finish his food. But he was a firm believer in leaving the tastiest part of a meal until last, so right until the final bite he could look forward to the best bit. Sometimes he discovered that the savoured morsel had become too cold or dry by the time it was reached.

Zeb chewed his food more times than was strictly necessary to swallow, and always ate his favourites first. After which he would sit sulkily and grudgingly toying with the rest. Or, if allowed, he would put his plate down for Oscar's over-enthusiastic, chomping chops.

Zeb's looks came from his mother: dark hair, brown eyes, skin that tanned at the mention of sunshine. But Terry had always secretly hoped that in teenage years his son was going to show that his character came from his dad. Not that he believed there was anything wrong with his wife's character: she just no longer seemed to care about things the way he did. Only about money and work.

She was personal assistant to the boss of a big construction company. She did his filing and his appointments, typed his letters. And eventually was persuaded to clutch him to her in regular, rough, stock-cupboard sex.

When she told Terry this, his fingers clawed into the paisley-patterned cloth of the sofa on which he'd been sat. He felt like he had been battered, and had to fight to suppress his own violent thoughts. He threw a figurine of Buddha at the wall, where it smashed and left a dent in the plaster. Only the plump, pink, smiling face survived, of what had been one of Terry's most prized possessions.

'Why?' he had asked her.

'I don't know,' she said. 'Maybe because you seem to care more about your work, about vicious little thugs, than you care about us. Than you care about me.'

He said: 'You know that's not true,' and she admitted that she did. But it was the best she could come up with. Other than that she didn't seem to love him anymore.

Terry wanted details, and he kept digging until he got them. Cutting himself deeper each time, like a self-harmer – the kids in the home who had discovered the only way to take away pain is to find a fresher, nastier pain. Which works, until the shock dies off and you need a new wound to concentrate on.

He ran through the images in his mind of the boss, the best lover the world has ever known, never failing or even straining to make his wife scream to climax. And the two of them, laughing in the contented aftermath, about the shoddy second-rate sex she used to have to make do with.

And he pictured everyone else he knew, all their mutual friends, who surely had been keeping a pitying silence about the affair. Who at best must have felt sorry for him, through the ridiculous small talk of dinner parties he'd been to, as the oblivious straight man to a charade of a couple. But who might have been sniggering behind his every word.

So they went their separate ways. Agreed a blameless split, for the sake of Zeb. There seemed little need for him to learn the sordid details of his mother's overtime duties. She didn't want to be with her boss anymore than she wanted to be with Terry, and soon moved company, with a glowing reference and a golden goodbye.

Terry moved to a small flat with few furnishings but a 24-inch TV, a video player and a settee which could turn into a bed, for when Zeb came to visit. The sofa-bed didn't get as much use as Terry had anticipated. He watched a lot of movies on it, but rarely his son sleeping. Another of life's pleasures had gone. He could no longer just look in at Zeb's peacefully heaving chest. No more see such calm, such protected contentment on his face.

Unable to break his promise and tell Zeb the full facts, Terry came to feel that he was taking the blame for the separation in his son's eyes. When they saw each other they didn't talk like they once had. There was no family dinner to engage over, just tinned food and takeaways. And as the weekends started to become more and more important to a teenage boy, his father began to see him less and less.

Finally Terry realized that he had been robbed. Not just of a wife, but of a son. He was not going to be allowed to partake in what he had relished for so long. He was not going to witness his boy's transformation into a man. Only from a distance. Only as a casual bystander. He was not going to be allowed his youth again, to live vicariously through his own genes. He was never going to hear what happened at the parties and the pubs. Never going to be a mate, a support, a friendly ear, a person to turn to, to depend upon. He would just be another absentee father, like the fathers of most of the boys in his care.

G is for Garden. Garden Party.

The people in the sunken garden are cheering again, when Jack gets out of the toilet. As he navigates his way back, he rolls his sleeves up like a sailor's, to hide his wet cuff. Jack feels like he's been a long time. He's relieved to see that Chris and Steve the mechanic are still there at the table. In fact they've been joined by someone, someone large and longed for. A red spotlight shines from behind her, illuminating like a halo.

'I was beginning to think you were avoiding me, Jack,' Michelle says. 'Remember, this was going to be our night first of all.' Her words are bold, but she seems less certain than normal, more coy. Or maybe the drink has made Jack more confident. Michelle tilts her head in a deliberately sexy way. Like Jack's a camera. Like she's a young Marilyn Monroe, size 16, from Salford.

'Come on, Chris, let's go for a wander,' says Steve the mechanic, winking almost imperceptibly at Jack.

Chris looks unsure, but goes when Steve the mechanic nudges his shoulder. Jack takes a slug of his beer, which is slightly flat but very welcome.

'So, you having a good night, Jack?' Michelle asks. She is stroking her plump hand up and down her tall thin gin and tonic. It takes a minute or two for Jack to construct this as carnal. He was thinking how the fluorescent lumps of ice look like the undersea shots from polar documentaries.

'Yeah, really good. Best night in ages,' he says.

'So what d'you know, Jack?'

He's come across this before, it's an invitation to converse. He knows that, but not much more. He knows that she has a place inside her, a space that it's possible for him to be in; and he knows that this thought is bizarre, and yet compelling.

'Luton are playing at home tomorrow.' Idiot, *he* doesn't even care about that. Why's he telling her?

'Come on, Jack, what d'you know?'

She's teasing him this time, he can see it in her smile. But, fuck, it's a lovely smile. Come on, say something good, say something clever. What would Chris say?

'Have you got a mirror in your knickers?'

Michelle laughs. 'Jack!' she says, feigning indignation. 'That's not the Jack I know.' Then she leans across the table and strokes a finger down the back of his left hand. 'What makes you think I'm wearing any knickers?'

Jack swallows, and looks at his hand. He almost expects to see a line down it. He can still feel where she traced, a tingle that stops at his knuckles. He plays back her words, 'what makes you think I'm wearing any knickers,' expecting to be unnerved by them, but finding them quite comfortable, finding that they fit somehow. In fact the words start to float. Washing up and down his chest with his breathing. Spreading waves of pleasure. They're mingling with the tingling in his hand. And that's flowed right up his arm now. And across his chest. Down the other side. Is this love? It must be. It must be love.

Trembling with delight, Jack looks deep into Michelle's come-to-tea eyes. He sees her looking into him too, and she seems even to like what she finds.

Jack has become intensely aware of the music. He can't stop his toes tapping, and his hands, moving like they've got minds of their own. He manages to push his mind back to Michelle. He loves her, he must do. Rushes of it flood him now, every time he exhales. He has to tell her, no more wasted opportunity, no more men in suits, he has to tell her.

'Michelle,' he says.

'Jack,' she says.

'I love you,' he says.

'Oh my God,' she says.

'I love you,' he says again.

'You're drunk, Jack.' She ruffles his fine blond hair. 'And those words are over-used. You don't really mean it.'

'I do, Michelle, I love you, I really do. I can feel it all over. I've never felt anything like this before.'

She takes his hand, which is jigging about on the table, and holds it in both of hers.

'Stop moving a sec, you little nutter. I mean, you just said a massive thing. I wasn't even sure that you fancied me, and then you say that.'

Jack smiles at her. He can feel the grin spreading, taking over his face, releasing even more waves of pleasure. Being in love is amazing. No wonder they make so much fuss about it. 'All you need is love,' someone once said. He's pretty sure it was Jesus. This could restore his faith. That ginger bloke in the toilet was right: it is heaven in here tonight. Being in love is like heaven, it's like total fucking ecstasy...

Oh shit.

'Oh shit,' says Steve the mechanic, as he returns to the table to find Jack maniacally drumming on it.

'Oh shit,' says Chris, as he sees Jack's giant pupils and monster grin. 'We were starting to think they were duds. I guess not, heh, Dodger.'

'You shit,' says Michelle. 'I should have fucking known. You're off your head, aren't you! You don't even know what you're saying.' She turns and walks off, leaving her drink, not once looking back.

'Oh shit,' says Jack.

'Leave it, Jack,' Chris tells him. 'They're best left when they're like that. I don't think you're in a frame of mind to talk her round now anyway.'

'What happened?' asks Steve the mechanic. 'You decide not to chunder it?'

'I thought I had. Now I've blown everything.'

But Jack doesn't feel like he's blown everything. In fact he feels like it wasn't that important after all. Michelle's sure to come around, isn't she. She doesn't understand at the moment, that's all. And every time he moves, he still gets a bolt of joy along his limbs. He can't not move, really. It's like the music's making him move.

'Plenty more fish, Dodger,' says Chris. 'Come on, let's hit the floor. I feel like I'm coming up now.'

Jack is drawn down to the sunken garden by the footsteps of his friends. Chris selects them a place in the spotlight shade of a pillar, and immediately starts to dance: weaving a wild Spanish style, out of keeping with the House that's playing. He grins like he's taking the piss, and spins about to eye the birds that dance behind him.

Steve the mechanic dances more tentatively, small gestures to the beat. Which is getting stronger. His feet look rooted to the ground except for occasional sideways slides. Jack watches him. Clumsily copies him, diluting already modest moves.

Michelle has not returned to the little group she was dancing with before. Jack finds that it really doesn't matter. He feels on top of the world. Dancing is easy, he's a natural. He knows he's high but he couldn't help it, could he? And all the pain has gone now. He is not threatened by anyone. Since it can never happen again he might as well just enjoy this once to the max. There'll be plenty of time to make up with Michelle. He's got the rest of his life, hasn't he? He's got his whole life ahead now. Steve the mechanic pats him on the back, and clenches into a half-hug. And Jack is sure that this moment will never fade. Everything is possible and wonderful. Nothing can ever go wrong again.

But the ginger bloke from the toilet is poking into the air at Jack. Moving towards him, bewildering him, shaking his confidence just when he thought he could dance. Just when he was slipping some new expression into his rented routine. Jack thinks that ginger bloke is laughing at him, pushing hands towards him, mocking him. He tries to copy ginger bloke's moves, mirroring to make himself less vulnerable. Ginger bloke seems to like this. His eyes sparkle and he exaggerates his dance: hands all over the shop, like an orangutan doing kung fu. Jack keeps copying, really loving it, realizing that ginger bloke was being nice all along. Not laughing at him; dancing at him. Friendship floats between them, Jack can feel it. Like he feels the strobe lights in his hair.

He spends two hours at this elevation. In this state of elation. Buoyant in a world populated by dancing strangers, who are no longer strange. With his friends Chris, and Steve the mechanic, and ginger bloke, and girl with flares, and other girl with blue highlights and a vest that looks like fish scales. There are others too who may not quite be friends, but must at least be acquaintances because they dance nearby.

They all clap and cheer when the music finally stops, and by the power of their collective will they force the DJ to play two more tunes. It is generally concluded that these are the best tracks of the night. And Jack is happy to agree with ginger bloke, that the evening has been: 'Well pucker.'

'Listen, mate,' ginger bloke goes on, shielding his eyes from the sudden rise of the house lights. 'I'm mates with the organizer, and there's going to be a massive after party. You gonna come?'

'I'm with my other mates,' Jack says, thumbing behind him to where Chris and Steve the mechanic have got an arm around each another.

'Bring 'em, man, bring 'em all. Look, I'll give you a wodge of tickets, you're all right you.'

From the back pocket of baggy trousers, he produces a stack of tickets like a TV gangster's bill-fold. He peels off six and hands them to Jack.

'If you need more come back to me, yeah,' ginger bloke says. 'I'm s'posed to have given 'em all out anyway.'

He saunters off into the thick of dazed clubbers, to distribute more tickets among the hardcore, some of whom are still dancing, oblivious to the fact that the music has died.

Chris is chuffed with the news of the party. He takes two tickets from Jack, and sets about finding a female who might be receptive to a last-minute panic chat-up. Steve the mechanic tells Jack that Michelle is still inside. And leads him to where she and Claire are sat, on a section of dark velvet sofa that runs a whole wall.

Claire and Steve the mechanic move to a table a few feet away, leaving Jack standing in front of Michelle.

'You can sit down, Jack.' She says, 'I'm not in a mard with you.'

Jack places himself beside her. His legs still want to move, but he's fighting it.

Michelle laughs. 'Look at your jaw going,' she says. 'You're gerning all over the place. I'm the idiot for not seeing it.'

'I've got tickets for a party,' Jack says. 'Do you want to come?'

Michelle shakes her head. 'I want to spend time with you, Jack. But not now. Not when you're like this.'

'But I'm all right, I feel great.'

'I bet you do, Jack, I bet you do. And you love me and the sex would be fantastic and you'd think that we have everything in common. But none of it would mean anything. You go to your party, Jack. I'll see you Monday.' She gets up, and with the palm of her hand wipes his sweaty forehead, and then she kisses it. Just once she kisses it, but she holds the kiss for a second or two, before she goes to get Claire. Jack touches the spot, sure it is glowing. He tries to remember the last time anyone kissed him, but can't.

'Haven't you got a home to go to?' a bouncer asks.

Jack has got a home. Even better is the fact that he's not going to it. He rejoins Steve the mechanic, and the two of them set off to find Chris, before the bouncers lose their patience.

A beige Nissan Sunny gypsy-cab drops them at the site of what the tickets describe as an 'After Hours Extravaganza'. They are still just three; unable to locate others from work to share their fortune, or women without a better offer. Their location is just a house, albeit huge. It's in a wide leafy grove, an inner-city suburbia.

The two brawny black guys at the door are not as fussed about the tickets as they are about a 'contribution to security'. Steve the mechanic is informed that security is more expensive than he obviously thought, and asked to donate again.

Chris leads them about from room to room, too quickly for Jack to take in as much as he wants. There are beers in the bathtub, so they grab one each, and queens in the kitchen, out of which Chris whisks them, almost as soon as they step in, with a mumbled: 'Let's check upstairs.'

Upstairs is not much cop. Bedrooms are either locked, or flocked with sitting, spliffing student types. Jack has no wish to be around more drugs, and to his relief his friends don't seem to fancy it either. The lengthy lounge is a dance-floor, but all three of them agree that the time for dancing has passed. Even Jack's virginal rushes have slowed to a lingering, easy pleasure; and the lounge is too packed anyway.

The dining room is home to DJs and decks, but through it, and out of a set of bright white plastic patio doors, they discover the garden. The night is still balmy; positively un-British, but the garden is green and pleasant.

There are fewer people out here, most of them sitting or lying on rugs or the lawn. A dreadlocked white bloke is breaking up wood from a stack of pallets to feed the fire.

'I know where you could get a fiver a piece for them pallets,' Chris tells Jack.

The fire is in a side-turned shopping trolley raised on bricks. It and the pallets look out of place in the neatly kept garden. There are dark trees and a board fence at the end. Someone's taking a piss down there. Everyone else is near the fire, many are not even talking, just staring into the flames.

The three of them sit down on a free patch of grass, in the vague circle around the fire. The beer Jack sips feels like a blanket. The can is comforting to the touch and the brew warms him.

'I'm going to try a few lines with that lass over there.' Chris nods in the direction of a blonde elf, sitting on her own.

'I thought you didn't believe in chat-up lines, oh great master,' Steve the mechanic says.

'This is different, not chat-up; foreploy.'

'Foreploy?'

'The plan that gets you into foreplay. Look and learn, boys. Look and learn.'

Chris gets up and, with Apache stealth, makes his way around the rear of the ring. He says something to the girl that Jack can't hear, but she smiles and says something back and Chris sits down.

'I can't bear to watch,' says Steve the mechanic. 'I'm going to get another tin, d'you want one?'

'Cheers,' Jack says.

The pill must have increased his tolerance, he thinks. He can't even begin to work out how many drinks he's had tonight, but he feels all right on it. More sober now than he was when he went into the club. What time is it anyway? It's too late to ask Steve the mechanic. He's nearly inside.

Chris looks as though he's doing all right. He's lying back on one elbow and the girl's laughing a lot. Jack is at once envious that Chris can have such an easy way with people, and proud to be his friend.

Two guys come out through the patio doors together, forcing Steve the mechanic to take a step back and wait for them to pass. They don't acknowledge him. They both wear hugely baggy jeans, crotches hanging almost to their knees. It's supposed to be a prison thing, where trouser distribution is haphazard, and the screws won't let you have belts. Jack doubts these two have been inside, though. Clothes that don't fit mean you have no respect. No one would advertise that.

There's something about the way the two guys walk so directly to Chris and the elf-girl that straightens Jack's back. Brings his thoughts to the moment. One of them, with a shaven scalp, says something to the girl, and she shakes her head. Then he says something to Chris, who just shrugs. The guy kicks out the arm that Chris is leaning on, so that he falls on his side.

Jack feels his balls being winched up close to his body, and his hair prickle upright.

Chris gets up as well. Leave it, Jack thinks. Please let him leave it.

It looks as though he's going to. Chris starts to walk away. But then the shaven-headed guy grabs the girl by her arm, tries to pull her to her feet. She yelps. Chris turns around. Jack stops breathing. The shaven-headed guy drops the arm and takes a step so that he's toe to toe with Chris. He's shouting. Or the adrenalin's pumping to Jack's ears.

'Do you not get it? Piss off, is basically what I'm saying!' There's a vein standing out on shaven-head's neck.

Come on, Steve, how long's it take to get a beer? Jack thinks. He doesn't need this, he can't afford this; where the fuck's Steve the mechanic?

Chris doesn't reply to the man, but he doesn't back away

either. Jack can see that there's really nothing between the two of them in height. The girl pushes herself away with her hands. It's OK, Jack thinks; if it's an even fight I don't need to get involved. He's got the impression that Chris would be able to handle himself. But maybe that's the impression Chris wants people to get. It doesn't necessarily mean a lot.

'Piss off!' the shaven-headed guy shouts.

'Fuck it, you warned him.' The other guy punches Chris on the side of his head, connecting on the 'f' of 'fuck'.

Totally blind to the blow, Chris is dropped like a sack of charcoal on a garage forecourt.

Jack is looking round, but there's no sign of Steve the mechanic and no one else looks like intervening. 'Let that be it. Let it be over.'

But the shaven-headed guy kicks Chris twice in the stomach, and his friend is lifting a foot to stamp on his head.

'No!'

Jack is not fickle. He's had few friends in his life, and he won't watch his friend's face get stamped on. He's on his feet in an instant.

Jack is not clumsy. He closes the distance fast, dodging between people. He launches himself over a brace of sleeping hippies. And lands on his feet, still in stride.

Jack is not big. He's skinny in fact, by nature. But weightlifting in prison has put dense muscle on his light bones. His momentum carries him straight into the shaven-headed guy. He ducks his shoulder and uses the force of the impact to stay on his feet. Not expecting the collision, shaven-head is knocked to the floor, landing in a tangle on the girl.

Jack is not a fighter. But he's been in enough fights to know how to take a punch. As the second guy swings, he steps forwards, inside the blow. It barely catches him, glances the side of his head. He steps in further and locks his hands together, behind the man's neck.

Jack is not dirty. But he fights dirty. Fighting is dirty. Distinctions are made by people who haven't had to fight. Jack head-butts, grunting as he does so, face tight with the effort. He feels something crunch under his forehead. The man tries to hit back, but he can only reach the back of Jack's head, and knocks him into his own nose again. Jack sees a blur of red in front of him. He doesn't know if it's blood or adrenalin. He butts the man again anyway. And again before he's recovered. The man tries to pull him off, but Jack just keeps slamming his head forwards into the same spot. His head hurts and his neck hurts. But it isn't him that's squealing.

'Jack, leave it!' Steve the mechanic pulls them apart. The man drops to the floor when Jack lets go of him. He's got blood all over his face. Jack has too.

The other guy, shaven-head, is lying on his back.

'Steve smacked him with a tin of Stella,' Chris says. The can is nestled in the grass, gently fizzing from its side. Chris is on his feet, holding his stomach.

Some people are staring at them. Other people are staring anywhere but at them. Jack wipes his face on his shirt. Trembling like old age.

'Let's get the fuck out of here,' says Steve the mechanic.

He and Chris start running for the end of the garden. On auto-pilot Jack follows them. He's faster, they all jump on to the fence at more or less the same time. It collapses under their weight, sprawling them down into an alley. They can't see anyone following them, but they leg it anyway. They don't stop until they're almost knocked down by a cruising mini-cab driver. Who eyes Jack's red-stained shirt, but is willing to take them for twenty quid upfront.

'What the bloody hell have you lot been up to?' the driver asks, when they're in the back.

'You should have seen the other fellas,' says Chris. Him and Steve the mechanic laugh with the safety.

Jack does not laugh. Jack feels his whole world crumbling around his ears; sees the prison gates opening up in front of him – reaching out for him, like the long sticky tongue of a frog. Of a filthy, gloating, wide-mouthed frog.

'Come on, Bruiser.' Chris puts his arm round him. 'You should be on top of the world. You're a hero, son. A proper hero. It's just the come-down making you feel crap.'

'Yeah, I reckon it's time for bed,' Steve the mechanic says. 'We'll drop you off first, heh, Bruiser. What a night. What a fucking night.'

H is for Home.
Home Help.

The screw that brought *A* back from the infirmary took him to a new cell, on a different landing, a different wing. It looked just the same as the old one, although the door was painted in a primary-school yellow. The screw told him he was now in cell 17, threes, Kestrel wing. His new pad-mate was called Hacendado-563.

'Cheers, sir,' said Hacendado to the screw, when he saw *A*. 'Twoing me up with Quasimodo. Thanks for that one.'

A knew he looked a state. His face was purple, his lips busted and swollen, one of his eyes sealed shut, the good one blackened and bloodshot.

'Sorry,' he said to his new pad-mate.

Hacendado looked at *A*, and raised a dark eyebrow.

'Sorry is a large word, my friend; and apologizing to someone you don't know looks weak.'

'I'll leave him for instruction in your capable hands then, Hacendado,' said the screw. 'He's fresh in, first timer.' And he locked the door.

A stood, holding his bed-pack, all he had: two blankets; two T-shirts; two jeans; two jumpers; two pants; two socks; one jacket; one sheet; one pillowcase; one shoes; one toothbrush; one toothpaste; one razor; one soap; one shaving brush; one comb; and one property card to list the above.

Hacendado chipped himself slickly on to the top bunk and turned on his radio. *A* walked to the lower bed and sat down on it, still holding his bundle. With his tongue he felt the raw gap where his front teeth had been. He could have done with a dump, but the toilet was at the end of the bed, in plain view. Unsure of etiquette he thought it better to wait.

The lights went out before he had moved or spoken.

During the ten days that he'd spent in reception *A* had heard the nightly chorus of conversation from remote windows. Isolated down in the lowest coldest cells. Locked up alone for twenty-three hours a day, he had longed for this human contact. Voices, too faint to hear the words, spoke to him of solidarity. And singing, there was often singing, he could make out nursery rhymes. Though he feared what Feltham was going to fling, *A* was sure that he'd be better off up on a wing. In a paired cell where the shared hell could be halved. But his first pad-mate had nearly killed him, and his new one was ignoring him. When the voices started *A* began to believe that there was no amity left in the world.

Suck your mum. Fuck you. Batty boy. Batter you. Fucking kill yous. Sing you shit. Arren sucks screws. Baa baa black sheep. Window warriors. You'll be sorry. Quarter in the morning or I break your fucking arm. Bitch had a rape alarm. Fresh Fish threes 17. Eighteen. Yes sir, yes sir, three bags full. Stop when I say so. Lay low. Tomorrow Jethrow. Kenny says he'll chivvy your throat. Your mum's so fat, so ugly, so broke. Your mum fucks old bald Pakis. Gives hand jobs outside Stakis. I'm a soldier. One for the master and one for the dame. You ain't getting no older. Cut you a slash like a gash. Like your mum's. One for the little boy who lives down the lane. Sing it again, bitch. Again.

A could hardly believe what he was hearing. Threats and insults and bullying and bragging aggressed his ears. Some messages echoed as they passed along whole wings of barred windows. Some were aimed close to home. Live and direct. Live and kicking.

'Fresh Fish, threes 17, open your window,' someone shouted.

'That's you,' Hacendado said from above.

'Fresh Fish, threes 17, come to your fucking window.'

'Open the window, Fresh Fish.' this time it sounds real close, like the pad next door.

'You'd better go.' Hacendado said impassively, 'They won't let up until you do. You might as well go right away and not look scared.'

A was scared. But he put down his bundle, got up, and trod the four steps to the wire-crossed pane of glass.

'Fresh Fish, threes 17, open your fucking window.'

'Wait till I'm under the blanket before you open it,' Hacendado said. 'It's gonna be cold out there.'

A was shivering already. There were brown splatters all over the glass and the once-white ledge. Three truncheon-thick bars divided the world beyond them. He opened the window and the choir outside was immediately amplified. Calls bounced about like crows, squawking from place to place. Ugly, murderous, bare-faced and loud. Claims to have done things to each other's mothers, that *A* hadn't known could be done at all.

'Fresh Fish, threes 17, open your fucking…'

'It's open!' Hacendado shouted from his bunk.

'What's your name, Fresh Fish?' someone nearby asked.

A told them, told them his fake name anyway. His stage name for this cage.

'What you in for?'

Terry had said that question was against the rules; and said that everyone would ask it anyway. They'd practised together, dates and details. Facts learned so well that one day they would become Jack's: another young man with a similar history. Another young man who was not a nonce.

'You a nonce? Why ain't you answerin'?'

Not a nonce. Joy-rider. Happy car theft. Care-free crime. Pleasant escapism. Entertainment not evil. Everyone well-insured, everyone's a winner. No victims, no violence. Not a nonce, oh no, not a nonce. Nothing like that.

'Speak, you nonce! What you in for?'

'Taking and driving away.' A realized that he was squeaking a bit, his voice going involuntarily high. He tried to calm himself, stretched out his fingers by his side to give him something to concentrate on.

'Suck your mum!'

'My mum's dead.'

'Suck your mum RIP.'

There was laughter at this from all around. A was momentarily taken back to a time when he always seemed to be encircled by mocking laughter. But his present was so pressing that the memories quickly crumbled in on themselves.

Emboldened by a successful strike, the same voice ordered A to sing.

'Sing what?' he asked.

'Mummy had a little lamb.'

More laughter. Some people were banging on their bars to make noise.

'Sing it, Fresh Fish, or I'mna break your fucking legs in the morning.' The voice was shouting. A could imagine its huge owner, spittle flying from his enraged lips.

'Don't sing,' said another voice, softly from in the cell. Hacendado was sitting up, blanket still over his lap.

'But you heard him, he said he'd do me if I don't.'

'And if you give in he'll make you sing it again and again until you can't do it anymore; and then maybe he'll do you anyway. You've got to keep your fucking dignity in here, man. It's all you've got.'

'Sing it, you fuck!'

'Don't do it, mate. Trust me, I'm telling you the truth. Shit, I don't want a muppet for a pad-mate.'

A went to close the window.

The voice started screaming at him: 'You shut that and I'mna fucking do you tomorrow. I'll fucking mash you up. Don't shut that window, you little shit.'

Then it was done. The window was shut. And a door shut with it, to what might have been.

'Now what?' *A* asked his pad-mate.

'Now we go to sleep. People are always making threats in here, chances are nothing'll come of it.'

A roughly spread one of his two blankets and lay down under it fully clothed. Course fibres scratched at the welts around his neck. Though he knew he couldn't sleep, somehow he did.

Shrill shrieks joined *A*'s dream, turning to the scream of a girl who could never now become a woman, though in the dream she somehow might have been his mother. But the shrieks continued even after they broke him into a world of musty, grey morning light. He was immediately aware of where he was, but the noise was still dislocating. It told him that he could not go on like this, that something had to give.

'Fucking peacock.'

A recognized the voice as Hacendado-563's, great start to the day, wake to an insult.

'They're supposed to be calming, I think. But they make that noise every morning. Some governor's brilliant idea to bring them in when they changed all the wings to bird names.'

'Sorry?'

'The peacocks.'

'Ah.' A realization sinks in, a slim relief: the day's first bump just driftwood.

'But what was it going to achieve anyway, changing the names? They're still the same fucking buildings, still filled with the same scum and the same screws. Was it meant to be a joke? Like "wings", or "jail–bird"; or is it supposed to rub our noses in it, remind us what real freedom is? What goes through these people's minds?'

Hacendado dropped himself over the side of his bunk. His bare feet landed with a squeak on the lino floor. 'You are a mess, aren't you?' he said, looking at A. Then he hitched up his prison issue, white Y-fronts, which looked at least a size too big, and walked the four feet to the seat-less steel toilet. Hacendado's piss pounded against the thin metal, sounding like rain water down guttering. His hair was cropped close to his scalp. From behind, like this, you could see lines where it wouldn't grow, scar tissue.

He turned around and carefully washed his hands. Then he walked over to a locker, which was lying on its side. Not as if it'd been knocked over, but set precisely in the centre of the longest wall.

'You smoke?' he asked.

'No.'

'Don't start. You've got an advantage in here if you don't smoke. Most of the guys spend three quarters of their pies on burn. Look at this.' He pulled a neatly folded pair of jeans out of the locker and put them on. Then carefully, one by one, he took out sixteen identical bars of soap and placed them on top of the cabinet. Four perfect rows of four. Then he put beside them six unopened packets of Juicy Fruit chewing gum and four Whisper bars. 'I've got everything in there; phonecards, crisps, razors, hairbrushes, deodorants. The soaps look the best though.' He stood back to admire them.

'I always put my lockers on their side, nice to display your stuff. Also, it makes the pad look bigger if everything's below waist height. It's all about presentation in here. Look smart and clean, and keep your pad smart and clean. It shows you respect yourself. Which is the first step to getting respect.'

Breakfast was served at the hot-plates at the end of each wing. Hacendado had taken a wrap of toilet paper, from one of five fresh rolls, none of which had ever seen a toilet. He used half of it to wrap a stack of bread in, and gave *A* a section to do the same.

'Take a few slices back to the pad to eat later. You keep it clean and fresh this way.'

To *A* the bread tasted out of date already; there was a varicose vein of mould running through one of his slices.

Because they were on the third landing, the threes, there was netting strung about beyond all the railing. It looked like the stuff of circuses: springy, for capturing mis-timed trapeze leaps. But it didn't seem to protrude far enough to stop a determined jumper. *A* was sure you could clear it. He could imagine himself taking a run at it, legs tensed to spring, soaring, headlong, head first, fearless beyond that netting. The picture remained in his mind of himself suspended, just before the instant when the glorious dive would become a terminal plunge. He was handsome in the picture, wholesome, and though he was static he was active. Frozen forever in a position of decision.

When he asked Hacendado about the netting, later, he was told it wasn't meant to stop jumpers, just to stop people being thrown.

After breakfast they were locked in again. Everyone but *A*, who was taken to meet his Personal Officer, PO. The screw he was supposed to go to with his problems. The man had sweaty jowls, and a greasy brush-over.

'Just call me sir,' he said. 'I prefer the inmates not to know my real name. Rather like yourself,' he chuckled a joyless laugh. 'But make no mistake about it, that is where any similarity between the two of us ends. Right there.'

A shifted his weight on the moulded plastic chair, and nodded, not sure what response he was expected to make.

'This is your Wing flimsy,' the screw said, opening a brown manila folder, with shiny metal clasps for putting in a filing cabinet. 'Everything you do inside goes in here. You're not doing badly so far. Less than twenty-four hours and you've been beaten and changed wings. These sorts of things can create work for me. Please try to avoid them.' He put down the file, folded his arms and looked straight into *A*'s eyes. 'I've read your full file, by the way. I know who you are.'

A felt a squirt of breakfast and bile try to rise up to his throat. He could taste the acid.

'But I am a professional,' the screw continued, 'and regardless of the utter disgust I have for you, I will treat you like any other of my personal charges. There are those, among the officers, who would not be so understanding. Who might share the information with the prisoners. I am sure you are aware of the possible consequences of this.'

A nodded.

'Because of this your file has been placed in the care of the number one governor. Anyone wishing to see it must approach him. But since this in itself is so unusual, it would still arouse some suspicion.' His voice moved up a level. Stiffly, almost angrily, he said: 'Your best chance is to stay so bloody low profile that none of the officers bother to check your file at all. Do you understand? No fights, no complaints, work hard, but not too hard, obey their every word, but don't crawl, and you might just get out one day more or less intact. You got that?'

A nodded again.

'Don't just nod. You say "Yes, sir".'

'Yes, sir.'

'We've had them all in here, you know: Rat Boy; Spider Boy; Blip Boy; Safari Boy, every one of those tabloid touted toe-rags has passed through Feltham. And do you know what? None of them was any different to any other little thief. But you, you and your young friend were responsible for a genuine bloody national tragedy. Don't, for one second, ever make me regret helping you to hide in here.' His mouth twisted as though to let A see what it would look like in rage. 'Because they would tear you apart.'

Then in an instant the screw's entire countenance changed. He closed the folder in front of him, and with spread fingers, pushed it to the side of his large desk. 'Oh, on the governing governor's orders you're going to continue to see a psychologist once a month. Looks as though I should probably get you to a dentist too. Now, have you anything that you would like to raise?'

A looked at the man. How he leaned forward with a deliberate smile, as if he cared. He didn't care, A knew. But he also knew this might be all the help he was going to get.

'I don't know whether I can make it,' he said finally. 'I don't think I can take years of this. I don't see how I can do it.'

'That's not a problem.' The screw laughed his little joyless laugh again. 'You just do what you can.' He pushed a button that buzzed the door open. 'I'll see you do the rest.'

I is for Insects.
As Flies to Wanton Boys.

Time flies when you're having fun. When you're young. Days passed *A* and *B* by, in the days when they were together. There was no maths and no spelling; Fridays were pretty much the same as Tuesdays. And though there were plenty of games, there was only ever one team.

They would meet at the same crossroads where their ways parted again at night. The first there would hang around on a bleached bench that had been presented 'With love to the memory of Bernard Debbs'. Once *A* tried to erase those words while he waited, scribbling over the brass plaque in a stolen red marker. But the engraved letters collected more ink than their surroundings, and became, if anything, more defined. Usually he would hold on until *B* arrived before doing much. No point in using up a good idea on your own. Most things he found were much better now he had a friend. And it was together that they carefully carved their initials all over the bench. Using the powerful retractable blade of *B*'s Stanley knife. Stonelee knife he called it.

Sometimes *B* brought other tools with him, borrowed from his brother's box. Pliers, screwdrivers, spanners, wrenches. On days like these they would spend their time looking for things that could be undone, in acts of careful vandalism. Other days they just smashed and stole stuff.

Once B brought with him a ball of thick wool, a trowel and an old darning needle.

'For killing eels,' he told A. But he wouldn't tell him more until they got to the right bit of the Byrne.

A had never been down to the Byrne before. He'd watched it from a distance, seen the water run red then white. Leaving Stonelee stained with iron and aluminium salts. It congealed nearly to black in the flatter sluggish section, flowing under the unfinished ring road. It was here that B wanted to go, under the bridge like trolls. It was where eels lived, he said.

This was the Byrne at its worst, concreted like a canal. But disused, overgrown, steep stone sides crumbling and dangerous. Clogged with weeds and lumped with dumped mortar from building the road a decade ago. Blocks of stone still uneroded by the slow flow. A had been forbidden ever to approach this part of the Byrne. Which was in itself reason enough to go there. Some mothers preferred to say that evil lurked under the bridge. And sometimes it did.

B picked up a used condom with his trowel and wafted it at A, making him shrink back from it. But not actually trying to get him with it. Not like when he'd been held down and smeared with shit from a nappy that the boys in his class had found in a skip. Although he could tell it was to be avoided, A wasn't really sure what the condom was.

'Is that from an eel?' he asked his friend.

B laughed and dropped the skin-like tube at his friend's feet, so that he could inspect it unafraid. 'It's a rubber-jonny,' he said.

A nudged it with a scuffed school shoe, not much the wiser, knowing only that he had on occasion been compared to such a thing.

'You put it over your dick so you don't get slime all over you when you shag a woman,' B explained.

It looked impossibly large for such a purpose to A, but he knew his ignorance next to his worldly companion. He kicked the jonny into the Byrne. Where it floated, no doubt due to its slime repellency, on the water's dismal skin. Watching the jonny's sorry progress was like trying to see the minute hand of a watch move. The debris-choked channel drifted at the precise border between flow and stagnation. It wasn't long before they took to trying to sink the rubber-floater with rocks. The Byrne swallowed them with disdainful ease; eventually sucking down the jonny too.

'Come on then,' B said, brandishing his trowel. 'We're going to need a lot of worms if we're going to go eel-bobbing.'

'Eel-bobbing,' A repeated, hoping this wasn't going to resemble the apple-bobbing he had done one Halloween.

B selected a spot where the earth was soft and began to dig. A joined him when he'd found a flat lump of wood and a rusty six-inch nail, which he used as shovel and pick. The worms came quickly, it had rained early in the morning, and B placed them all on a plastic hubcap, so they couldn't escape. He tried to divide them into big ones and small ones, but the two groups kept squirming together. One worm they found was so large that, as it clung in its hole, it stretched in B's hands to well over a foot before its flesh ripped and it snapped. Even shrunk back and in half, it was the biggest worm they had. So they carefully excavated its other section, which still burrowed frantically, shitting out the dirt it ate through the wound where the rest of its body had been.

When he judged they had enough large worms B showed A how to thread them. He selected a fat one, which writhed in his grip, growing and twisting, and poking its blind head all around; in what seemed to be either pathetic attempts to escape, or else very proficient attempts to be so disgusting that it might be thrown away. The efforts were futile. B lifted his threaded darning needle before his glinting eyes and worked it through the whole length of the worm, so that it hung on the thick wool. He repeated the action with a second worm, and continued until a good three-foot section of string was covered entirely by worm.

Often the worms he pierced splurted a clear liquid which would fly on to his bomber, or his grubby school shirt. *B* would laugh at this, and assured *A* that it was good luck if some landed in your mouth. *A* kept his mouth firmly closed and took his chances with bad luck.

Next *B* wrapped the worm-coated wool around the span of his hand, and tied all of those loops together at the top. To create a big clump of dead worms at the end of a long piece of string.

With the Stonelee knife they turned a green branch into a rod, and then attached the heavily baited wool. *A* still couldn't understand how they were going to catch eels with no hook. But he didn't question his friend.

B's patience was amazing. Normally he got bored of any activity after a few minutes. But he sat there for half the morning on the bank of the Byrne, gently bobbing the clump of worm carcasses just off the water-bottom. *A* sat beside him, occasionally, as directed, throwing in a couple of the smaller worms as ground-bait. A few times he was allowed to take the rod for a while, on the strict condition that he pass it straight over if he felt a bite.

'The strike's got to be just right,' *B* explained. 'You got to be quick, but really steady, and then eely's little teeth get snagged in the wool, and if you're good you can get him over the bank before he untangles his self.'

A didn't feel a bite, but he felt a bit like Tom Sawyer when he held the rod; with his friend as Huckleberry Finn, whose adventures he'd seen on TV. The feeling would have been stronger if they were allowed out in the sunshine, but *B* insisted that eels liked the darkness under the bridge.

Periodically, articulated lorries would labour over the road, and everything would rumble as if the whole world was going to come down on them.

While they waited, *A* watched an ant dragging at a lump of dead worm, six or seven times bigger than itself. It was making slow progress, but it wouldn't give up, just kept pulling, a millimetre at a time, in the direction of an unseen nest. On a generous impulse, *A* pushed the prize forward a few inches, careful not to harm the ant as he did so. The ant went frantic. Leaving the worm-meat altogether, it ran round and round in panic, and then fled, in the opposite direction. *A* didn't understand what had happened, why his attempt to help seemed only to have flung the ant into the throes of insanity. He figured that the ant must have seen his hand as the hand of a god, something huge and powerful. And for a moment he felt huge and powerful.

A realized from *B*'s face that he hadn't really expected to catch the eel. Even so, *B* struck just as he had described, smooth and steady. But when he swung the eel over the bank they both realized that they had nothing to put it in. They had reached the end of their plans. The end of the line. But they couldn't just let it go, not after all that trouble. The eel felt danger, it thrashed on the woollen trap to free its teeth, and dropped to the concrete. Both boys just looked on, as it started to writhe its way back towards the water. Flecks of rust and brick-dust sticking to its lithe slimy body. It must have been able to smell its home, just feet away. But it saw the boys in front of it and changed its tack, heading left towards the deeper shadows, and the softer foe.

'Grab it,' *B* yelled.

And *A*, knowing that he had to, did. Disgust twisted through him with every twitch of the thick, slick, fish-snake. But he held it, with one hand around its throaty gills and the other on its tail. It struggled and glared and gasped at him, showing tiny dagger teeth tangled with streams of red wool.

'Get something to hold it down, quickly,' he said.

B appeared, with their digging tools. He slid *A*'s flat wood beneath the eel, and pushed the point of the nail just slightly into its oily back. Then, with a half-brick, he banged it home. The eel hissed wetly, and bucked its head upwards, as the nail passed through it and into the wood. Fatty blood splattered. One small drop went in *B*'s mouth.

The eel fought for an hour, while its tormentors shared *A*'s pack-lunch. They always shared. *B* got free school meals, but the scrap-saving, flap-armed dinner ladies didn't do take-outs. He tried to feed the eel a bit of Mighty White crust, only for some reason it wasn't hungry. It twisted around to bite at the nail though, tearing the hole in itself larger and larger, yet still unable to get free.

When it finally gave up the ghost, *B* ripped it from the board and threw it into the Byrne. It sank for a moment, and then inexplicably rose to the surface again. They pelted it with stones like they had the jonny. But it wouldn't go away. Eventually it drifted out of sight.

Even after lunch, and half a flask of lemon-barley, *B* was sure he could still taste the drop of eel blood. It moved somewhere inside him. And his hands felt dirty from where they had touched it. Like when he'd had to touch his brother, who was also slimy. Sure that the sticky secret was still on him. Sure that the next day's light would reveal where translucent globs had clung while in the dark.

They left the rod where it lay, and climbed back up to the road.

B had always been an Outlaw, just like Just William. But somehow high jinks are not acceptable from certain people. If your hair isn't ruffled, but greasy and uncut. If you're dirty, not from climbing trees, but because you don't wash. If you have thin pursed lips instead of a cheeky grin. But there was more than this too. He could sing the lyrics, but he couldn't understand the melody. There was something missing from this boy called *B*, something broken maybe, or never allowed to grow. People could feel the empty bit. And they were wary of it. He was a starer, *B*, and his stares created discomfort. Uneasy himself, he was a vector of unease, spreading it in slow ripples. His teachers tended to ignore his absences, because everything became much pleasanter when he wasn't there. The tension was gone, the thick heavy air that you get before something happens. This is what they said afterwards, anyway.

On *B*'s estate all the buildings were fused into termite rows of tenements; unevenly heighted, with tunnels twisted through their midst into unseen yards and further blocks. Washing hung from tightrope lines, which traversed above the streets at unnatural angles. Most of the clothes were too grimy with age to ever be properly cleaned, and the air felt too cold and damp to dry them. Technically the area was condemned, due for regeneration. But the project, like Stonelee, had run out of money. There were hardly any children still living there. Families were prioritized for escape.

B's brother liked it, though. And as the bread-stealer of the house, his views went. The estate was almost impossible to police: a lattice of courts in which you couldn't be trapped, because each was linked by alleys to four others. The permutations were simply impossible to investigate. So many flats were disused that there were always plenty of holing places, even for those too knackered to keep running. Once inside the estate you were safe. Provided of course that you could ever feel safe in such a place. The brother did. He ran with a gang, who didn't seem to like each other much, but who worked as a co-operative for burglaries and beatings. They called themselves the Anthill Mob. After the cartoon, not as admission of their insignificance.

Like a Satanist, *B* hated the one he worshipped, his brother. A brother that taught him, protected him and used him. To whom he was soon to have been apprenticed. The inadequate, that boasted about the women he conquered, and the faggots he bashed. Who called *B* maggot, when drunkenly fucking him one night. And swore him to a secrecy so deep that he hardly dared to think of it again.

B tried to use the secret to fill the gap in him. But found that it jolted around, wearing away at the sides, and making the breach even bigger. So instead he buried it. Down beside the Byrne.

J is for Jonah.
Just Jinxed.

Chris puts his mobile back down on the van's cluttered dash. Driving while on the phone is not one of the offences for which he routinely abuses other road-users. Jack had never seen a mobile before he went into secure accommodation, maybe on the telly. Now they're everywhere. Even scally little kids have them. Terry gave one to Jack, to go with the panic button/pager, so they can stay in touch, for safety. Chris' phone is perfection, a slim Nokia, an ideal of scale and beauty. But Jack already knows enough of the world to see that newer, smaller, comelier mobiles will be created; to make this goddess an ugly and embarrassing hag.

'You hungry, Jack?'

'I could eat.'

'There's a McD's at the next drop. Let's do brunch.' Chris says the last bit in his London Luvvy voice.

It's all about getting from A to Z, this job of Jack's. Not so much map reading, more making time pass. But they have ways, him and Chris. They have the radio, they have the games they play and they have the delights of the service stations they service. If they unload quickly, with the time saved by Chris' shortcuts and fast driving, they generally have fifteen or twenty minutes spare at each stop.

'You've got to take plenty of breaks,' Chris had explained on the first day. 'If you don't then the office'll shorten the journey times, and before you know it you've got three more deliveries a day, and they're laying people off.'

They pull into the slip road that guides them around to the services. The yellow brick road to McDonalds. They have to eat first, so the time signed on the delivery sheets approximates their ETA. It takes a while to park. Chris always wants a space where he can back the van against a wall, so no one can force the doors open.

'I'll get these, Bruiser,' says Chris in the queue, when Jack starts to hunt around his pockets for change. 'I reckon I still owe you for saving me from a beating the other weekend.'

Jack has felt a difference at work over the last week and a bit. As people gradually heard about the fight they warmed to him. He asked Chris and Steve the mechanic not to tell anyone, but it was too late, they'd both already let it out. They couldn't understand his reticence, when he'd done the right thing. No one thought he was a monster. Couldn't he see? Everyone respects someone who stands up for a mate.

It's true, it was all smiles at the unit this morning. Jack the lad, that's what they thought. But Jack had wanted to keep it quiet; Jack is still terrified that this could come out. That it will all come out, and he'll go back in. Or worse. Tell me I'm not a monster, then.

He agonized all weekend over whether to talk to Terry about it. But Terry is an official, even if he is much more; and Terry is too moral to trust on something like this.

Every day for the past twelve, Jack has expected a knock on the door. A gang of fierce blue uniforms to tell him his licence is revoked. And, although he's scared of returning to prison, some mornings when he wakes, he almost wishes they would come. To put an end to the waiting and the fear.

In a way it wouldn't be so bad to be back inside. He knew where he was in there. He had routines. All right, they were routines that he hated, but they divided his time neatly. There was no wondering how to get through the day. No decisions of any consequence to be made. Only that biggest one.

But his confidence grows each time the knock doesn't come. Every evening that he goes to sleep in the same bed he woke up in. He's adjusting.

'So what you having, Jack? Bacon sandwich meal?'

Jack nods.

Even McDonalds has had to adjust. Chris told him that when they started doing breakfasts in England, they tried to sell pancakes and maple syrup and muffins, and all kinds of crazy American shit. Brits just didn't go for it. Mass advertising campaigns said that fifty million Americans couldn't be wrong. But they were ill judged. Not everyone believes what they read. Bollocks, said England, more people than that go to watch baseball every week. You can dictate our foreign policy, but you'll never dictate our breakfast. So Ronald conceded, and invented the McBacon Roll with McBrown sauce. Though he still served it with a hash brown.

They take their paper-blanketed trays, and sit down on the hard-backed plastic chairs. Jack is sure they used to swivel, once upon a time. McDonalds is at its best in the morning. Everything is freshly cleaned. Like in his memory. Like in the adverts. Jack loves McDonalds because of those adverts. He watched them for years in secure accommodation and prison. McDonalds was a land where everyone was happy. Even some of the meals were happy. And the food, when he finally tasted it again, didn't disillusion him. It's not so much cooked as chemically generated to be delicious. You can tell that teams of scientists have worked on every detail. Getting it just right.

But there's a gherkin stuck on the wall. Marring the immaculacy of the white tiles. It must have been there since yesterday; they don't serve burgers yet. It's wrong of the cleaners to have missed it, and their failure makes Jack feel slightly let down.

They time their breaks flawlessly, heading back to the unit at precisely 2:30, to pick up more stock. It's crisps today. Their firm does local distribution for a company that makes snacks, seemingly just for garages. At least Chris says he's never seen them sold anywhere else. Big bags of salt and vinegar sticks, bacon balls and cheese puffs. The piles of identical goods make Jack think of Hacendado. It's a long time since he last saw Hacendado. It's getting to be quite a while since he saw Michelle too.

'Don't be ignorant, come and sign the stuff out, Jack. You haven't seen her since the party.'

Up North ignorance is a social thing, not intellectual. Manners are more important than knowledge. Normally Jack likes this.

'I just…'

'Come on. What are you going to do, never go in the office again? You've got to face up to it. What are you afraid of?'

Who knows? Jack doesn't. Confusion, upheaval, humiliation, even happiness, perhaps. Putting his head above the parapet. Climbing high enough to fall. To fail. But he follows Chris into the office.

They pass through the doorway which marks the distinction between two worlds. On one side of it the floor is concrete and the walls are whitewashed breeze-block. On the other there are carpets, corridors, computers, Café Costa cappuccinos, women. The only women in the yard-side are on the calendar, they arch their naked backs and smile with promises and tease their own breasts. The women in the office-side don't do any of these things.

Michelle doesn't even smile when she sees Jack.

'Hi, Jack,' she says coldly, then she files something away.

'Hi,' he replies, aware suddenly that his fear has hurt her. There is no sparkle in her eyes when she turns to him.

They all perfunctorily perform to sign out the snacks. Even Chris doesn't try a joke. Although the atmosphere is as dense as Kev from accounts, and probably warrants one.

'Look, Jack,' Michelle says abruptly. 'Do you want to go for a coffee after work, talk about it?'

'I, well, Chris, I get a lift off Chris.'

'I'll take you back after,' she says.

'OK.' Jack is sheepish. Collared like a bad schoolboy. In the days when that meant scrumping apples.

The last deliveries are nearby. Regular haunts, where Chris laughs with the staff, leaving Jack free to think. When he was young, the petrol stations had a few cans of oil and a cash register. Maybe some peanuts if you were lucky. Stuck to a board that gradually uncovered a woman; always disappointingly more clothed at the end than seemed likely at the outset. Garages now are like supermarkets were then. Supermarkets are like towns, as alien and alluring as Las Vegas, only with strip-lights instead of neon; parades of goods you didn't even know existed, built next to things similar, or identical or absolutely distinct. It's the choices that overwhelm Jack. Consumerism in prison was limited to short printed lists. Now he can lose an hour reading the ladverts in the back of *Loaded*. There are too many choices in the world.

He has no option but to meet Michelle. The deal has been done. Chris wishes him luck, before shredding the van out of the yard. Jack's work boots feel heavier than normal as he heads into the office. The air in Michelle's room is lighter though.

'Just hang on a minute, can you, Jack? I'm still finishing up.' Michelle's cheeks are flushed and there is the barest hint of a smile on her lips.

Jack wonders why on earth he has been avoiding her. Now that he sees her again he can think of nothing better than to be near her. He watches her efficient, pale, hands flirting their way through the final few forms of the day. Her nails are painted the briefest pink, just scarcely darker than they would be if they were left. He imagines those nails stroking his face. Feeling its post-shave smoothness, like in a commercial.

Michelle walks quickly on the way to Café Costa. Jack has to slightly extend his normal stride, to stay up with her without seeming to hurry. A jogger comes towards them. He wears the absurdly tight track suit bottoms that serious athletes wear to define themselves as such, to show they are unfettered by fashion. Jack has to step close to Michelle to let the man past, and in that tick-tock, where he can smell her, and feel her hair against his cheek, he starts to grow hard.

The swish pseudo-Italian coffee shop seems incongruous coming from the industrial estate. But behind it are gold and chrome-mirrored offices that front on the ship-canal. This road is another border between worlds. Michelle looks longingly at the bold new blocks, filled with solicitors and ad-execs, not crisps and white vans. But there's also determination in her eyes, and Jack suspects that one day soon she will be there.

She orders a mochachino, which Jack doesn't manage to pay for. He has a coke, overpriced and weak, in a kid's cardboard cup.

'So why have you been ignoring me?' is her blunt opening gambit, once they've sat down.

Jack is grateful for the distance they are away from the nearest people. 'I don't know,' he says, in all honesty.

'Is it because you were embarrassed about the "I love you" thing? You don't have to be. I know you didn't really mean it, I thought you were rather sweet.'

Sweet is something that Jack is unused to being; he wipes

his sweaty fingers on his blue nylon trousers. They have seven pockets, these trousers, all the lads at the yard are forever losing keys in them. Most prison trousers have none, they're cut out for visitors: hand-jobs and hand-overs. Jack feels a bit like he's on a visit. Just the two of them, sat across a low table. But only Terry ever visited. Never a woman.

'I think I'm a bit scared,' he blurts, amazed at his own openness. But still only revealing in order to remain hidden.

'Scared of what? Of me? I know Chris' nickname for me, but I'm not a nympho, Jack.'

'No,' he says, a bit too hurriedly. 'No, it's not that. It's just. I don't know. I've never really been in a relationship,' he nearly says 'before.'

She laughs, 'Jack. I'm not asking for one. I'm not even after one at the moment. I just want a bit of fun. You know what they say: "All work and no play makes…" ' She stops herself. 'Everyone thinks they're the first one, don't they? I guess you've had that all your life, haven't you?'

'Something like that.'

'I can't believe we're talking like this anyway. It's not like anything's happened. We haven't even had so much as a snog. What are we discussing?'

Jack shrugs, and smiles. He feels safe with her, he really does. And he wants that snog like he could burst with it. But he knows he could no more do anything about it than he could tell her the difference between a mochachino and a latte.

'Look,' she says, 'I said I'd go round mum's after work. I'll have to drop you on the way. But why don't we do something tomorrow night? Watch a film or something? If you fancy it.'

'That'd be cool,' Jack says, feeling anything but.

Michelle's car is a Clio. Chris said that 'Clio' was meant to make you think 'Clit'. Otherwise they'd spell it with an 'e', like normal, wouldn't they? Clever advertising, he reckoned, sexy, supposed to appeal to strong women. It doesn't make Jack more comfortable.

When she drops him, and he starts to open the car door, she beckons him back, leans forwards and kisses him ever so softly, at the join of his lips and cheek.

Kelly isn't in, and Jack races to his room to watch Michelle manoeuvre the curvy turquoise car out of the space and off down the street. He feels bizarre, at the edge of excitement and in complete turmoil.

Terry calms him down. He offers to come over, but Jack says that he's fine. Just wanted to tell him what had happened. Terry tells him to take it slowly, reminds him of the consequences of a relationship. That it must, by necessity, be built on falsehood. But he encourages Jack as well, says that this might be what he needs. As they put the phones down, Terry wishes him luck, just like Chris did.

Creeping like a thief, Jack steals into Kelly's room. He knows she shouldn't be back for hours, but still his frame is tense, with a furtive sort of adrenalin. The long Simpsons T-shirt, that she sometimes uses as a nightie, is draped over a chair. On her pine dressing table are arrayed the unctions and ointments used to apply and remove make-up, and hair, and wrinkles and bags. But Jack is not interested in these. He moves to her waist-high bookcase. Where, among the novels and books on nursing, he knows he has seen... And wanted to look at, but was too nervous to try... And there it is. Centre shelf. *The Joy of Sex*.

Still in his work clothes, lying in the upstairs hall, lit by the skylight, close enough to Kelly's room to slip the book back in its preserved nook should he hear a key in the front door, Jack is studying, as if for an exam. At first he was aroused by the line drawings of the hippies in their carefully constructed coitus. But quickly this is replaced by worry, as he realizes the enormity of his ignorance. He practises, where he can, when descriptions of movements are given. He moves his fingers, gently beckoning a dove, or stroking the underside of a cat. He balances upon his knees and one elbow, so that his pelvis and hand are free, and he tries to synchronize their action. Often Jack finds himself gripping his tongue in his teeth with concentration. Though he's aware that it too might be needed in a practical.

The evening is spent with Kelly, *EastEnders* and bad sit-coms. But Jack is not really watching. He is studying again, rehearsing. Running through the unfacts that he has learned about his life. His legend, as the protection squad call it. Things that Michelle may ask about tomorrow. Things that he might have to tell her in order to make her fall for someone that he is not.

This is the house that Jack built. This hide of twigs and leaves. A little extra camouflage added every day. Another little sprig of lie, that he must himself remember and believe, or die. He can't do anything other than stay inside his hut, and hope he's safe from prying eyes. Except to pray, if he still can, that no one kicks the sand foundations. And no one checks the brittle sticks that support the straw roof. And most of all, that no one huffs and puffs.

Michelle's house is a flat really. Town house, she calls it. But it only has a kitchen-cum-living-room and a bedroom, just that they're on different floors. It's new though, and Jack suspects it's probably slightly beyond her comfortable means to rent. It's also meticulously kept. Seat cushions perch on their corners like card-pack diamonds. Magazines and newspapers are neatly racked. Even seemingly chaotic elements show the underlying order. Strands of bamboo stick out of a glass vase, intimating a random spray. But each stalk is exactly equidistant from the others, confirming pride and precision.

Jack had assumed they were going to the cinema when

she'd asked if he wanted to watch a film, yesterday. But when she picked him up she brought him round here instead. Two Blockbusters boxes are stood on a stocky coffee table, next to a three-photo frame. One shot of a woman who must be Michelle's mother by the resemblance, kind eyes, broad shoulders. A schoolgirl Michelle, thinner-faced, innocent, but something slightly sly in her smile. Then three laughing friends, threatening to flash flesh from their skimpy party tops.

'Do you want a drink?' Michelle asks. 'I bought you some tins of lager. Or you could have wine if you want. Or a soft drink,' she adds, with an edge of disapproval.

He goes for the lager, and examines the videos while she gets it. One is an action film he has seen advertised on telly, the title of the other means nothing to him, and the box looks battered, older. She brings the beer in a glass, expertly poured with an inch of froth.

'I'm good at head, aren't I?' she says, and laughs guilelessly.

Jack can feel himself blushing, but tries to laugh as well. She asks which film he wants to see, and only knowing one, he expresses it as his preference. The other, $9\frac{1}{2}$ Weeks, sounded a bit boring to him in any case.

They sit side by side. Watching the surprise on the bad-guys' faces, as they gradually realize that the refuse collector, improperly tied up, turns out to be an ex-Delta Force, kung fu master, crack marksman, down on his luck. There is not much opportunity for talking, of which Jack is pleased. But in the tense final stand-off, between the bin-man and the chief villain, who turns out to be his old Delta Force colonel, Michelle takes Jack's hand. And she strokes it while the hero kisses the rescued hostage, who turns out to be his childhood sweetheart.

'What did you think?' Michelle asks, as the credits roll.

'Good story line,' Jack says. 'You never knew what was going to happen next,' which is a strange thing to say, because he did, all the way through.

'Do you like surprises, then?'

She turns to face him, and her eyes are beautiful, but with a seriousness that Jack has never seen before. Not just in her, not ever. And there's a heaviness to her breath. And, he realizes, to his. And then that is it. They are kissing. He is kissing. He can feel her lip on his lips and over them and between them, and she draws away, only to push forwards to kiss him again, and again, and her fingers are on the back of his neck, and her tongue is with his and beyond his, into him and his trousers are tight against him with twelve years of waiting, but he wants to wait even longer, because he wants this moment to last as long as it should.

And then they are in the bedroom. On the bed. On a duvet. Which is soft and pale like Michelle. She frees her breasts, which immediately capture Jack. They mesmerize, hypnotize, entrance him; seem to give him greater pleasure than her. And as he cups them, she cups him, through his jeans, and he believes that there cannot be any more to life than this. But even in the intensity, he feels a strange detachment, as if he is watching them both. As if he is not Jack at all.

Which he isn't.

Still spectator, now to his own increasing nakedness, Jack's mind reels around the fact that someone else wants him this way. Not for a strip search or a medical. He sees his own slapstick struggle with bunched-up jeans. Hears his mournful gasp, as a hand which is not his, for the first time in his life, grips him and pulls back his straining uncut skin. He feels for her, and having suddenly no memory of what his studies taught him, he kneads the whole plump, parted mound, which seems to somehow work. Michelle tries to kiss him through her moans, but he has to turn to watch his hand at work. To see his fingers through her hair. Which is so blond as to be hard to see at all, and strangely soft, almost fleecy, unlike his own. Her hands keep working too, both of them, wrapping and enclosing and working him, with a proficiency that makes him sad. And at the same time happy, almost beyond his physical endurance of pleasure. And he realizes that his endurance is indeed coming to an end, because he is coming to a point which he knows well, though not in circumstances such as these. He doesn't want to reach this point, but every nerve ending in him says that it is not only desirable, but necessary, and inevitable. One more stroke and there will be no going back in any case.

'I want you, Jack.' She stops and looks at him.

Taking his returned gaze as some sort of answer to some kind of question, she rolls away from him, bending her body over the side, to reach below the bed. Her beautiful bare flesh flexing away. Not so much a whale as a dolphin. Arched in the instant before diving beneath the duvet waves. She surfaces with a smile, and a fist-full of condoms.

'Pick a colour,' she says. And Jack picks the black one.

She tears it from its packet with her perfect nails. And, checking its direction, she pops it in her mouth; and smiles again, to show it sitting there. She is too practised. Jack feels suddenly like he's in a performance. As she bends her head down to him, he feels himself retreat from her, lolling to the side. With her lips she tries to coax the condom on, but he falls away. She grips him in her hand, and attempts to tease him back to form, stroking the underside of his balls. He tries to concentrate on the sensations, but finds himself just watching, and thinking, and shrinking. Until she is working him with just two fingers, in the gesture people made in prison to be really offensive. It's too much, and he stands up.

'Jack, wait, it doesn't matter. It happens to everyone. You'll be fine in a minute, we'll watch the other film.'

But he's already got his clothes on, and he feels stronger in his clothes. He just wants to be out of this situation. He just wants to walk, to think. And it seems to him that maybe he isn't supposed to be happy – which isn't unlikely, or probably even unfair. And he can hear that it's raining outside, but he doesn't care. He just wants to get away. So he tells her he's sorry. Because he is. She's wrapped in the duvet now, being naked is suddenly wrong. Like the serpent's come along. She asks him to stay, again, just for a while. But he won't. So they hug. Then he leaves.

K is for Kangaroo.

The interior of the vans didn't have windows. Not that anyone could look in or out of. Just narrow arrow slits of toughened Perspex. Translucent rather than transparent. This was probably for the best. The driver's windscreen was smashed when one of the boys was brought to court the first time. Spread into shattered cobwebs with half bricks and bottles. The mob broke through police lines. Officers were swept to the floor by the force of the anger, which washed over the barriers and banged on the vehicle sides. Rocked stationary wheels, blocked by people baying, screaming, wanting a lynching. Faces contorted in rage and despair that such a thing could happen. That such little animals could have grown up in their midst, unspotted. So they howled and scratched at the van, and vented bestial threats about wearing entrails and eating hearts, and snarled at the 'pigs' for trying to stop them. For trying to prevent their brand of justice, which was only natural, only human.

Once inside the building though, order returned. Where Court and Queen, Crown and Country, honour and majesty prevailed. Procedural relics of an earlier, more dignified, age.

Though they were old enough to be tried as adults, in this country if not in most of the western world, the toes of the defendants did not quite reach the ground from their seats. Which, both boys being slightly less than four and a half feet tall, had been placed on low plank scaffolds, so they could look around the room. Or be looked at. They did not look at each other. Some of the many concerned and curious, who queued to watch every day of the trial, would maintain that not once in the four weeks did either of the accused glance at his former friend.

The older boy had his parents behind him. His dad sat hunched by the strain, often with his head in his hands. The mother, high-backed, carried a kind of nobility. A bodily assertion that, whatever her faults, she would not be broken by this shame. She met the eyes of those who stared at her hoping to have a glimpse into the soul of one that makes monsters. She listened intently to every word that passed the plummy lips of the barristers and judge. And just as closely to the thick Durham drawl of the witnesses, though no doubt she found them easier to follow. She wore dresses which were smart and plain and similar. To each other, and, in a way, to those of Mrs Thatcher.

By the side of each of the boys was a social worker. Appointed by the state to support and help two children teetering on the edge of an abyss. Though they weren't allowed to talk with them about anything related to the case, for fear that this might taint the evidence. For the same reason, British justice felt, psychiatric help should not be given, at least until after sentencing. Though many in the gallery whispered 'psychos', when they saw the boys brought up from the holding cells.

There should have been a revival of phrenology in fact, around the courtroom: so many people could tell, simply by looking, that the boys were born evil. Some said just one was; acknowledging the unlikelihood of finding two such freaks of nature in a school so small. Concluding that the other must have followed, though they divided on the choice: child B being from a gene-pool clearly predisposed to crime; but the other, an academic year older, was brighter and had the mark of the beast, in his face and teeth. Folie à deux was the theory of the better-educated onlookers, frequently expressed in the eleven o'clock breaks. Where they tended to stick together, huddled in the fog of other people's Berkeley 100s and Lambert & Butler's. They would sip bad coffee and agree that each boy had egged the other on, gradually, like wading into a pool; until both found they were up to their necks in it.

The victim's family also watched from the gallery. In the front row, which was their rightful place. There sometimes subtle jockeying for other seats, but nobody would have willingly taken the bench the Miltons sat at. The whole nation felt the sadness of Angela's death. It brought people together, bonded them, like a royal wedding. Angela was blameless, beautiful, classless – a true people's princess. She was normal, knowable and yet extraordinary. Ten years old. Would never be any older. And already the sweetheart of a country. An entire people in mourning, for the passing of a girl they never knew existed, until she didn't. But the public couldn't feel the heart-rending personal loss of someone who lit their lives, like those in the front row did. There were traces of Angela on many of those faces. Faces fixed in anger and undiminished grief. Some had her hair, some her delicate oval chin. But none seemed to have all the things that made her. She was the treasure and measure of this clan, all its parts were exemplified in her. She was its chosen one, its representative to the world, and the world itself. Its darling, daughter, scholar, student and future teacher.

The teachers who gave evidence at the trial mostly said they'd seen something coming. Though strangely, they hadn't alerted authorities to the fact that neither boy had been seen in the classroom for some time. One in particular, a Ms Grey, gave a frank and eloquent account of a number of occasions on which she had been forced to punish Boy A. Which tended to take the ground from those who claimed an old-fashioned clip around the ear would have prevented the tragedy.

The ears of the jury were assaulted with hours of audio-tapes. The sobs and squirms and barefaced lies of children telling tales on each other. The acts of brutality gradually weaned out, over weeks of police interviews, each blaming all on the other. Boy *B* constantly changed his story, until eventually he accepted he had played some part. The older child, Boy *A*, stuck throughout to more or less a constant path of guiltlessness. But the transcripts pointed out his slips and inconsistencies. Both were still pleading innocent, on the grounds that their friend alone was guilty. Sometimes the tapes that most upset the jury weren't the ones about the crimes. In the twisting devious way they both feigned innocence, the accused were easy to condemn; but not when they described robots that turned into racing cars. When they talked about childish things not yet put away, it was hard to pretend that they were not just children.

The younger boy, alone but for his counsel and social worker, had curled hair, chip-gravy brown, and wore a tracksuit throughout the trial. The other wore new clothes, that fitted perfectly, probably for the first time in his young life; bought for an occasion, not to grow into. Smart trousers and a selection of shirts, presumably purchased in a different town, where his mother would not be recognized. Even the trial had been moved to Newcastle, for fear that feelings ran too high in Durham. He also wore a tie, tiny, probably a clip-on, that stopped at an elasticated snake-fastening belt.

The appointed pastel artist found that he couldn't get the colours right for the sickly pallid tone of this boy's skin. And it was hard to draw his features, without seeming to satirize or exaggerate. In the end it didn't matter. Only views which hid the accuseds' faces were shown on the nationwide nightly coverage.

Two weeks into the trial the entire circus went to

Stonelee Byrne. Out of the court, under police escort, the judge, the jury, and all the court officials, the press, the prosecution and two defence counsels, their aids, and their aids' aids, expert witnesses and associated staff. The boys stayed, on the decision of their lawyers. So did the spectators' gallery, except the Miltons, for whom accommodation was made. A coach carried all those that left, like a charabanc trip with uniformed outriders. From the tour bus the Newcastle Law Court building looked imposing. Itself new and castle-like, with towering stone pillars, moated by the Tyne. On a quayside, which had been caught, as if in undress, halfway to becoming yuppified.

The waters of the Byrne would join the Tyne, but at Stonelee they remained a different course. Sluggish, stained, glutinous. Less fresh than some of the flowers which still lay under the bridge. The ground had been cleared to discourage the morbid. Which made it hard for the forensics witness to point out spots distinct in evidence of pain. The pain was visible enough in the eyes of the Miltons, who hadn't seen this place before. This dirty, murky, cave under a two-lane road. They held on to each other, as it was explained about each specific torment that Angela, their pride and prize, had suffered. If one more of them was taken away, it looked like all would have fallen. But by the Byrne-side they survived. Stood like a pyre, with each stave of wood supporting every other.

The judge led the jury round, almost incognito without his wig and his scarlet and ermine robe of office. Out of his red leather chair, he looked like an ordinary chalk-striped citizen, a businessman or banker, if they are ordinary. The jury was five men and seven women, mostly working class, all white but for one of the ladies, who was Asian. Even she became pale, as the cloudy water edged past, and the police described what the drag-tracks on the tow-path had meant. One of the other jurors, a former stranger, took her hand, though he had a fading NF tattoo on his own, and cried by her side.

Although there were usually only two minors present, the court stuck to school hours. Starting at nine, breaking at eleven, and then again at one and two-thirty, closing for the day at three-thirty-five; or sooner if the judge felt an apt natural pause had been reached. Sometimes there were other children. Three boys testified separately, via video link, about a time when they had all been set upon by the two defendants. They were clearly still upset by the experience, because their faces were anxious, and they stumbled during the gentle cross-examination, getting confused and contradicting each other about exactly who had said and done what. But the jury got the gist of this unprovoked assault.

The televisions were kept in place to play the CCTV footage. Most of those watching had already seen the highlights, shown in the first days after Angela disappeared. Damning slowed-down frames of children, already formed into premeditating monsters, darting from alley to doorway, as they followed an angel down the street.

The pathologist's mortuary report came last. When it was hoped that the jurors and the gallery would be already steeled to what was going to be revealed. A Stanley knife, in a neatly labelled clear plastic bag, was handed to the foreman. Some jurors touched it gingerly, as if an evil genie might erupt, should the knife be rubbed or the bag burst. The photographs that passed around left many of the twelve clutching their eyes to their palms, rubbing, like that or anything else could erase what they'd seen. The pathologist concluded that he remained unsure, in the absence of DNA, the boys being hairless and seedless. He couldn't confirm for certain that one or both had entered her. But it sufficed for him to say that something had.

To sum up the summing up. A girl named Angela, ten years old, perfect as the world might ever know, was molested and murdered on the bank of the Byrne. Under clear skies, in broad day, she had been trailed, trapped and dragged along a gravel path. She was slashed, with many strokes, and slung into the filthy water. Not even the prosecution had the stomach to dwell on what may have happened between her capture and murder. It was enough to think of Angela, alone and afraid, at the mercy of creatures that had none.

And so, before it reached its verdict, the jury knew the facts at least, if not the truth. Having tried every ruse in a child's repertoire, every lie and weakling wile, it was doubtful if even the boys could remember the real truth. But then a court isn't necessarily there to find the truth. Its purpose is more about finding a wise solution.

In his verdict the judge seemed shrewd enough: a seven-year sentence was passed; severe, but not unfair, considering the gravity of the case. The Home Secretary, however, more at the mercy of public will and already a tabloid-painted fool, made detention indefinite. Prompted, perhaps, by a coupon campaign. And because governments in the terminal spins of election years know far better than unaccountable officials the necessity that justice is damning. No doubt the Minister felt vindicated when the Courts of Appeal, all the way up, kept to his line. They too contended that justice must be *seen* to be done. But they also upheld the decision of the trial judge: that other than one photograph of each, the boys themselves should never be seen again.

L is for Letters.
Love Letters.

Jack and Chris play a game of 'Old People's Shoes' while they do town-centre deliveries in the morning. The rules are simple: you take it in turns, street by street, and get a point for every pensioner you spot wearing trainers, two if they have a tartan trolley as well, which is more common than you might think. In the advanced game you also get two points for any young people that you see wearing sensible school-type shoes with tracksuits. Jack is winning 15–9, when they have to suspend the game to head off the A roads and on to Bs, and bizarre country drops. Jack has never been to most of these village garages, but Chris still knows his way. They're delivering air fresheners and learner plates today.

'So what happened with you and Michelle last night? How'd the date go?' Chris asks, manoeuvring round a tight curve. There are dark woods to one side of the road, and a fenced bank down the other.

'It wasn't really a date, as such, we just watched a video.'

'Oh yeah, round at hers, was it? Any hanky panky?'

Jack looks ahead while he considers his response; an old blue Cortina is in front. He doesn't really want to get into this. But Chris is his friend and he knows that this is something friends talk about.

'Just tell me, did you get a go on those tits? Steve the mechanic reckons they're so big she has special bras, cos they ran out of letters and had to start using the Greek alphabet.'

Jack shakes his head, but can't help a laugh. The Cortina is pulling away from them, too fast for the roads. As a general rule of thumb anyone that drives faster than Chris is going too fast for the roads. Jack knows this because Chris has told him. The Cortina driver must be a real local.

'You don't give much away do you, Bruiser? I don't think you need to worry about protecting Michelle's honour…' Chris stops talking when he sees what Jack sees.

A deer jumps out of the wood. It's suspended in a split second of sunlight. Then it lands on the road in front of the Cortina. The driver brakes, and the car skids. Locked wheels send it careering. It smashes through the fence, with a whip-crack. Disappears from sight. Chris hits his brakes too, but pumps them when the van starts to swing. He steers into the skid and brings the Mercedes to a stop. Less than a child's length in front of the motionless deer. It looks at them with watery brown eyes and tilts its head to one side. Then it turns and scrambles back into the wood.

Chris and Jack look at each other.

'Shit!'

They jump out and run to where the car disappeared. The fence is wooden, and jagged lumps of it lie all around. The blue Cortina is at the bottom of a long steep bank. Its roof is dented down, almost to wing-mirror height at the front, and its crumpled bonnet is wedged against a thick, partly uprooted, tree.

Chris shouts that he's getting his phone and the tyre-iron from the van. Jack is already starting down. It's hard to keep his footing on the grassy incline. There are huge chunks of red earth showing, where bits of the car have dug in as it rolled. Jack slips on a lump and finds that he's rolling too. Spinning down the bank on his side, like he'd done as a child. But with fear. He is going much too fast, and he can't see, but he knows there are trees about. He tries to open his arms, to stop himself, but wrenches his shoulder and carries on rolling. He has no control over direction or speed.

Jack only stops spinning when the terrain lets him.

When the ground does level out, he is virtually next to the car. Other than aches he isn't injured. Judging by the state of the Cortina, the driver will probably not be so lucky. Its flattened roof is scattered with green leaves. Flung down like tickertape by the impacted tree. Jack can't see inside.

'Hello!' he shouts. 'Are you OK? Can you hear me?' There is no response.

The driver's door-handle is coated in the same rich red mud as the scars on the slope above. Jack strains with it, one foot pressed against the car's body, but he can't open it. He tries the rear door, to the same effect. A glance tells him Chris is coming down the bank now, occasionally resorting to sitting to keep his balance. The passenger side door is completely crumpled, twisted into the frame. But behind it there is a chance. The last door is the least damaged, and not trapped by the dropped roof. Jack can even see into the car, through the tatters of glass that cling in the window. There is a baby bucket-seat in the back, strapped to the battered matt-black upholstery. In it there is a little girl. Her dress is pink-gingham, her hair is blond and alice-banded, and her face… Her face is blue. Still and blue.

Jack is shouting to her to hang on, as he wrenches at the door. It moves a little but he can't get it open. Chris arrives and shoves the tyre-iron straight into the small crack that Jack's efforts have made. The two of them groan together. Speaking only to count from one to three. Until the door speaks too, and falls open with a metal whimper.

Jack knows his ABC. He studied it in the secure unit, they all did, as part of education. Airways, Breathing, Circulation. Airways, Breathing, Circulation. Airways,

Breathing, Circulation. He repeats it like a mantra as he crawls into the small space on the back seat. Her blond head is tilted forwards. He takes it beneath the chin and by the crown, and moves it gently back. Her lips are a pale powder-blue. With crossed fingers he parts them. He can't feel a tongue initially, then it appears and he draws it forwards, tries to check for other obstructions. She gags. A beautiful retch to Jack.

'She's alive,' he shouts. Then he checks to listen to her breathing. It is too gentle to hear, but he can feel her chest rising with his palm. ABC. Circulation. He feels a pulse at her throat. A tiny throb of life. He is overwhelmed, almost in tears.

'You're going to be all right,' he tells her. 'It's all going to be all right.' He can hear Chris outside on his mobile. Describing their location. The little girl looks at him. He hasn't been this close to a child since he was one. She doesn't cry. She asks where her daddy is. Jack remembers the driver. The front seats are squashed together. There is barely a gap between them, and the roof is flattened to their top. They won't get to him from the back.

'They're coming,' Chris says. 'It stinks of petrol in there. Shouldn't we get her out?'

'You got your knife?'

Chris passes in the Leatherman that he always wears for work, with the blade already opened. Jack slices through the webbing that holds the child-seat in place, and eases the little girl out. Still in her padded bucket, in case of back injury. He talks to her awkwardly, and monitors her signs. Chris keeps trying in vain to open the driver-door, until the fire brigade arrives to take over.

With the firemen come paramedics. And shortly after the police arrive. Two officers, with batman utility belts and flak jackets. They question Jack and Chris separately about what happened. Mercifully they don't ask them to make statements at the station. One ambulance disappears to take the little girl to hospital. The other waits for her father. By the time the fire crew manage to move the cutting equipment down the bank it is too late for him. Maybe it was always too late for him. Jack and Chris never see his face. He is strapped under an orange blanket when he's brought back to the spot where the deer landed. The second ambulance doesn't use its sirens as it pulls away.

The policemen shake Jack's hand after they have questioned him. They tell him that his quick thinking and first aid almost certainly saved the girl's life. Then they radio for a WPC, to help them tell a wife and mother she's a widow.

Most of the day is gone by the time Jack and Chris are back on the road. They have explained the situation to the office, but with Pony Express valiance they opt to complete the drop they started.

When they get back to the yard they are clapped in through the storerooms and loading bays. Most of the guys are quite obviously joking, but there is still an unmistakable feeling of pride around the unit. Jack has never felt a sense of belonging anything like this. They are heroes. He is a hero. It's a sensation almost strong enough to pierce his wall of unworthiness.

There is a letter for Jack in the whitewood pigeon-hole, below the sticky label inscribed 'Burridge'. He can remember the faint thrill when he first noticed that his name had appeared there, alongside the ranks of his workmates. But that is nothing compared to getting a letter in it. Not on a day like today.

'It's from Michelle, Jack,' says a bloke he can't remember even having seen before.

'Love letters straight from your window,' Chris starts singing. Two more lads join him, leaning in to each other like a barbershop trio, but crooning like Max Bygraves.

They peter out quite quickly, when it becomes apparent that none of them knows beyond line four, but the spontaneity and effort of the attempt has a lot of bystanders laughing. Jack grins as he puts the letter in his pocket, not wanting to read it so publicly.

'You two can go when you've unloaded the stuff you didn't deliver,' says the yard manager.

'Nice one,' says Chris. 'Time off for good behaviour, hey, Bruiser. Be like old times for you.' Then he says sorry when he sees Jack's expression.

But it doesn't bother either of them for long. The life-savers invest their early finish in a pint stop. In the sunny garden of a pub that they pass every day and have never before been into.

'Lager tastes better in the daytime,' Jack says. Realizing this is the first time he's tried it.

'It's the sunshine,' says Chris. 'It's what they make it from.' He laughs and sips his pint. 'You know, Jack,' he says seriously, like he's conveying a state secret, 'that guy, the dead guy, he was busy going about his life this morning. Now he's gone. It's weird, isn't it? But we're happy, because we saved the little girl. Just goes to show, doesn't it?'

'Goes to show what?' asks Jack.

'I don't know, that's the thing. Goes to show you have to grab every pint in the sunshine you can.' Then, as if realizing the implication of his own remark, he says: 'You're a good friend, Jack. A good person. The thing today, and you being ready to take a kicking for me the other week. I haven't really thanked you for that. I just want you to know that if there is anything I can ever do. Anything you ever want to tell me. I'm here.'

And for a moment Jack wants to tell him. To tell him everything, and he can imagine the weight lifting. He can feel what it would be like, for the first time in his life, to have a peer who truly knew him. But his sense of self-preservation cuts in. It could mean the end of their friendship, moving town, leaving Michelle. It could be suicide. All to lighten the load.

'Maybe it only goes to show you should drive slow on country roads,' Jack says. And there's a feeling of relief between them. A realization that it was getting too heavy for a day like today. You don't get many days like today. Most people don't get any.

'Yeah, there's some pretty rough stuff around. But it's not such a bad world, is it?'

And Jack thinks maybe it's not.

As it's a Wednesday, Jack goes for a pizza with Terry. Terry is excited by the story of the accident. His excitement gives him energy, and makes Jack remember what he looked like when he was younger. In the days when Terry had no grey in his hair and fewer lines on his face, with more of them caused by laughter. When he had a wife that he lived with, and said he loved, and a son that lived with and loved them both. And a dog that Terry said loved everyone. Because all Labradors do. It makes Jack remember when he envied that son. Now he almost feels sorry for him, because he spends less time with his dad than Jack does.

'Don't you see?' Terry says. 'It means that you've been forgiven. You being given the opportunity to save that girl's life, and with the first aid you learnt in the secure unit. That's divine intervention, or fate, or something. That's someone saying you've been forgiven.'

Jack isn't sure. He's not a great believer in God. But he usually believes Terry, and he wants to believe him now.

After he gets home he reads Michelle's letter again. It says that she hopes he's all right, and that it doesn't matter about the other night. It says they were probably just rushing things, and that she cares about him a lot. It asks if he wants to go round for dinner tomorrow.

★

She cooks tiny conches of pasta, with oil and fresh chicken, and a lot of herbs which are sharp to the taste. They eat with two bottles of a posh red wine. Which cleans their mouths and stains their teeth.

When they kiss he can still taste the herbs. He calls her Shell, and finds that her pubis is like a shell as well. Softer in its crinkles even than the pasta, and more salty. He believes she must be a mermaid, half woman, half sea. And when he enters her he can feel the water washing him, claiming him. Waves rush over him, and he hopes that he's drowning, so that this might be the last thing he ever knows. But living is even better. They have sex again and again and again. Until he's sore to the touch, and still her touch arouses him. When she finally falls asleep, with his arms around her, he prays for the first time in more than a decade. His prayer is of thanks, and he thinks that Terry is right: he must be forgiven.

M is for Mother.
Mothering Sunday.

The children at school were probably reminded. Maybe they made cards on Friday afternoon. With pots of stiff white glue, one between two. *A* hadn't been there, so the morning started like any other Sunday: with cereal and cartoons.

His mum got up unusually late, well into *Inspector Gadget*. She looked at *A* expectantly, purple towelling dressing gown wrapped tight round her. It had brown stains on the shoulders, from when she wore it for dyeing her hair. Getting no response but a 'Morning, Mum,' she started on the washing up. *A*'s father had generously told her to leave it, the night before. But had not gone so far as to touch it himself.

A thought that something was wrong, in the way she banged the pots around in the sink. He presumed she'd had an argument with his dad. He never heard them fight. But sometimes they could be mercilessly silent to each other for days. An uncomfortable quiet would come over the house, making it impossible even for *A* to speak normally. Every basic task, requiring a little communication, became a chore, and felt like it created further friction.

When *A*'s dad got up, though, he stood behind his wife at the sink, and patted her back.

'You shouldn't have done that, pet. I was going to wash up.'

A knew he wasn't really going to, even if his dad didn't. But such attention showed this wasn't one of the silent times.

Something was wrong, though. The cold in her tone was unmistakable when she said she was going to have a bath. Normally she would fuss around the house while the water ran. Maybe make a cup of tea to drink while she soaked, if she was feeling decadent. That day the bathroom door shut with a sharp slap that was near enough to a slam. And the bolt, that was hardly necessary in a household of three, was drawn heavily across.

A and his father were both looking for blame in the other's face, when the TV provided the answer.

'Because it's Mother's Day today,' the excitable blond presenter said, 'we're going to show a wildlife special, on how different creatures care for their young.' The camera panned in on an audience section of hand-picked cool-kids, who erupted into spontaneous cheers.

A's dad started tiptoeing to the front door, and motioned *A* to follow him. They eased their way out, into a cold May morning. Co-conspirators, in matching brown, Christmas present slippers. Closing the front door with the stealth of spies, and hurrying along a frosted pavement as fast as their footwear allowed them to run.

Their out-of-breath mouths bellowed steam by the time they reached the corner shop. But they both allowed themselves to smile. And *A* felt close to his dad in their crime of kindness. A fellowship he had only ever found with *B* before.

His dad paid for a card from *A*, and the last bunch of paper-wrapped pink flowers from himself. He borrowed a biro, so that *A* could write a message in his careful print before leaving the shop. The paper-shop man grinned too, because he was in on a plan.

When she got out of the bath, *A*'s mum was sat down and

presented with a tray. The flowers were in a vase, and the card was propped up against barely browned toast and fresh tea.

'Oh,' she said, 'I thought you'd forgotten,' and *A*'s dad slipped him a wink.

B's mother hadn't lived with them for years. She had left a pound for a bag of chips each, and a note, that *B*'s brother said meant he was in charge. No one disputed it now. Their father was a drunkard, who had been made a coward by the booze. Once he must have been strong, fearless, ferocious. He was a Glaswegian, a man who'd fought in razor wars. Who had clawed his way out of that gutter. Into this one. He had arrived in England with nothing but a bag of burgled gear, and a desperate need to disappear. Stopped in Stonelee, when he discovered it was as far South as they still sold Buckfast. And stayed when he married *B*'s mother.

The wedding photo still sat on the mantelpiece. Showing that he was not always this shrivelled, sausage-skin of a person. Cowering in the corner of his own lounge. Cooking for a monster of his own creation. *B*'s brother. The great provider. Who would chuck his dad a tenner at night, to get food on the table. But would usually be gone before the lion's share was spent on Buckfast, or Special Brew. Whisky and Irn-Bru on dole day.

None of them knew where *B*'s mum had gone. But on Mothering Sundays, it seemed, she wondered about them too. Within a few days they would always have a postcard from her. The only one of the year. Nothing for birthdays or Christmas. *B*'s dad slurred that it proved the slag thought only of herself. It was when *she* wanted attention she contacted them. The cards came from all over England, one from Wales. They contained nothing traceable. Nothing factual about her life. And also no emotion. They said nothing at all, in fact. Except that she was alive, somewhere.

But still they held the family fascinated. Each of them would pour over the words when the others weren't there. Even *B*, who could only read a part of it.

So Mother's Day meant anticipation. It marked the start of a short wait for something they all pretended not to care about. From someone who clearly didn't care about them. But then, when any one of them looked at the other two, they could see her point in not giving a shit. Which made them hate and miss her all the more.

A's mother was the daughter of a miner. This led her to believe that she knew what she was doing when she married a rigger. She thought that she could handle the months apart, and the needling, nagging worry. Always wondering where he was and what he was doing. At least she knew he wasn't being unfaithful, not out in the North Sea. Mostly she could handle the rest, too. But sometimes, in the heart of winter, she'd felt alone. Rattling round a cold house that it didn't seem right to heat just for one. And when it got dark so early, when the streets were so silent, she could believe there was no one left in the world but her.

Him working on the rig, though, it had made the times they had together more valuable. Every instant anticipated, enjoyed to its utmost and then lingered over for weeks. They cheated time in their way. Made it last threefold, by revelling in the expectation and the memory, as much as the moment. She used to plan every hour of his visits, long before he came. Had to be careful to leave space just to be together. But she did, because this was the best part of all: when they did nothing but hold each other.

She hadn't made any preparations, the weekend their son was conceived. Her husband wasn't supposed to be back for months. But someone had been injured on the rig, and he'd cadged a lift in the chopper. Just appeared at the door, still in his denims. Like he'd bust out of a jail to see her. They made love on the stairs, didn't even make it to the bedroom. He smelled of oil and tasted of grit and made her forget about the sharp, carpeted edges in her back.

That weekend was the last time she would ever feel his passion as such an unabatable force. Something changed not long after. Perhaps when he stopped working on the rig, time became less precious. Maybe it was the pregnancy. Or the death of his father: their final family link severed. What ever the cause, his feelings dwindled in its aftermath. Not disappearing altogether, not something you divorced over, especially with a baby boy. But his love changed, it became dutiful rather than wonderful. They had to make time pass, instead of savouring every second. There was a blockage between them. Something they never talked about. That still lingered in every conversation.

'We aren't what we once were,' she wanted to say. 'Why? Why aren't we? What is it?' But she never did. And he never gave her enough cause to argue, so she could shout it at him. Which she knew was the only way to get it out.

So they went on, from hour to day to year, until the baby was a boy. A boy, she knew, who imagined everything was all right. Who couldn't feel the tension that was sometimes in the house. They had a lot to be grateful for, more than most in Stonelee. And it's easy enough to ignore a little, when you have so much.

It just seemed better to play along, and hope that everything would turn out for the best. That's what she'd always done. That's why she pretended not to see the damp and street-dirt on their slippers, as they handed her the tray for Mother's Day. And those years of practice helped her to carry on as normal, when the CCTV images were on the nightly news. She washed up, and cleaned and made packed lunches for five days. While inside she shrieked and screamed and wept. Until, at last, the detectives came to the door. They didn't say what the call was about, they didn't have to. After she'd asked them in, she went upstairs to fetch her son. Then, holding hands, on trembling legs, they came down together; and a second boy was created, on the same steps as the first.

N is for Newspaper, Negatives and Neckerchieves.

They're going to Alton Towers. Chris and Steve the mechanic are discussing the merits of the new A50 dual carriageway, on which they have sped from the M6. Jack is listening in the middle. It's odd to be in the van on a Saturday. The windows are open, and he can smell the dust and dirt, whose scents have been awakened by an earlier light rain. Chris is taking it slowly now they're on these little country lanes. It's only days since the accident. It's still on Jack's mind too. But the air is fresh out here. The skies are clear. The sun is shining through the trees, scattering strip-lights on the road before them. And they're going to Alton Towers.

They pull in, past the big purple billboards, along the park's road. Which has a single unbroken dividing line, to show you are in a different world now. Chris continues straight on, when the way splits, to the branch marked 'hotel' not 'entrance'. Jack waits a moment or two before he says anything. Hoping that Chris or Steve the mechanic will notice they've gone wrong. He doesn't like to point out mistakes in others, particularly in Chris, who rarely takes a bad route. But there is no getting round it, they have certainly missed their turning.

'Chris,' he says, 'I think we might have gone past the entry back there.'

Chris laughs, 'Don't worry, Bruiser, we've got a special way in. I told you we could do this on the cheap, didn't I?'

Jack suffers a slight sinking feeling, but the unstressed grins on Chris and Steve the mechanic's faces tell him there is nothing to worry about.

'It's mostly public footpath where we're going,' Steve the mechanic says. 'It was there before the rides.'

There's a big brass statue of a flying machine in front of the building. Jack would quite like to look at it, but Chris swings the van into a parking space beside a gleaming people-carrier, almost hidden from the hotel. They walk together down the gently inclined field that flows down the left-hand side. Steve the mechanic says the slope reminds him of a hill he used to go sledging on, when he was little. But the field is too lushly green for Jack to picture it covered in white, and he tries but fails to remember the crunch of snow under his feet. Here the ground bounces with the thickness of the grass. At the pasture bottom there is a barbed-wire fence. Jack finds barbed wire repellent. He saw someone trying to climb razor wire once. He'll never forget that.

Over a stile they go, into a wood. Sure enough there is a small green sign that says 'Public Footpath' and points along a beaten hard mud path, which they follow. It's quite beautiful in the woods. He wishes Michelle was here. Jack feels close to nature somehow along this path, with trees all around. Like a woodsman. Like Davy Crockett. His dad took him to see the film once. When the other boys had played cowboys and Indians he had often played Davy Crockett on his own. Watching the cavalry and the Comanches fight, out of sight, not quite one thing or the other. Living on the frontier.

The path ends abruptly at a border of green mesh fence, though Jack can see it continues on the other side.

'What now?' he asks.

'A quick shimmy, and we're in,' Chris says. He pulls at a section of the fence, by the bottom of the post nearest the path. It lifts to produce a gap just bigger than required to squeeze under.

'They keep trying to fix it,' Steve the mechanic says. 'You can see the new wire, but it's always been cut again when I've come here.'

'I reckon they figure that not enough people know about it to matter. They must make millions anyway. Go on then, get in there, Steve.'

While Chris holds up the fence, Steve the mechanic drops down to a press-up position, and pushes one leg through the gap. Then, careful not to get dirt on his clothes, he eases his whole body past it.

'Come on, Bruiser, your turn.'

Jack can't see what else he can do. He can't get home without them. Is this illegal anyway? They're only going under a fence. Other people made the hole. The sign said public footpath. Fuck it.

It's only when Jack and Steve the mechanic are holding up the mesh from the far side that they see the spying camera mounted behind a tree above them.

'Bugger,' Steve the mechanic says. 'That wasn't there last time I came. Hurry up, Chris.'

Chris gets up, and sees what they're looking at.

'It's probably for catching the guys doing the cutting. But we'd still better get lost in the crowds pretty quick.'

And that's it. They're all belting along the path. Jumping over logs and puddles. Arms raised to knock branches out of their way. Running for it once more. Jack tells himself that he's never going out with these two again. But he knows that he will. He has to, they're his only friends. Chris runs ahead of him, sure-footed like an Indian scout. From behind him he hears Steve the mechanic let out a rebel yell, as he clears a fallen tree. And Jack finds that he's laughing. How could he not go out with them again? It would be like never seeing Shell again. He couldn't bear that.

The trees finish and the three of them drop to a trot on concrete, among ornamental gardens. There are no security guards to be seen, but they file into the midst of the largest group of people, and keep pace with them up to a ride of giant, swirling, chintzy-china teacups. It looks about as adrenalin-packed as a cup of tea. But there is no queue, so the three climb aboard a blue and white cuppa to keep their heads down and get their breath back.

An hour later and they have forgotten all about caution. They are in the heart of the park, in the throng of thousands, indistinguishable from any other group of jean-clad lads. They ride the Black Hole first. Chris and Steve the mechanic talking about how they used to be scared of a ride that seems so tame now. Jack is not as complacent. Even the astronaut on the way up is unnerving: hanging there, suspended in the emptiness of space. Where's his ship? Is his lifeline severed? Is he just floating, waiting for his oxygen to end? When the ride has wound itself to the top, it plunges. Whirling downwards with bewildering speed and the clatter of rickety-sounding steel wheels. Like hundred of ambulance trolleys.

As they go out, they look at their photos, digitally delivered to the exit to entice. Chris and Steve the mechanic are laughing, in the picture; Jack looks pale like a ghost, like his own negative. He's glad he was a carriage back from the other two.

Three is a bad number for the park. One is always odd. Jack tries to be that one, so the others won't see his reactions, but sometimes Chris or Steve the mechanic volunteer. The rides get easier anyway. Quickly Jack finds that he enjoys the sense of fear that they provoke. It is foundationless fear, after all. And it leaves no space inside him for the very real fears with which he normally has to contend. He understands why people love these rides. There is something liberating about being terrified and still safe. Chris says that amusement parks are like drugs: they give highs to people who will never feel them through achievement; they give lows, without the need for real danger or despair.

'Imagine coming to Alton Towers on acid, then,' Steve the mechanic says.

Jack doesn't want to.

The Oblivion ride is as close as he wants to go. This is what it's like to fall, to finish. This is what it's like in his darkest hours, and in his dreams of release. They are in the front row as the car rolls forwards on its gleaming twin tracks. It tilts towards the brink, and over it. But stops. Holds them there. People are screaming all around. Even Chris shudders. But Jack feels utterly calm. This is what it's like in mid air.

The drop, when it comes, is a true drop. A vertical, terminal velocity plummet into a void. A smoking black pit that looks like a wall. Looks like the end. But you don't end. Even though your body screams that you must. Even though evolution tells you, you are dead. Genes produced by billions of successful breeds say that you have failed. You haven't. Not yet. The pit catches you, changes you and sends you somewhere else. Takes you to the end of the line. Jack is smiling when the ride is over. No more than two minutes from when it started. He is alive. It's everyone else who looks like ghosts.

Sunday is spent in bed. Except when they get up to have a bath. The water sloshes over the side with their two bodies' movement. She looks perfect to him like that, with soap suds not quite concealing the pink of her nipples. When he tells her this she says: 'You can take a photo if you like.'

Jack laughs.

'I'm serious,' she says. 'There's a camera in the top drawer of the dressing table; I'll give you the shot when I get it developed. But I keep the negatives.'

Jack hesitates before he gets out of the water. Slick with oil and coated in soap suds, he drips to the drawer. He feels more naked when she is not. Embarrassed, even though she has explored every nook of him. The camera is where she said, next to a teddy bear worn eyeless with love and two books: *Demystified Accounting* and *The One-Minute Manager*. Before he touches the camera, he dries his fingers on his T-shirt, lying where it was thrown, at the bed's end. Incongruous in the neat room. He has noticed that all clothing migrates to the bed's end, part of some law of motion. Jack studies the camera, trying to familiarize himself with its workings. It's a disposable; there's only a winder, flash on/off and the button for taking the picture. Long-termers, like himself, were allowed to have two pictures a year taken by the screws, to send to friends or relatives. He usually didn't bother, thought it safer the fewer shots there were of him. Once he sent one to his dad, and one to Terry. Terry still has it in his wallet, Jack's seen it. Who knows what his dad did with his one. Probably threw it away. He never got a reply to the letter.

'Come on, Jack. What are you doing?'

He slides back, flat-footed, so as not to slip on the wet wood-laminate flooring of her bedroom.

'So how d'you want me?' She giggles.

'Just like you are.' He raises the Kodak to his eye.

'You don't want these in it then?' She lifts her breasts out of the water, holds them together like the calendar models'.

'What?'

'Just take it, Jack. I'm saying I trust you not to show it to those *little boys* at work. Or don't you think it's sexy?'

He uses up the rest of the film on her. He can see that she

enjoys it. She's a natural actually, a lens pleaser, she *is* Monroe. Or maybe Madonna in her Monroe phase. She takes Jack in her lips for the last shot. Gazes up wide-eyed while he looks down at her through the steamy plastic viewfinder. He tells her to smile, and she bares her teeth around him. Like an animal showing it can bite. She says something. It sounds like 'trust me,' but could be 'fuck me,' it's hard to tell with her mouth full.

Jack's Monday-morning-tired. It's raining. Raining so hard the wipers don't ever clear it.

''Bout time too,' Chris says. 'You haven't had a proper taste of Manchester weather yet. It's been practically tropical since you've been here.' But he swears a lot on the way to the base, and peers through the windscreen like an old lady.

Jack always calls it the 'base' now. 'Unit' feels like it needs 'secure' to be whole; 'yard' smacks of 'exercise'. 'Base' is cool; it's got a military feel, it makes their missions important. The crack DV Deliveries team, with their precious cargoes of chocolate and charcoal.

'Dave wants to see you two,' the yard manager grunts at them, when they enter the building.

Chris tucks his shirt in as they walk to the office. Dave Vernon is the owner/MD of DV Deliveries. It's amazing that anyone who lacks the vision to even make up a proper name for their company can keep it going. He's a mole-like number-cruncher. Most of the lads slate him non-stop behind his back. Jack kind of likes him. Maybe Jack's more grateful for his job than the others, respects the trust he's been shown. Even though his background's invented, the legend lists plenty of prison time.

Dave's office door is open; it usually is. 'Hi, it's the heroes of the hour,' Dave says, ushering them in. He's a bit too eager to ingratiate himself, slightly slimy. Jack's noticed it before, but it's in spades today. There's another man in the office. He's sat down, with a coffee from the exclusive pot that permanently percolates in here. Everyone but Dave has to drink instant, or go to Café Costa on their break. Shell says the smell drives them all mad.

'This is Felix,' Dave says, gesturing to the man in a way that is slightly effeminate, and seeming to realize this, correcting it to a more manly posture. 'He's from the *Evening News*. They're going to run a short piece on your quick thinking and bravery. And DV Deliveries.' He turns to look at Felix, as if to check that this last point is correct. 'Felix is going to take some shots of you.'

Jack sees that there's a camera on the desk, by Felix's elbow. It's a fierce-looking, futuristic piece. Long-barrelled and deadly. It looks like it could blow holes in people, spaces you could fit your fist in.

'Look,' Jack says, 'why don't you just take Chris? He's the real hero, he's the one that thought of the pry bar and phoned the ambulance.'

'Nonsense, Jack,' says Dave. 'You both did it. You're both shining examples of our team. Now where d'you want them?' he asks Felix. 'I thought beside one of the vans, maybe.'

Jack tries to protest. 'I really would prefer not to. I'm not really one for publicity.'

'But I am, you see, Jack, I am,' Dave says quite firmly. 'Now what do you think, Felix?'

'Is it not going to be too wet to get them by the van? I think we're going to be doing indoor stuff. Why not just a shot against the wall there?'

'It would be nice if we could get the logo in, though.' Dave shoots Felix a smile, so sickly it would make Jack want to retch, if he didn't want to retch anyway.

Perhaps sensing his discomfort, Chris tries: 'Maybe we could get Steve the mechanic to stand in, if Jack really doesn't want to do it. Who'd know? Steve's a good-looking bloke!'

Jack nods vigorously; there's a chance here.

'Look,' Dave turns on them, with a face like breeze-block. 'We are not getting some bloody grease-monkey to pretend to be Jack, when Jack is standing right bloody here. Now, Felix and I are trying to organize something. Chris, would you go and find out if there's space to fit one of the vans under cover at the moment. Jack, would you wait outside, please.'

Felix gives them a sympathetic shrug from behind Dave's back.

Jack trudges to the allotted place with the compliance of the condemned. He and Chris are lined up in front of the van. Chris looks at Jack, and winks.

'Hey, Dave,' he says, 'maybe we should wear our caps for the shot?'

Dave's eyes light up. 'Good idea, Chris. Have you got them with you?' Chris and Jack shake their heads. 'Hold on a minute would you please, Felix. I'll just go and get you a new one each.'

He returns from the locked uniform store with two brand-new baseball caps. They still have the cardboard shape-savers inside them. Normally none of the lads wear their caps. Dave, proud of his initials branding, had DV put in large letters on the front. It's a bit too close to 'divvy' to warrant much wearing in public. Jack's pleased of the cap now though, he pulls it right down on his head, so that his eyes barely see beneath the brim. Chris wears his at a jauntier angle.

They don't really speak until they're on the road again.

'What is it, Jack?'

'What d'you mean?'

'Come on, you really didn't want your photo taken. That was more than just being camera shy. You didn't want to be in the newspaper. Do you owe people money? Surely your mates are all down South? No one's going to see it up here.'

'Yeah, you're right. I just don't want my old crew

catching up with me. I don't want to get dragged into all that again.'

'You're being paranoid, Jack. It happens. Shit, I thought for a minute I was being followed the other night. But this is a different world. You've got new friends. You don't have to worry.'

And maybe he is being paranoid. He hardly came across anyone from Manchester inside. Probably that's why they chose it. What are the chances of someone seeing that shot who could recognize him? And even if they did, putting two and two together to figure who he really is? But he's tired of all this. It's making him weary. The pretence. All the lies. Like Shell, on Sunday.

'I just want to get close to you,' she said. 'It feels like you didn't even exist before you came to work here. I mean it's nice to be with a lad who doesn't just want to talk about himself, but I have to do *all* the talking. Tell me something about you, Jack. Tell me a story.'

So he told her one. He's getting good at them. But that's the thing. That's all she's ever going to get. Just stories.

O is for
Once Upon a Time.

She wondered if she would recognize him, if she didn't know. He had changed a lot, of course, he was nearly eighteen. His face seemed to have changed for the better; maybe suffering does ennoble. There was no mistaking those teeth, though. She could remember the headline 'Monster' underneath his picture, suggesting what the editor didn't quite dare state: 'He must have done it, look at how ugly he is.' Would it have been different if the girl, Angela, wasn't quite so lovely? Would he have been quite the same embodiment of evil; if it wasn't so Beauty and the Beast?

She made a note on the paper she had before her, to disguise the fact she hadn't given her full attention to his last sentence.

'You know of course that I can't help you while you remain in denial?' she said. 'I've replaced Dr Bittlefield because he felt he wasn't getting anywhere with you.'

'I wasn't there. I can't tell people any more times. Yes, we took her and we walked with her down to the bridge. And I knew he was going to do stuff, but not that stuff, not kill her. But then I left them, I was further down the Byrne. Do you want me to admit to it, now? After all this? Admit to something I didn't do?'

'I want you to come to terms with what you did.'

'They get it wrong, you know? Judges and juries, they get it wrong sometimes.'

She had worked in a prison, when she first qualified, where everyone was wrongly convicted, or so they said. It doesn't matter: innocence is not considered sufficient grounds for an appeal. This young man was not innocent, she was sure of that. The court case took thirty-three days, the jury was unanimous. Dr Bittlefield believed the boy had repeated the story so many times that it had become true. He had come to believe in this version of events. A story he had clung to like jetsam after a shipwreck, and could not now be persuaded was waterlogged, would drag him down. Which was one of the reasons she'd been asked to take over: they hoped it would be easier for him to tell the truth to someone he had not told the same lie to for so many years. No, he could not be innocent, or this would be one of the gravest miscarriages of justice ever. That didn't even bear thinking about.

Not innocent then, but not psychopathic, as her new colleague Dr Webster believed the other boy might be. She allowed herself a little smile as she thought of Dr Webster; he had been utterly charming on the phone, so easy to talk to.

The initial results of Elizabeth's evaluation did not produce fresh insight. As with the tests Dr Bittlefield had conducted, there didn't seem to be anything extraordinary in the young man's responses. If unusual at all, the results showed a slightly younger level of thinking than one would have expected from a seventeen-year-old. But even this was perhaps not remarkable, for one who had not seen any degree of freedom throughout his formative years. Since adults made all of his choices, he had probably been kept in a more childlike role.

She had plenty of time to think about it on the drive home. It was a long way from the secure unit to where she lived; a couple of hours by car. But it was only once a week after all. Besides, this was a prestige patient. She had thought there might be a book in it, some scientific articles at least; but Dr Bittlefield had warned her that secrecy was such it was doubtful this would be allowed for many years. Still, she knew it could be alluded to if the need arose. It was definitely not going to impede her career.

The Range Rover's tyres chomped into the gravel, as at last she pulled into their driveway. She liked to look out at her lovely garden as she drove up to the house. Actually it was nice peering out of the Range Rover anywhere. You felt so secure, so safe, so aloof; three feet above the other motorists. All right, so she probably didn't *need* a four-wheel drive, but she did at least live in the country. She wasn't one of those urban housewives who just used it for the school run. Thomas wasn't quite old enough for school yet anyway.

Saturday was glorious. She lounged in the garden under a sky as blue as any they had enjoyed in Medina the previous month. She could see her husband upstairs in his study, catching up on missed work. Consulting one volume after another of accountancy law, and typing away into his computer.

She couldn't help feeling jealous of his success. She was always the clever one, the one destined for greatness. When they had got together at Cambridge, she could tell that people thought he was beneath her. Yet somehow his hard work had eclipsed her brilliance. She took a break to have Thomas, and when she returned to work, she found that his basic salary was more than triple what she could earn. It wasn't even about the money. It was the way his colleagues and new friends treated her: as though her psychology was a hobby. A means to keep busy, like their own wives did charity work or coached badminton. Sometimes Elizabeth felt that he was complicit, that he too had begun to see her career as secondary to childcare.

Thomas was playing by the wheelbarrow the gardener had left out. It was tin, and had showed it could hold water after the storm on Thursday. Elizabeth had topped it up with the hose, so that her son could float his boat in it. She should probably get him a paddling pool if it stayed this hot. She watched his head bob about as he collected ants to crew his ship. His hair was blond, but darker underneath where she had the barber shave it, like a basin cut. He looked beautiful. He was the most beautiful child she knew; not just because he was hers. She was sure, even impartially, he simply was the most beautiful. He looked like a page-boy with his hair like that. She could hardly bear the thought that one day he would want it shaved off, or quiffed, or long like a hippy, or whatever else was in style which would look awful.

She also knew if that was the worst that happened she would be a very happy woman.

She could remember at the time of the trial, everyone she knew was horrified, imagining what it would be like if their child had been murdered in such a way. In such a brutal, senseless, godless way. No one had stopped to think about what it would be like if their child was the murderer. That was why the boys had to be evil, they had to be alien: other, demons. They could not be something that normal children could have become given the same set of circumstances.

Thomas had started to shake the boat around in his makeshift sea. He made roaring noises like the thunder from Thursday's storm. Again, she wished he could stay this way. The larger an animal's brain, the longer its childhood has to last. Maybe if he was a genius he'd wait a little longer to grow up. He didn't seem unusually bright, though, whatever she told her friends. Who could say how quickly he'd develop? She noticed that he seemed to be squashing the ants now, crushing any that were washed by his cruel waves on to the edge of the barrow. She went and stood by his side. He didn't look up at her, continued to torture the marooned insects. He rolled them on his perfect thumbs, so that their bodies crumpled in on themselves, became a ball of abdomen and head and legs.

After a few minutes she stroked the back of his neck and said to him: 'You know that hurting the ants isn't very nice, don't you?'

He nodded.

'Why are you doing it then?' She wasn't cross, just curious.

'You didn't stop me, Mummy. I thought you'd stop me.'

On the first meeting with Dr Webster they just discussed the cases, compared notes.

'I'll show you mine if you show me yours,' Dr Webster, Michael, had said. And she had laughed, even though his joke was both inappropriate and childish.

They found the meeting very useful, however, and thought that it was something they should do regularly. Since they were based so far apart they agreed that the Travelodge, where they had first rendezvoused, was the most sensible place to get together. A neutral place to meet, to discuss people who would never meet again.

After a couple such summits they took to booking rooms at the Travelodge, so that they could continue their talk over dinner. Soon it became clear that two rooms was an unnecessary extravagance.

Elizabeth did not actually enjoy sex with Michael as much as she did with her husband. Michael rarely made her come. But she enjoyed his desire, she enjoyed his attention and she enjoyed his stories. She didn't have to pretend that she hadn't heard every anecdote, as she did with her husband at the numerous dinners they attended.

She found that she was surprisingly good at stories herself. She stayed near the truth at all times when she discussed Michael with him, leaving out only the details that would matter. She discovered that by distressing the edges of the facts, most of the gaps could be very neatly covered. Not sturdy enough to step upon, but pleasing from a distance.

Her husband's initial admiration, that she had been selected to work on such an important matter, seemed to have faded rather quickly. Now he only ever asked about her work in terms of whether or not she had made the breakthrough. As if dealing with a damaged child was as straightforward, as cut and dried, as winning a corporate court case.

Elizabeth began to dream of being carried around on a sedan-chair, by her husband and Dr Bittlefield. Sometimes with laurels on her head. She did not, as a psychologist, set much stead by dreams. But hers was hardly difficult to decode. Michael said the other boy suffered intense nightmares. To which, in her opinion, he was devoting far too much attention. Elizabeth believed the primacy of dream in the Freudian school to be ascribable to the Viennese middle-class habit of eating large quantities of cheese after dinner. She cut out dairy products altogether. Nonetheless her sleep continued to be disturbed.

The sessions in the secure unit were not proving fruitful. While he remained in denial about his culpability in the crime, little other development could be made. She was beginning to see why Dr Bittlefield had handed the case to her. There did not seem to be any realistic chance of a career-enhancing study without even an admission of guilt. She reminded him that in a little over a year he would not be able to remain in the secure unit any more. He would be forced, by law, into a young offenders' institute, a prison, and she told him quite bluntly that he would never be paroled from prison whilst in denial.

'Will any of the staff be able to come and see me when I'm in the young offenders'?' he had asked her.

'That is not normal procedure,' she said. 'I believe it is within my remit to advise that contact could be maintained if a relationship was particularly beneficial to stability, and as you have no family in the country. However, since you do not appear to be making any significant progress, I can only think that no such relationship exists.'

'It does with Terry, I've told you. You know it does with Terry.'

'I believe that your reliance on Terry, and his unconditional support, may actually be detrimental to your eventual mental health, since it is impeding your ability to confront your guilt.'

'And if I said that I did it? Would you say that he should see me then? If I said what you want?'

'It's not what I want. It's for your own well-being.'

'If I said it?'

Elizabeth smiled; this could be the watershed moment. 'I would certainly recommend, in the strongest possible terms, that Terry be allowed continued contact if he was contributing to such a substantial leap in progress.'

The boy let out a sigh, almost a shudder, and his shoulders slouched. He looked up after a minute or two, and she could see the pain in his eyes.

'OK then,' he said. 'I did it. I killed her too.'

Elizabeth turned to a fresh page in her notes. So that she might have this new story uncluttered by what had come before.

P is for Pictures.
Past and Present.

Marble the cat is vibrating with its own purrs on Jack's lap. He and Kelly are watching *The Forsyte Saga* on TV. Jack is not keen on these sorts of shows. Hacendado used to say that 'period drama' was called that because it was woman dribble. It's nice to sit here with Kelly, though, stroking a cat with one hand, a beer in the other. He only allows himself one or two beers on week nights, conscious that he can't allow alcohol to become a crutch. Kelly met Shell yesterday. They seemed to really hit it off. Everything's well with the world until the news comes on.

The chimes always strike deep in Jack. They're too loud, too impersonal, too powerful. It was from the news that he had first learned his appeal to the European court had failed. Somehow the BBC had managed to get the information to the studio before his lawyer could phone the secure unit. Europe means nothing to Jack, a place even more distant and abstract than the picture of parliament behind the presenter. A newscaster who is himself supposedly a part of national heritage, a grey statesman, an honest broker, telling Britain about how 'sleaze takes a new turn tonight'. Jack hasn't trusted the news since John Craven.

The next item shows bodies in the Balkans, then crisis in

the Middle East. It's hard to understand how this can be called 'news'; the same things happen time after time. Repeating with monotony, like the tired plots of American cop films. But in the pictures polar-opposite partners always reach a grudging friendship. It doesn't happen in the real world. People who seem to have more in common than apart just keep on killing each other.

'News just in,' says the anchorman, with his most serious expression, normally reserved for British disasters. 'A man has been hospitalized, and a house set on fire in a vigilante attack, believed to be a case of mistaken identity. The twenty-three-year-old man, who had recently moved to Nottingham, was reported to resemble the artificially aged photograph the *News of the World* released of the surviving murderer of ten-year-old Angela Milton. The Press Complaints Commission are still considering whether the release of the image contravened guidelines. It is not known whether this attack will affect their decision.'

'And finally,' the announcer says, although his words are lost on Jack. He realizes that his fingers are clenched into Marble's fur. The cat is not protesting but has stopped purring and stares at him through the same fierce eyes as the rest of the world. He puts the cat down and goes through as if he is going to the toilet. He finds it difficult to walk, because he's concentrating so intensely on walking naturally. When he gets in the toilet he slumps down. It makes it so hard, living with Kelly. Having to have his guard up all the time. But the beating shows that they were right to be careful. At least with Terry as his only link to the past there are fewer things to go wrong; he should be untraceable. It would be too easy to track him to a halfway-house, where most long-termers start freedom. He knows the plan, it's just so testing. It requires so much strength. He's not sure he's got enough left to see this through. But then what options does he have? Only that one other.

He washes his face in cold water, and inspects it in the mirrored cabinet. He should look old before his time, but there are hardly any lines beneath his eyes. They remind him of his dad, his eyes. It's bizarre, but he can remember that same clear blue looking down on him, like the sky. A time when adults and gods were indistinguishable, all powerful, peering from above. Maybe one day he can do what his dad did: go abroad, leave it all, have only a future. Imagine if he could have a future with Shell, somewhere where no one had heard his name. His real name, the one he keeps hidden in the dark. The one that sounds like a stranger to him now. Not a stranger, an old enemy. Someone who fucked his life up once, for ever.

He slides the door of the cabinet. Its shelves are stacked with pills, stuff Kelly gets from the hospital; half-used, high strength. A bottle of any would send him away more finally than a plane. You always have a choice.

Chris has got the paper on the dash, yesterday's *Evening News*.

'Check it out,' he says. 'You had nothing to worry about. Rather a fine shot of me, though, I feel.' He licks a finger and smoothes down his eyebrows like a medallion man.

He's right, the famous Chris grin beams out of the grainy black and white, but you can't see much of Jack under the cap. If you knew what you were looking for you'd recognize him, but not at a glance, not without close examination.

He sits back and breathes easy. 'Yeah, you were right. I was just being paranoid. Took me by surprise, is all.'

The article is short, and makes them sound a bit more heroic than they were. What's a hero anyway? Either they had to help, or pretend they hadn't noticed.

'I'm amazed how well you're adapting,' Chris says. He's obviously been pondering. 'It must be quite a culture shock, getting out and then moving up here. Starting a new job and everything.'

'It's definitely been strange.'

'Getting a bird, as well. Jeez, Bruiser, you're probably the best sorted out of any of us. How is the White Whale, anyway?'

'She's all right. I'd rather you didn't call her that anymore.'

'Ah, Jacky-boy, you've got it bad, don't you? You know I don't mean anything by it.'

'Yeah, I know. But it's not the nicest of names.'

'So what do you suggest? "The White Rabbit", I bet you two are always at it. I know, "The White Hole" – in Michelle, no one can hear you scream.'

'Chris!'

'Sorry, can't help it.'

'Why does everyone have to have a name anyway?'

'That's just the way the world works, I'm afraid, Bruiser. Everyone's got to have a name.'

'Now I know you trust me, Jack,' Shell says, drawing the razor across his windpipe. She wipes the foam and bristle on a towel, and rinses the blade under more hot water. 'Why do you shave with one of these anyway? I bet you're the only man in the country under seventy that uses a cut-throat. It is kind of sexy, though. Especially tonight.'

They're going to the cinema. A special showing, *Casablanca*. Shell was appalled when she realized he hadn't seen any of the classics that her mum had shown her as lessons in life. Then she noticed, in the same paper as the story on Jack and Chris, that the Odeon was starting a run of old movies: every Tuesday a different gem. Jack had to phone Terry and find out if it was all right; Tuesday used to be their night.

'No problem at all,' Terry had said. 'I'm glad to see she's educating you. We can just change to Wednesdays. Am I going to meet her one day, Jack? Maybe I could come to the cinema some week. You know I love films.'

Of course he could, Jack had said. But they'd left it in that limbo.

He's still in his towel now, clean from the shower, his face smooth and caressed. Shell massaged in moisturiser when she'd shaved him. She had to use Kelly's.

'You'll have to buy some of your own,' she says. 'It's not good for your skin to just leave it, specially if you're shaving with some sort of medieval weapon.'

He grabs her and pulls her down on to his lap, rolls back on the bed with her weight, pretends he meant to do it.

'Get off,' she shrieks. 'You'll scrunch my dress.'

She looks stunning: red dress, bright red lipstick. Jack is pretty sure that she's wearing clothes that go with the film, 1940s style, but he's not sure enough to ask. She looks glamorous anyway, he told her that.

'We're going to have to take you shopping one day soon,' Shell says, looking in his wardrobe. She's decided that she's going to dress him tonight.

'I haven't got much money saved yet.'

'Well, we're coming up to Christmas soon. We'll have to see what Santa brings, won't we?'

She could be Santa's daughter in that dress. Jolly, in a desirable way, and white hair rolling over her pale shoulders.

In the end she's forced to select his Ralph Lauren shirt; it really is all he has that's smart. He was relieved the blood came out of it. But Shell must be getting quite sick of it by now. Maybe he can speak to Terry, see if his son's got any other old clothes. He's moved in with Terry permanently now, come to Manchester, lost his job in London. Terry said his son was always losing jobs, took offence easily and bore grudges. But he'd said it almost proudly. It was obvious Terry's been looking forward to him coming. Jack finds it almost impossible to comprehend how any son of Terry's could be physically equipped to take offence. Terry's generosity of spirit rubs off on almost anyone he talks to. It will be great when Shell and him meet.

Shell seems at home in her car, more even than her home. She's told him driving relaxes her; she drives when she needs to think. She reverses the Clio into a tiny space virtually outside the movie-theatre. She's in first go, no messing. She's a good driver, Jack thinks. Not as good as Chris, no one's as good as Chris, but he's never seen her make a mistake. Jack would like to learn one day, still be Chris' driver's mate, but have a licence himself. It's nice to have plans.

The cinema's almost empty. They're a little bit early, but it doesn't look good for the Tuesday night classics programme. They get a seat in the back row, which is deserted. Shell wouldn't let him buy popcorn, 'because it's a rip-off', but she's brought along a pack of Minstrels in her handbag. She says they're her mum's favourite; she always talks of her mum proudly, as if she's a celebrity.

Casablanca turns out not to be a sloppy love story, as Jack had feared, nor a crime story, as he thought it might be. It's about people running, and people hiding and people trusting. OK, it's about love too, but the sort of love that you have when someone else's happiness means more than your own. Not the sort that sings songs and sends flowers.

Jack wants to be able to do something to prove his love. Some noble deed that would show the world what he is capable of. Or at least show himself. But the self that needs the proof, the doubting undermining side, says that if he really loved Shell he would give her up. Walk away like Bogart, rather than condemn her to a life with him. He's not the noble Rick from the end of the film; he's the cowardly, duty-shirking Rick from the start. The man hiding from his past in Morocco.

'Have you ever been abroad?' Jack asks, when they're outside the pictures again.

'Magaluf,' she says taking his arm. 'Tenerife, Gran Canaria, just girls' holidays, with my friends.'

They're walking up to a pub that Shell knows, since the

showing finished so early. Jack is pretty sure there was a short film on before the main one, when he'd been to *Davy Crockett* with his dad. They obviously don't do that any more. It's odd really, because *Casablanca* was made years and years before the last film he saw, all that time ago. It's like he's moving backwards when he should be moving forwards.

'Have you ever thought about living abroad?' he asks.

'What, you mean Wales or somewhere?'

Jack is about to say no, when he looks at her and realizes that she's pulling his leg.

'I've never thought about it. I mean, this is my home, Manchester. My family's here, all my friends are here. I've never wanted to. I'm not saying I wouldn't, but then I don't know if I could, really. It would be so hard to start totally from scratch. I mean even you've got your Uncle Terry here, and we speak the same language.'

'You reckon?' Jack says.

She digs him in the ribs, and they go into the pub. A man that Jack's been vaguely aware of behind them looks as though he's about to follow them in. But when Jack holds the door for him, he changes direction suddenly, and turns his head so Jack can only see the back of it. He's a big guy, built; he hurries up the road, walking much more quickly than he must have been when he was behind them. Jack stares wildly round for signs of anyone else.

'What's the matter?' Shell asks, coming back out of the pub again.

'Oh, nothing.'

'It's not nothing, you look uptight.'

'Well… I just thought this guy was following us. Of course he wasn't,' he adds quickly. 'It's just the film, probably.' He's trying to make light of it now. 'I'm thinking I'm a secret agent or something.'

'What did he look like, Jack? Was he a big bloke?'

'Yeah, dark hair, big white guy, with dark hair.'

'The fucker, it's my ex, I'll bet. The bouncer I told you about. He's done it before when he's seen me out with a lad.'

'Great, a bouncer,' Jack says, though really he's relieved. He still finds himself unconsciously touching the panic button/pager on his belt; but of all the bad things someone pursuing him could be, an ex-boyfriend is not in the top ten.

'Don't worry,' Shell says. 'If we see him again, I'll give him a piece of my mind. I'm not scared of him. He's got another suspended sentence already. If he touches anyone he'll be inside like that.' She clicks her fingers.

'Very reassuring,' says Jack. 'I'll die happy knowing he's going down.' But he's actually smiling again now.

'Are you going to stay over, Jack?' she asks, back at hers.

He plays with the coffee mug on his knee. 'What about my stuff? I haven't got my uniform and that for work.'

'I'll take you round to yours early in the morning.'

'OK, yeah.'

'I've got something to show you, then.' She pulls open a drawer on the low lounge table, and produces a small parcel, wrapped in red tissue-paper. 'Happy birthday, Jack,' she says.

He's confused. He hasn't celebrated a birthday in many years; occasionally with Terry, but this isn't it, not his real one or Jack Burridge's. 'But it's not my...'

She places a finger on his lips. 'I know. This is for all the birthdays we've missed.'

He turns the present over and over, looking for an easy way in, before he tears the tissue slowly away. There's a wallet inside, leather, the colour of caramel. He lifts it and sniffs it, understanding suddenly how people get turned on by leather. It smells lavish, lush, of lust.

'Look at it,' Shell says.

He takes it down and does so. His name is on it, Jack, burned in like it was branded on the cow. More final, more real than anywhere else he's seen it. This is the proof of who he has become. The wallet opens out like a book. There are slots inside, lined sheaths for crisp notes. She's put a penny in one of them, as shiny as he's ever seen, like it was made on the day they met.

'It's got a secret compartment, too,' she whispers, her hand sliding on to his thigh.

He studies it, and sees what she means. There's a credit card section which looks as though it might lift. It does; there's a brass pop-stud underneath. It flips open to reveal a plastic-covered photo. It's a shot he took himself. Shell, naked, coated in bubbles, holding her breasts out to him. She's cut off the picture so that it fits in; her nipples are just out of view. She looks like a goddess to Jack, unblemished as soap and snow.

'Shell, I don't know what to say. Thank you.' He can hear his voice croaking, feel his eyes glistening.

'You like it then?'

He nods.

They go to bed.

Q is for Queen.
Pleasuring Her Majesty.

Dorset. Portland Young Offenders' Prison. Induction wing. Smith-678, they had called him. Smith stank as a false name, too obvious. Might as well have called him *B*-678.

It stank in the cell too. A bowl, as basic as the Victorian prison itself, swam with his piss and shit in the corner. Yesterday they had let him empty it twice. The door hadn't been opened at all yet today.

He started pacing again. He wasn't the first, there was a trail worn into the tiles around the cramp, cold cell. Turn left by the steel bed, around the blue table, reach the door, and to the bed again. He had paced his way through last night, shouts all around him, unwilling to sleep. Sometimes burning toilet paper had fluttered past the mucky grilled window. He had masturbated for an hour, dully, unexcited by it, just trying to numb his thoughts. When he finally jizzed on to his belly, he had left it there, because it made him feel stronger somehow. Not for long.

The tiredness was creeping in now. When he sat down on the solitary wooden chair he started to nod, drifted towards oblivion. Only it wouldn't be oblivion, that was the problem. He knew the dreams would come. Sometimes he didn't know which was worse: to live in constant nagging fear, or to sleep with the risk of terror. His psychologist at the secure unit, Michael smug-wanker Webster, had said the dreams would go if he talked about them. Lying fuck. They only became worse, more real; alive in his waking mind as well.

He could picture the two dogs: hideous, pig-like bodies and tiny spiky legs. They faced each other, in one of the dreams, growling and threatening, and opening their huge snot-drooling jaws. But the dogs never moved, like their stunted little legs had lost the power to carry them. Then one of the beasts would eat the other one, swallowing it whole. Jerking its head to shake the vast meal through its throat. Snorting with each stage of success. Until only a fat, black sausage-tail, still writhing in panic, hung from its teeth. Then *B* would feel the panic too. The abject terror of the devoured beast, and also the sudden rising fear of the victor, as it understood that the thing it had eaten was too big. *B* would see the blood that squirted out of its arse and ears. Not its prey's blood, its own. Organs ruptured and squashed by the thing that still shook its death throes inside. Just one dream of many.

The slot slid open in the door, dark eyes peered through, nodded slowly. The slot was closed again.

B coughed. The cough made him feel sick, reminded him he needed a cigarette. As if he didn't know. They gave him ten with his 'welcome pack' when he got his clothes. He had four left. He didn't know when he could get some more. He figured with four he was fucked anyway. Decided he'd smoke a half of one. It tasted acrid and exquisite. They reckoned smoking was bad for you, but he never coughed when he smoked, only when he didn't. He doubled the value, by breathing out through his mouth and sucking all the smoke back in again through his nose. It looked beautiful, he knew, like a reverse waterfall, but there was no mirror to watch it.

Breakfast came on a tray, from a trolley that a trustee wheeled along. He was with a screw, who was there to unlock the door and watch him, but watched *B* more. The screw snarled disgust as he left. *B* pulled his knees to his chest on the bed and closed his eyes, surrendering to the urge to sleep.

The chaplain came to see him later. He spoke with a slight Dorset slur that suggested cider and straw sucking.

'They tell me you've been a regular chapel attendee.'

B nodded.

'Are you any particular denomination?'

'I don't believe in God.'

'You don't believe in God, then why would you go to chapel? I warn you, inmates here are not given a Bible, so if it's the fine paper for rolling tobacco you're after, you'll be wasting your time.'

'I want to believe. I just don't.' His voice sounded drained, even to himself, weary of this place already.

The chaplain put his hand on *B*'s shoulder, cautiously, like the first pat of a pit-bull. Then firmly with a squeeze, when no bite came. 'Well then, maybe that's something we can help you with; if you have hope, then faith may follow. I'll find out if we can get you out of induction on Sunday, for the service; I'll ask the number two governor.'

Even the governors have numbers. Screws wear their numbers on their shoulders, three digits. Cons have six. Doors have numbers, floors have numbers, wings and keys and bins have numbers. Everything you own is numbered on a property card, itself numbered in case of forgery. Forms are numbered, complaints are numbered and punished with numbers: 'Allegations against a prison officer not upheld can result in up to 156 extra days,' read the signs all around. So days are numbers, nights are numbers. Nonces are numbers: section 43. Suicides are numbers: code 1. Even the public can become numbers: 200,000 coupons had been sent in from the *Sun,* demanding *B*'s sentence be a longer number. Blame was a number: three months younger and he couldn't have been tried at all. Would not have been demonized. But God has his numbers too.

'Luke 23, 43,' the chaplain said. '"Today you shall be with me in paradise." Jesus told Dysmas that – one of the thieves – and he was saved at the eleventh hour. There is always time, you see, if you have the will there is always enough time.'

Time was the only thing B didn't feel short of. He had no watch and no release date. Time is meaningless unless it's numbered.

He was escorted to service on the Sunday. A prison officer to himself, the only one on induction going along. They walked side by side through the corridors, not looking at, or speaking to, each other. B's gait had altered in the secure unit years. He discovered that the stride he had adopted to ward off monsters provoked inside, instead of protecting. He learned gradually and painfully to saunter instead of strutting, to stroll and then to shamble.

The officer stopped at the door of the chapel, motioning B to continue in. The other prisoners were there already, seated on old plank benches. As B entered they stood, and there began a slow hand-clap. Not an applause, an identification. We know. Getting louder as more found the rhythm. Until it seemed like everyone inside was clapping. To his horror B saw that one of the screws was doing it too, hitting the wall at his back with the flat of his hand. The unhurried ovation continued, even after B had found a seat on an empty row. He knew that it was out. He'd been fingered already. He would have to hide under section 43, but he was strangely unafraid, as if his body no longer had the energy for fear.

The noise had died by the time the chaplain entered, wearing a dress and a look of piety. He was middle-aged, of middling height, with mid-brown hair. But he had an exuberance that was for some reason undented from his

years at Portland. He scanned the ranks for *B*'s face, as he
mounted the pulpit, and smiled when he caught his eye.

'Thou shall call his name Ishmael,' the chaplain said,
'because Jehovah hath heard thy affliction. And he shall be as
a feral ass among men; his hand shall be against every man,
and every man's hand against him; and he shall be set against
all his brethren.' He rocked back on to his heels, and tilted
his head, as if in this quotation he had asked the room a
question. 'Genesis 16, 14,' he continued. 'Many of you here
may have felt like that. How many of you have thought that
the whole world was out to get you, as it was out to get
Ishmael? Who among you has believed himself completely
alone?' With this he looked at *B* once again. 'You are not
alone. You are never alone. Because the Lord is with you.'

The number one governor concurred with *B*'s request for
protection. He was sent to F-wing, when he came off
induction, to where the wild things roam. The fraggles: kid
fiddlers, grave diggers, grey rapers, nonces, bent coppers,
shower hawks, snitches, chesters, cho mos, the retards, the
radio rentals, the snotters, the scunners, the diaper snipers,
baggawires, grasses and all the rest who were hiding from a
hiding. And there, among the chevvy dodgers and shank
skankers, he was given a one-person cell to call home. At
least it had a flushing toilet in it, though in spite of this the
mattress was stained with piss.

B began to spend most of his time in his pad, even when he
didn't have to, occasionally emerging to watch television.
He had made a couple of attempts at conversation, but the
fraggles repulsed him. They were all freakish, ill-composed,
put together from oddments. Survival of the fittest had been
suspended on F-wing. These were the people who couldn't
even fit in prison. Nothing fitted, every part of them
seemed grotesque. At the bottom rung of the laundry

pecking order, even their clothes either hung off them, or left mocking gaps at the cuffs and ankles. *B* would flinch whenever one of them brushed against him. He paced his cell all day, doing push-ups and chin-ups on the fat pipe that wound around one wall. Bulking his short, stocky body.

He realized he needed a new charm, a spell to keep people from him. He tried to ask for it, from the God that the chaplain knew. But He was never there, or the radio was too loud from the cell next door. *B* lived in a state of depression and tension for so long, it became normal. He felt like he was in a bunker, with a grenade on the floor. But he knew he could never get to it in time, so he didn't bother. He just stood there watching, waiting for the explosion.

In the TV room he saw a programme about Vietnam veterans. It was explaining how constant fear could rewire the brain, when someone turned it over to *Coronation Street*.

B told him to switch it back. 'Can't you see?' he said. 'They're talking about us.'

The youth was part of a group who considered that they ran F-wing, multiple rapists mostly, who would have been bitches in the main gaol. He told *B* to fuck off.

B floored him with a flung chair, and fought off two of his cronies until the screws broke it up. They dragged him back to his pad, and banned him from any association time for a month. *B* didn't much care. He figured he might have found his spell. And, while pacing his cell, he discovered that his walk had recovered too. The shamble strolled into a strut, and though his concrete hut was only four strides long, he began to feel it was enough.

He had learned to read in the secure unit, and in the unmissed absence of company he requested books. He liked biology. The books he was given had many pages missing, where pictures had been removed for masturbatory consumption. But he discovered other subjects of fascination. For example: did you know the human eye sees everything upside down, and it's only some trick, with mirrors in the mind, that makes the world approach the shape we believe it to be? *B* knew that. And he reclaimed the slow hand-clap that had started his descent into this place. Practising it as he paced, ever further each day, around his tiny room. Sometimes he would sing, just to remind himself of his voice.

'If you're happy and you know it clap your hands,' he would bellow, thinking that this further proof of instability could only help his cause of solitude.

He was smacked once, as a child at primary school, for refusing to clap at the right point in that song. He could see now the injustice of that, because he had not been happy. Except for some few weeks with *A*, before even that soured to an impossible poison.

Because he was restricted to his cell, *B*'s meals were brought to him by another prisoner. A trustee from a different wing, who had grown fat, or at least remained so, by stealing the choicest bits from all the trays on his trolley. *B* had never spoken, or moved a muscle in protest. He sat impassive when the line of grease next to his lone sausage revealed that there had once been two. Or when three fat finger trails streaked through his baked beans. But when he heard the unmistakable sound of someone hoiking up phlegm and spitting it, outside his cell, just a moment before he was given his dinner, he coldly asked for another one.

'This is all you're getting, you little queen,' the fat guy said, and he stirred his finger into the ice-cream-scoop of indeterminate veg. 'Enjoy your greens.'

B rose and took the tray from him. Then, staring straight into his eyes, tilted it so that all the food slid between their feet. The fat guy looked down, and when he did so *B* smashed the tray up. It wasn't that heavy, but the blow was hard enough to make the guy stagger back, and allow another shot. *B* held it by the sides, above his head, and slam-dunked it down onto his opponent's hairline. This time, the guy's legs dropped from under him.

He had a flap of skin hanging from his forehead, like a mangled second nose, by the time the prison officers could take *B* off to the segregation wing.

Back to where he had begun, almost. There was only a mattress in segregation, no bed, a chair but no table, a pot and a blanket. Only now he found he could sleep unafraid on his mattress. When the dreams came, he could take control. If the two dogs faced each other, slavering away, *B* found he could reach his arms into their world, and bang their heads together. They whined and whimpered and turned against him with their snarls, but they became friends, and both were saved. Other than the indignity of the pot, *B* was happy in segregation. He didn't count the hours or the days. There was only him, no numbers, he just was.

It was an evening when the numbers came back. There were four of them. They opened the door and rushed in. They wore pillowcase hoods with ragged eyeholes. They looked like Klansmen. And by the noose of blanket-platted rope one carried, it was clear they meant to have a lynching. *B* knocked him down, and leaped like a power-surge for the emergency button on the wall. But he was blocked by two more. They wrestled him to the floor, and while three gripped his thrashing body, the fourth placed the noose around his gnashing, spitting head.

It was all they could do to hold him beside the grill, as the rope was threaded through it. Twice he got a hand free and punched pillowcased faces. Then they pushed the chair under his twisting feet.

Though his wrists were still held, *B* saw his opening to land a kick. He launched off the chair, and it toppled backwards to the floor. But he had exploded with sufficient force to ground his foot with a crack of broken jaw. And as the rope went tight he thought: 'I got you, you fucker, I got you.'

R is for Rocket. Reward and Resolve.

I see no reason, Why gunpowder treason, Should ever be forgot.

It's the 4th on Tuesday, when Terry comes around to pick up Jack. The cinema's classic reshowing attempt has flopped, so they're back to the arranged night out. Terry's serious; his lips barely flicker into their usual smile when he sees Jack. It's obvious there's something on his mind. When he finds that Kelly isn't in, he sits them both down on the sofa.

'Jack,' he says, 'something's been brought to my attention today. I've debated with myself, but I think you've got the right to know.'

'What's the matter?'

'There's been a bounty posted on the Internet.' He lets the words sink in. 'For information about your whereabouts. The police are investigating, but it looks at the moment like it's been posted in the States, in which case there isn't really much we can do.'

Jack always knew that something like this could happen, but that hasn't lightened the blow.

'This doesn't necessarily affect anything. There's no information about where you might be, no pictures. It just confirms what we already knew; that there are people who will never let this go. But they don't know a thing. In a way this just proves how successful we've been, how successful you've been. They wouldn't have to do this unless they really didn't have a clue.'

'The reward,' Jack says, 'it's just for information.'

'Just for information. There's no explicit threat of violence.'

'How much am I worth?'

'Thirty thousand dollars, about twenty thousand pounds,' Terry says.

'Maybe I should turn myself in.' Jack laughs a dry damned laugh.

Terry puts his arm around him. He can smell Brut aftershave, and beneath it the safety of the special Terry smell.

'No one but me and the protection squad police know where you are, Jack. They're not going to find you, I promise. Nobody's going to find you.'

Jack wonders if he should tell Terry about the man he thought was following him the other week. Shell said it was just her ex, though, didn't she? And nothing's come of it. Maybe it wasn't anything at all, just paranoia. If he says something, and Terry takes it seriously, they might move him. He'll lose everything: Shell, Chris, Steve the mechanic, the job, his room, this whole world. He'd rather take his chances. He doesn't feel like he could do it all again even if there was another Michelle out there.

Neither of them much feels like going to the pub after that, so they ring for a pizza. It arrives with a pubescent on a moped, and a free bottle of coke.

Jack guesses closest to the time they get back to the yard. Under the rules of the bet, Chris owes him a pint. A small victory in a grey day. Someone's written *www.washme.com* in the thick city grime on the side of the van. Chris thinks it's funny. It aggravates Jack's Internet anxiety.

'Are you coming to the fireworks tonight?' Chris asks. 'I'll buy you your winnings.'

'I said I'd go somewhere with Shell.'

'Bring her along. I'm meeting Steve and his mate Jed in the Crown at eight, and then we're going over.'

Fireworks sounds like a good idea. So does company, Jack's feeling too broody to want to be alone with Shell. She'd know something was up. 'OK, let's go and ask her.'

Shell agrees, but Dave shoos them rapidly out of the office. He's got an angry red boil on the side of his neck, which is threatening to go volcanic. The office is erupting too, into pandemonium over some lost stock.

'Ungrateful bastard,' Chris mutters, when they're back on the unit side. 'We were heroes a few weeks ago. He's forgotten that one pretty quickly.'

Three children, wearing faces like film orphans and dragging a go-cart, intercept Jack, as he starts to walk home from the drop-off.

'Penny for the Guy,' their leader says, in a plaintive voice that suggests some illness could take his feeble life at any moment.

Unless Fawkes was a teddy bear in a babygrow, the Guy is not a close likeness, although they've tried to biro a beard on to its worn beige face. Jack finds himself giving the boy a pound anyway, before he's even thought about it. They all rocket off as soon as they have the money, as if afraid he'll change his mind. The cart rattles behind them on twin tow ropes. Guy Fawkes would be unseated if his stunted legs weren't sellotaped to the plank chassis.

The Crown's busy, being opposite the park. Actually it's called the Crow, the 'n' seems to have fallen off. Not a good omen, but Steve the mechanic and Jed have managed to secure a table. Jed's thick-set, olive-skinned, shaven-headed and could look menacing. Only he doesn't; he looks friendly and familiar. He stands up to give Shell his chair and goes off to try and find another one.

Chris arrives last, grinning like Scooby-doo, and holding a plastic bag full of fireworks and cans. He shakes Jed's hand, apparently he's never met him either, and kisses Shell on the cheek. They talk about work for the next pint, having to explain about people and events to include Jed. He doesn't seem to mind though, or else he puts on a good show of polite interest.

Shell says that Dave's been going mad all afternoon. Apparently the missing stock is worth quite a lot of money. If it doesn't turn up, then not only will DV Deliveries have to pay for it, but they could lose the contract with that company. It's sobering for a second, but Chris and Steve the mechanic crack with laughter when she tells them how she christened Dave's boil 'Mini Me', because it mirrors his bald, bright red head.

It's raining when they cross over to the park, just before the fireworks are due. Some scallies are selling disposable plastic macs for two pounds a pop. Chris hands out sparklers and lagers from his Asda bag, as they make their way to the chunk of crowd that looks the thinnest. The field is already thick with mud; Jack's glad he wore his work-boots, not his trainers, but realizes that he's going to have to clean them before tomorrow.

A bonfire, big as a house, is burning ferociously; but ropes prevent anyone from getting close enough to enjoy its heat. Two fit birds, with horsy waxed jackets, sit sharing a spliff on inflatable armchairs. He sees Chris eyeing them, torn between his friends and the potential pull. Jed and Steve the mechanic light their sparklers and this seems to sway Chris, at least temporarily.

Jack tries to write his name with his sparkler. The letters leave a brief imprint on his eyes, but the blackness quickly swallows them. Only by scribing into the air again and again in rapid succession can he reach the level of permanence required to see his whole identity at once. Jed slashes Zs in the air with his brand, like Zorro.

The display starts with a warning, safety instructions delivered through a loud speaker. Stuff that should be common sense, pounded out from fear of litigation. The last instruction is to not discharge any of your own fireworks. Chris manages to send off a rocket with a trailing whistle almost the second afterwards, and soft laughter ripples through the crowd nearby.

The official rockets shoot up in clusters. They crackle like high amp rice-crispies as they fire. Explode into bright, life-loving, punk-rock colours. Then drift slowly downwards like destroyed worlds. Jack is entranced. He holds Shell's hand, but doesn't murmur a word while volley after volley lights up the sky. When it's all over the darkness looks more dark because of what it's known.

'Which were your favourites?' Shell asks, as they meander back to the pub or the car, still undecided which.

Jack preferred the long bleached streaks, that flowed down like Tina Turner's hair, and he says so. Shell laughs and squeezes his hand.

'Best legs in the business, Tina Turner,' Steve the mechanic adds, with sham sincerity.

'What business, shipbuilding?' Chris says. 'She looks like she could carry a steel joist under each arm.'

Jack laughs out loud, and then again silently, when he hears Chris describe himself as 'in logistics', to answer the wax-jacketed girl he has his arm around.

But the humour is short-lived. Jack is suddenly struck with the sickness of his situation. Laughing at Chris for bending the truth in the hope of a pull, when Shell, the woman that he loves, knows nothing about him that's true. Not even a name. It all comes down to nothing.

The good mood vanishes. Jack tells Shell he thinks they should go home.

'See you tomorrow, Bruiser.' Chris winks.

'Yeah, see you,' Jack says. He waves goodbye to Steve the mechanic and Jed, and the two girls whose partially deflated armchairs they are carrying.

Jack says he's too tired to make love, when they get back to Shell's. It's the first time they haven't had sex when they've been together since that first time. Shell's brown-sugar eyes look hurt. Jack puts his arms around her and tells her that he loves her. He's never said it before, except when he was on ecstasy, centuries ago. He means it too. He means it with a sadness that could swallow him if he let it.

Jack's restlessness contradicts his claim of exhaustion, but that is the least of the untruths that bother him. He can't get comfortable on the mattress. He feels like he's lying on his lies. They niggle at his skin like fleas, trap nerves in his spine, infest his mind. When eventually he does fall asleep it is shallow and disturbed. Full of bitter dreams that are almost thoughts, they are so clear. Thoughts about her. About Angela Milton. He wakes in the morning more weary than he went to bed.

They're running late. Shell seems pissed off. He doesn't know if it's because they're stuck in rush-hour traffic, or because he didn't have time to clean his boots; they're dropping great lumps of dried mud on the Clio's carpet. He's trying not to move his feet, but Shell's jerking the car around, in anger or a futile attempt to make up ground. They don't speak when they get out. She kisses him, quite coldly, on the cheek, and tears off up to the office. Jack is left to trudge into the yard, leaving parts of a fireworks field in his wake.

It's another drab day at work. They pass a series of cardboard signs, tied to trees and lamp-posts, advising the world that Simon is twenty-one. Chris asks Jack what he did for his twenty-first, and Jack replies with a seemingly blithe trickle of lies, that turn out to pool around his feet for the rest of the journey.

On the way back to base, Jack finds his stories are smeared across the windscreen with the fumes and the flies. They spoil everything he looks at. Even tainting his view of the moon-blue motorway markers, which point to 'The North', as if it were a destination in itself, as if it were attainable. And suddenly he realizes that this can't go on. Maybe with Chris it can, at least for the moment. But not with Shell. If he loves her he has to tell her. Or what does love mean? And though he feels sick with the knowledge of what he has to do, for maybe the first time in his life he actually feels in control of the future.

He strides into the office, barely noticing a look of disdain from Dave, who asks what he wants. He just wants to see her. Of course he won't tell her now, but she'll know something has changed. One glance at his face will show Shell his resolve. He'll ask to come round tonight. He'll bring some wine. No, not wine, she has to see that he's telling her only because he loves her and trusts her so completely. And then they'll talk until the morning, in a way that he's never talked to anyone. He's going to be completely open with her, and she'll understand him, because this was meant to be; maybe this moment is the culmination of it all. Everything happens for a reason, that's what Terry says.

Dave says: 'She's ill. She's gone home.' His lip curls up as he touches the bulbous sticking plaster on his neck. 'Now get out, and don't come in here with your dirty boots on again. I'm not running a bloody escort agency.'

Jack has a strange sense of relief that Shell is ill. He won't tell her until she's better, so that will give him maybe a couple of days to try and find the perfect words. How do you broach something like this? There is no thing like this. If Shell's sick then that also explains why she seemed pissed off with him this morning. He whistles back to the van, and asks Chris if he minds dropping him off at her place.

Jack wonders whether he should have bought some flowers or something as Chris pulls away. Too late.

She's not answering the door. He rings the bell again. He can hear its shrill echo in the still inside. There's no sign of movement through the long linen-draped windows. He can see that the table where she places her bag and the hook where she hangs her keys are both empty. She must be at her mum's or something, which makes for a long walk home. Still, he's got plenty of thinking to do. He looks up at the sky. It looks like the rain should hold out for a while yet. And maybe a good march will knock the last of the muck from his shoes.

S is for Sand.
Sand Castles.

It gets everywhere, the sand. In your shoes, in your food, in your bed, in your ears. Sometimes it feels to him like it migrates inside his head through his ears. He'll poke a finger in and find the grains sliding further, grating as they go. How do they get out of there? They must go on to your brain. Glass is made out of sand, that's how sharp it is. It gets to you after a while. It's good to be out of Kuwait, he thinks, even if it's only for a holiday. It's good to get away from the sand.

It's still bloody hot though, worse really, with the humidity, and at least he's got aircon in Kuwait. He leans back to feel the pillow against his neck, and watches the slowly mesmerizing ceiling fan thudding in its lazy circles. Tiredness overtakes him and he eases into sleep.

He can feel the darkness when he wakes. It's night-time. Good, that's why he came. He showers in the white tiled bathroom, soaping the paunch that's been growing through his forties. It's still not as bad as some. He dresses in slacks and a plain short-sleeved shirt; smart but not over the top. It's best not to look too wealthy. Not that he is, but the US dollars they get paid in Kuwait go a long way in Bangkok baht.

'Tuk-tuk, Patpong,' he says to the receptionist, using most of his Thai vocabulary, and emphasizing with an imaginary driving action.

The man nods, says something to the boy that habitually sits in the corner and may or may not be his son. The boy gets up and runs to the end of the street, to hail one of the three-wheeled jalopies.

He remembers when his own son was that age, not long before it all went wrong. Went more wrong, anyway. Wrong, wronger, wrongest. Adulthood was supposed to be a reward, wasn't it, for people who'd had shitty childhoods? He supposed that had gone wrong for his son too. How could it not, after all that time in prison? You can't lie in a bin without getting litter in your pockets.

The tuk-tuk arrives at the hotel-guest-house, and struggles to turn around in the narrow lane. There are corrugated iron fences on either side of it. Not the most salubrious street in the city. He doesn't know why he came back here really, just that it was where he'd stayed once before. He supposes it's good enough: cheap and convenient. Basically clean or cleanly basic, depending on how you looked at it. At least you knew what you were getting, that's what he always thought.

The roads are full and fumy, even though it's after ten o'clock. The tuk-tuk, painted a New York taxi-yellow, weaves through gaps that don't look big enough for a bicycle. Its driver blots out the sound of the horns that blare at him by blowing his own almost continuously. Unnecessarily. It isn't like they're going far, and this passenger's not in any sort of a hurry. He's got all night.

Pasty crowds mill around at the bottom of Patpong road, arguing with the stall-holders over pence or pfennigs or francs, for labels that they know are fakes and hill-tribe artefacts that they don't. He works through them, sticking to the edges of the street, where bar doors beckon. Not just the doors, young Thai touts stand outside, trying to draw him in.

Beautiful girls, only beautiful girls. College girls. Clean

girls. Special show. Special room. Special price. Thai massage, you try. Hey, English guy. You English guy?

How do they know? he thinks. Dressed like a continental, with a tan like this, how do they know I'm a Brit? 'Later, later,' he proffers. He knows where he's going, further up the street. Take a right and the drinks suddenly drop in price. He's not just here to gawk at girls.

The bar's just like he remembers it. The tout outside shook his hand when he came in. Not through recognition, more in gratitude at such an easy customer, he supposes. He orders a six oz bottle of Mekong whisky, and a coke. This is what it's all about. Half the price of just down the road; and they're paying him to take it compared to the shady ex-pat drinking spots in Islamic bloody Kuwait. The bar surface is some sort of plastic, but dirt and dim lights have conspired to make it look more like wood than the manufacturers could ever have hoped for. The stools have seen better days too, battered bamboo legs and seats sunken with the strain of supporting a decade of bloated arseholes. He laughs to himself. At least he *knows* he's an arsehole. He knows the girls don't fancy him, and they aren't even interested in him. He'll pay for their company with every drink in these bars, and he'll pay again when he has sex. They are prostitutes. It's not just how they do it out here, an argument he's heard time and again from punters who believe themselves to be culturally sensitive. They are prostitutes and he is an arsehole, and he's not even doing the girls a favour, as some might tell themselves. Except maybe that they'd be doing it anyway, so a night with a man whose demands are not extreme, who tries to be gentle and kind, might be preferable to what they often get.

The girls are dancing on a two-foot dais. Draping themselves around chrome poles, or tilting their hips, stroking the skin nearest their cheap swimsuits. Only the oldest ones look like they really want it, probably desperate to be kept on by the bar another couple of years. The youngest girls look nervous, but it's to them his eyes keep returning, it's for them that *he* keeps returning. Just to feel young again, one more time.

He wonders whether his boy's lost his virginity yet. He's been out a few months now. Ugly little fuck would probably have to go to a whore as well, he thinks. And then he hates himself for thinking it. Takes a big slug of the Mekong without adding the coke. Feels the burn in his throat like it's a punishment. Though he knows it's not. The spreading warmth tells him it's not. The boy didn't look so ugly in the photo he sent anyway. His own dad hardly recognized him. Probably wouldn't have without the letter. The photo and the letter have a shelf in his wardrobe back in Kuwait; a secret little shrine they share with some baby snaps, and two stubs from a cowboy film they once saw. He stacks shoeboxes in front of the shrine. Keeps it in the family. Away from the eyes of friends, who are round so rarely he sometimes considers whether it's worth the rigmarole of them coming at all.

There's a game of Connect Four on the bar top; most of them have them. A little ruse to spare the girls from having to make conversation with men who probably wouldn't have to come to Thailand for sex if they had anything much worth saying. He swings the trapdoor, so that the much-thumbed plastic counters clatter into their tray, like a junior fruit machine. A bored barman asks with eyes if he wants a game. He shakes his head and goes back to watching the girls, just an urge he had, just an urge.

There aren't that many punters in. All falang – foreigners, western men. Mostly groups of two or three, some alone like him. None alone quite like him.

It's hard to have a son, but not to know or ever see him. Harder because when he had a son, he only half believed he did. Always looking for traces that would tell him it was really his. Or looking for another face in Stonelee that matched the quisling in the cot. He'd been working on the oil rigs when she fell pregnant. They'd had a weekend together, made love once; it wasn't impossible, just hadn't seemed likely. All the riggers knew they were vulnerable; they joked about it. Then every so often someone would get a letter or a phone call, and they wouldn't laugh any more.

'Nature abhors a vacuum,' she used to say.

And he knew she was right, knew she should know. The nature of women abhors most of all. There's more spaces in women than men, more places that need filling. Not just the obvious ones; it's in their heads and their hearts. If you don't fill them, someone else will. Money's not enough; if you're not offering something for those spaces, whatever else you do is worthless. That's what the guys in the bar don't realize. The gaps are not just in the Connect Four game.

First time he had sex, it was with a whore. It was different in those days, everyone did it. Up in Newcastle with the boys, first jobs, almost their first pay-packets. All of them saying they weren't virgins, all of them suspecting they all were. He mistook her professionalism for genuine interest, believed her when she said how handsome he was, when she said how she longed to feel his young body between her legs, after all the old, fat factory workers. He had tried to make her feel pleasure, excited by the moans his clumsy fingers extracted. The soft murmurs when his lips brushed upon nipples for the first time in sixteen years. He was lifted when he didn't come, like he'd feared, in the moments after she effortlessly fed him inside. Proud when his calculated thrustings seemed to bring her to the very edge of the drop that he neared himself. He watched with growing joy the thrashing of her bottle-blond hair on the sweat-stained pillow. But, as the joy juddered through him, he caught her eye, and in that intimate instant he saw her relief that he was finished. She clung to him and groaned, grinding herself upwards against his body, but it was too late, he'd seen. He never went with a whore again. Well, not until he started coming to Thailand.

It is these instants which change your view of the world; little moments when you can see into someone else. A few times, when he's been drinking, he's had those instants with himself. Drunkenly remembered half truths, or half-remembered truths, that seem to alter everything. Would it have all been different if he hadn't been a rigger? If he'd known the boy was his from the start? Would it have made him want to play football with his son like other dads? Would that have made his son like football? Would football have made him friends? Would friends have stood up for him, stopped him being bullied, stopped him making friends with that other boy?

Once, he asked, would it be better if his son was the murdered one?

Time for the show. The dancers get down and make their way out of the room. Into the little suites out back. He's been in one of them before. 'Suites for my sweet, sugar for my honey, your perfect kiss thrills me so.' That had been their song. Later. There's plenty of time for melancholy. Get a drink in first, before the show starts. He asks the barman for another bottle of Mekong. He's hardly dented the coke.

One of the older girls returns to the stage. She's long since a woman actually, beneath the make-up. She doesn't have any knickers on now, just a yellow bikini top, and her bush is shaved into one finger-thick line. She lowers herself on to a bottle of coke that sits on the stage, and drains the dark syrup inside her. A gravity-defying act of suction. Depravity-defining. How low can you go?

He's seen lower. Down in Phuket, in the South; middle-aged Americans, Dutch, Brits, Swedes, South Africans, men who have more in common with each other than anyone from their home countries. Their arms openly wrapped around eight-year-old boys. Not their sons. Though some do try and adopt. Some are no worse than the real parents perhaps. Here in Bangkok they buy boys and girls from the countryside. Set them up in one-room concrete cells; mattress and a sink, and a string of visitors each day. Paying off the pimp for what he paid out to their parents. Premium prices for the under-twelves and the uninfected. He's not one of the ignorant tourists. He knows what goes on. Understands, in many ways, these girls in the bars *are* the lucky ones. But he knows he's still an arsehole.

She's walking around now, holding the bottle, showing its emptiness, like a sandy-skinned, glassy-eyed Debbie McGee. She squats again, and the receptacle fills up. Not a drop runs over the side on to the painted stage. Holding the bottle aloft, itself modelled after a lady they say, she strolls to the end of the dais, as if promenading on a pier.

Hartlepool pier. The two of them, side by side in the rain. Her wearing his coat. Both with sand in their hair. He had something to ask her. She kissed him yes.

The audience is clapping. Three fat Aussies cheer. He takes another drink of his whisky. Suddenly the coke is less enticing. A waiter lifts his arm up to the stage, to help the woman down. As if, though knickerless, she is still so much of a lady that she can't drop two feet on her own. Or maybe it's just because the punishing heels she wears would twist her ankles, make her worthless. 'Hobbling', that's what they used to do to slaves that tried to escape: break their ankles, and set them crooked, so they could never run again. The girls can't run anyway. Not just because of their shoes. To escape you need somewhere to run to.

His boy was always running. He never realized till the trial that his son had hardly been to school in months. Why couldn't he have asked for help from his father? A father should have known, that's why. A father should have known. But he wasn't even sure he was the father. Kept that bitterness locked inside him all those years, like a parasite in his entrails, feeding off shit.

He remembers the day he realized. Looking into his son's eyes, he saw an instant of his own dad, and it was obvious, indisputable, the boy was his. Stumbling over words that didn't fit, shuffling best shoes in wet grass, he knew this was his son, his flesh and blood, and it was all too late. Too late to tell her he was wrong, to apologize for suspecting her of a thing she'd never even known he suspected. And too late to hold his son and tell him that he loved him. Really tell him. Tell him so he knew it was meant. The space between them was only a pace, but it was too far. Too much had gone before. He wanted to turn time upside down, to force back what had trickled through, to give his boy an empty chamber in which he could begin again. But he didn't know how to do any of those things. Instead he shook his hand. Watched him climb into a hearse with someone else. And ran.

There's a new act on stage. The waiter is handing out balloons to the audience. He takes one, a red one, blows it up as others are doing. He's surprised at the ease with which he knots it, an act that he remembers as fiddly, irritating. He sits the balloon in a clean glass ashtray, beside him on the bar. It wears it like a crown, but upside-down. There is a murmur from the crowd as the girl, younger this time, produces a fistful of darts and a short blowpipe. He's seen the act before, but doesn't suppose that many of the audience are surprised at where she places it. She's naked, but for a pair of gym shoes, her perky little breasts poke towards the roof, as she positions herself in a crab. She has to do it one-handed, so she can direct the blowpipe. He can see why she wears trainers. She's a good shot. The accuracy alone would be worth watching. The first balloon explodes into a damp rubber rag, and the audience bursts into applause. She edges herself around, pivoting on her one hand, while she reloads the blowpipe from the small pile of darts beside her. Occasionally she misses, but more often she pops at the first go. Until only his balloon remains. He's the finale, the furthest from her. He sees her swing her hips towards him, in a posture which should be stirring, but isn't, because what she's doing is so absurd. He lifts the balloon from the ashtray. Play by the rules if you play – and holds it out by its navel stub. Her expression doesn't change as she fires. It is as blank and beautiful as a doll's. And he is left holding the shell of what he once had.

Before he asked her to marry him they had spent the day building sand castles. Until they'd made what was more like a sand town, a sand land. She told him about all the people who lived in it, which house belonged to whom. Which was the baker's, and where the mayor lived; and she built a sand barracks for the soldiers, who were to line the ditches and the walls to fight the tide. At the top was a house she said belonged to them. It wasn't the nicest or the grandest, because she said she didn't want that. It was the furthest from the sea. It was the safest. But eventually, while they sat and watched, it sank too.

T is for Time.
Teacher and Trainers.

In time *A* and Hacendado discovered that their lives rhymed: both their fathers were abroad and their mothers dead.

Hacendado's dad was Spanish, hence the name, but he had three older sisters who often visited.

'I miss girls,' he'd tell *A*. 'It's not just about sex, I miss the softness, the laughter. You can't get that from a picture.'

Their pad was filled with pictures. Every wall a collage of cuttings expertly attached with toothpaste. Hacendado was the wing porn baron, which was to say that he had six magazines he rented by the night, with surcharge for stain or damage. He wouldn't put those glossy pages up, though, and not just to save his goods. The pictures on the wall were more concealing, selected to tantalize a little, but not to torture.

'Don't make it harder than it has to be,' was his motto, and he applied it to every aspect of his prison life. He taught *A* to try and take a zest in each little decision. Which radio station to listen to, what card game to play. He showed him that to stay sane you had to keep control over everything you could. Forget about the big choices you don't have, concentrate on the minutiae which are yours.

Hacendado was respected on the wing, not through fear, though he made it clear he would fight for what was his. But because he was a fixer, a hoarder, a helper. He had what others wanted. He didn't get dirty with drugs, where competition and robbery was rife, but stuck to sex-mags, sanitation and snacks. *A* was always happy to pool his slim weekly resources, to buy in to some scheme or other. Not only because of the profit share he would receive, but because it involved him in a venture. It was something to do. And it increased his bond with his pad-mate.

Hacendado never asked much about *A*'s life. It was another of his rules not to pry. And *A* was grateful, because it kept his lies small and straight, like his new teeth.

The dentist delivered. One of the offices was kitted out as his surgery. He was moustached, methodical and humane. He stood out in Feltham like a stick of chalk in a bag of maggots. By the time he came, *A*'s face was long healed. So all that was left of near death was a one-inch gap that sucked air when he spoke. The dentist made a cast of the hole, and returned a month later with an insert. It fitted so perfectly that it might have stayed sat inside, even without his skill with cement and drills.

A could not believe the brief view in the dentist's portable porthole mirror. But he had to wait until it went dark before he could properly examine his new mouth, in the reflection of the cell window. And there, with voices shouting the nightly flush of threat and shit, he realized he was changed. Not least because the voices couldn't touch him.

Not so long ago they had. The first night on Kestrel wing he'd been terrified after someone threatened to fuck him up. He hadn't believed Hacendado's claim that most menace came to nothing, having just been beaten to a pulp by a man whose warnings the warders hadn't taken seriously. Then on the way to tea, he was punched from behind, at the base of the spine.

'You don't shut your window till I say so,' the voice from before had said. 'I just wanted to hear you sing last night, now I want an eighth of snout. Or I'm gonna make your

face look even more like road-kill.' The guy pulled around
him and walked off down the stairway. He wasn't that much
bigger than A, but he had two groupies loping behind him.

'Now what do I do?' A asked his pad-mate.

'Probably you pay up,' Hacendado said. 'I'll get you the
baccy, on a strict loan basis.' He turned to A, eyes stressing
the seriousness of his words. 'But you don't just give it to
him, you make sure it's the hardest day's work the fuck's ever
done, then he'll find someone easier to pick on the next
time. You don't have to win in here, but you have to fight.'
He laughed. 'Maybe you're better off getting a battle out of
the way while you're still mashed up, save you getting
damaged twice.'

A hadn't laughed. But later he'd concentrated, as
Hacendado expounded moves. Learning how to fight up
close, so his opponent wouldn't be able to land blows on his
busted face. He shadow-boxed shin stamps, knee and elbow
smashes, ear twists and eye gouges. He locked his hands
together, behind a ghostly neck, and head-butted until
adrenalin streamed and he almost ached for a fight to come.
Almost. He knew his best chance was what his PO had told
him: to keep his head down, walk away from trouble. But
there's nowhere to walk away *to* in prison. Everything comes
back sooner or later.

The guy came for the baccy one association time, when
Hacendado was out striking a deal. A told him he didn't
have it, though he could feel it bulge in his sock. The guy
said he wanted it by dinner, or he'd bring his mates and
break him up.

Trembling, A had started to reach for his sock. But then a
cold clarity came over him, spread around him like a ring of
taunting children. He stood up and said: 'Fuck yourself.'

Neither of them was really winning, when Hacendado
came back. They were both bleeding. Hacendado pulled the
guy from A's lock, and flung him out the cell door. He

landed on the landing, sprawled against the rails. Sneered, as he wiped the blood from his nose on his sweatshirt sleeve, but walked off without looking back in.

'Yeah,' Hacendado said, thoughtfully. 'I reckon that'll do the trick.'

A wasn't troubled by the guy again. Sometimes he got a nod or a grin from him when they crossed paths. And he'd grin back with his new teeth.

Terry came after six months. Six months of forms signed and countersigned, winding like white eels around the country. A was freaked out for three days before the visit. Just like Hacendado said he would be. He was jumpy, pacy, couldn't settle down to play shit-head or pontoon. Stared out of the window instead, trying to see something of the world that was coming in to see him.

Terry said that A looked well, and he supposed he did. Terry seemed healthy himself, brown, though he said he hadn't been away. Just brown against the pallid indoor faces all the white guys inside wore. They talked about old times, which were not so long ago, in the way that people generally do, which is to forget the periods of pain. The chat blended in all around them, swirling together like the twenty brands of cigarette smoke that filled the room. A room already full, with mothers, girlfriends and kids. Few fathers, as most must have taken Terry to be, if they'd cared enough to notice. He had to be family, they would have said: by the way the two hugged when their time had elapsed; since there were tears in his eyes, as he made a sign to the boy to keep his chin up; because, as they filed their separate ways, the two waved in a manner that insisted they were tied by a deeper thing, a past that glued them, that collective stick-together sense that you only get in families. Or those who've shared other catastrophes.

When A was returned to the cell, Hacendado was once more admiring his soaps. He had his radio tuned to a pirate hip–hop station. He was told to turn it down, before the screw escorting *A* locked them in again. After he'd turned the volume back up, Hacendado started to clean his shoes, white Reeboks. Using a rag he meticulously massaged every crevice, although they didn't look like they had a spec of dirt on them anyway.

'You want to get some trainers sent in, now you've got a visitor,' he told *A*. 'Only gypos wear them prison issue shoes.'

A nodded, not sure how he could broach such a subject with Terry. Or if to do so would be abusing his kindness. Taking berties.

The Milton Keynes Organised Berties, MKOBs, ran Feltham. Less than the screws maybe, but more than the governors, who changed sometimes twice a year. STABS, St Albans Bastard Squad, had made a play that left two of their members chevvied. Slashed with razor blades melted into a toothbrush. Their leader was PP–nined. When *A* first heard this phrase he thought PP-9 was a form, a complaint or a transfer, or some other from the ream of arbitrary numbers that the screws bandied about. In fact a PP-9 is a radio battery, the largest allowed inside. A cylinder related to power only in terms of struggle, when swung within a sock.

It was in the shower that the STABS' director took his PP-9. Unaware, from behind. A blow that knocked him to his knees. Slid his redded face down the clean tile wall. And dumped him in the two inches of water that the faucet delivered faster than the plug could clear. The wet-armed attacker delivered one more blow, which made the naked body twitch. Then he strolled calmly out of the shower room.

A watched from the stall opposite, and stood by the general view, that the youth had slipped, when the screws came to take him to hospital. What other reason could there be for the blood that still swirled in the shower tray, if no one had seen a thing?

From then on *A* showered with his back to the wall. Not because he feared some soap-dropping come-on, of the sort that the boys in the secure home had nervously joked about. But because he wanted to see who was there. To know what approached. Since they were two, in a cell designed for one, he and Hacendado had devised a dignity-saving routine, where they'd try and schedule dumps for when the other went to get clean. But it meant he was always on his own in the shower room. Water washes away evidence, and confined in a stall and naked, there's little defence to present. But *A* was getting tougher.

They went to the gym most days, him and Hacendado. Whenever they were allowed their legal right to an hour's exercise. *A* still felt puny beside most of the guys in there. He wouldn't have kept going on his own. But, doing repetition-then-rest swaps with Hacendado, he was amazed at how quickly his strength grew.

It didn't feel like a wasted day when they'd been to the gym, because he was making himself bigger, harder, more resilient. He felt like he was preparing for what the world was going to drop next.

The whole world was almost within reach at Feltham. Only miles from Heathrow. With the window open he could hear the gas-stove burn of the jets that scorched the air overhead. Taking people away, bringing new ones.

Terry came one visit with a pair of new trainers. Like he'd read *A*'s mind. A pair of Puma Sunrise. Nothing special in the grand scheme of sneakers, but a million miles from pikey prison shoes.

'It's your birthday,' Terry explained, 'or at least it will be on Wednesday.'

A had forgotten about its approach. A meaningless date, twinned with a made-up name. 'They're perfect,' he told Terry. 'How did you know?' They were perfect, too, egg-white with a yolk-yellow stripe.

Terry just smiled.

The trainers made the prison floors less hard underfoot. They were something to keep clean, to take pride in. When eventually constant wear took its toll, Terry bought another pair. It became instant tradition, and Puma Sunrise became Reebok Classic. Then the blue-striped Boks became Converse One Stars. The Cons were the same as the pair Kurt Cobain was wearing when he placed his mouth around a brace of twelve-gauge barrels. But they served *A* well. When they gave up their spirit, they were superseded with a set of grey on grey New Balance, with a number instead of a name. They looked cool enough, but *A* was somehow relieved when his toe started to poke through the nylon. Then he got his first pair of Nikes, Yukon II, not the best of the brand, but Nikes were the undisputed champions. When Terry saw how pleased he was with them, Nike became the standard. Air Stab and Air Vengeance followed. Badly named, but beautiful shoes.

Trainers had become markers of time. They defined the events in *A*'s prison term as reliably as cell-mates.

Hacendado was ghosted halfway through the Boks: moved in the middle of the night to a different prison. No reason was given, but it wasn't an unusual occurrence. He was allowed only his essentials, so *A* inherited his wealth. And had the cell to himself for a while. He used to get the soaps out and dust their pearly skin while he listened to the radio. He never sold or rented any of the stuff. It didn't seem right. So he lost it all when he got starred up: sent to adult prison. Allowed to keep only the trainers that he'd had on his feet.

Adult prison was easier. *A*, obviously a graduate, was left alone. It was a much less aggressive place anyway. Three or four times less attacks than Feltham, they reckoned. Fewer men in for violent crime, and there seemed like less to prove. Most were pros, took a fall as a part of the job, same as watching *Antiques Roadshow.* Looking for tips, not looking for grief, just counting the days until release.

They moved him to Ford Open Prison, near the end, when his EDR approached. A wind-down, to adjust the institutionalized to freedom. The mattresses were still Rizla-thin, rumpling under him in the night, so that every morning started uncomfortable. They were still fenced in too, but freedom isn't about open spaces. It's about doing what you want to do. Most days were still like playing the same tape over and over; but the music was much better in open prison.

Some people had spent their whole sentences at Ford. Embezzle a bank and you get a different ride to robbing one. There was a disgraced cabinet minister in there, and a failed mayor. Both Tories, hard on crime and punishment. Both as famous as him, or the boy he'd once been. Mostly they kept their heads down and their mouths shut. In a way A felt sorry for the toffs that had it soft, because for everyone else Ford was the finishing posts. They had to watch while one by one all around them were freed. One of them said once that it cost the same to keep a man in prison as it had to send his daughters to Cheltenham Ladies College. It made A wonder about the money that had been spent on him over the years. What could have been done with it.

They tried to teach them skills at Ford. Skills other than weaving lines out of blankets to pass things between cells. A started to cook, which he hadn't done since the secure accommodation. He felt a pride when the steady crackle and bubble of pans was his to command. He was allowed to cook a meal for Terry once.

Terry came by quite often. Visiting was much more relaxed. Everything was more relaxed, even the screws. A supposed that the high cat. prisons punished the staff too.

A couldn't believe he was going to be freed until Terry confirmed it. It was too big, he couldn't grasp the idea. He was even allowed to choose his own first name. It seemed like a psychologist's game, another trick to try and get inside his mind. So he picked one that was straightforward, normal, that gave nothing away. Which were also things he wanted to become.

Terry gave A one last pair of shoes, on the day that he became Jack. A set of brilliant white Nike Air Escape. Top name. Top of the range. Top of the world. And on top of the box were some words of advice, from the goddess of victory, not Terry: 'Just Do It', they said. And he did.

And in the car, which might as well have been a plane, because it took him to another world, and travelled faster than seemed possible without taking off, it was explained that he had family again. Because Terry was now his uncle.

U is for Uncle.
Uncle Terry.

Terry groans awake. Alcohol is a curse, like something out of Dante. The more you drink, the more you want to drink, and still you're left dehydrated. That's a better torture than pushing boulders uphill. His hand clutches around the bedside table, hoping to find a glass of water. Failing to do so at about the same pace as his brain reminds him he forgot to put one there. He can feel the daylight beyond his eyelids, but wants to delay it a moment or two longer. The rude electronic abuse of his alarm clock is still going, though. There isn't any satisfaction in lying in bed with its torrent bouncing around the walls. He'd throw something at it, but it sits beside the desk his computer's on. Well, the police's computer. It's a lot of kit, and it's Jack's lifeline. You can't mess around with that.

He can hear his son clattering around in the kitchen, probably cooking him breakfast again. He's changed since he's come up here, or maybe Terry's just noticed it now they're spending a bit of time together. He used to be so surly, so uncooperative, like he'd been in teenage suspended animation. He'll be twenty-seven next year, Terry's pretty sure. How old does that make him? He staggers to the cheap wood-framed mirror on the bedroom wall. Not such a good plan.

There was an item on Radio 4 about how Mick Jagger was pissed off because they put his picture on the front of *Saga* magazine. Terry rubs at the yellow goo that lines his bloodhound eyes. If he looked as good as Jagger he wouldn't care where they put his picture. These days he feels as wrinkled as Keith Richards' bollock.

'Breakfast's ready,' comes a shout from the kitchen. 'Do you want it in bed?'

'No, I'm just coming,' Terry croaks.

Breakfast in bed. Zebedee's really grown up. It's taken over twenty-five years but he's finally there. 'Zebedee'; well, you can hardly blame the boy for resenting him a bit, saddled with that for life. He was named for the *Magic Roundabout* though, not the Bible. They were different times. Should have called him Ben, for Mr Ben, the number of different jobs he's had.

Terry crosses the hallway in his dressing gown and into the flat's kitchen. Zebedee grins and salutes with a spatula.

'You all right, Dad?' he says. 'We knocked back the whisky last night.'

He's wearing a Fred Perry shirt; the tight sleeves emphasize his probably steroid-enhanced arms. Old Fred must be back in, Terry thinks, for Zeb to be wearing it. Everything he wears seems to have someone else's name on it: Tommy Hilfiger, Ralph Lauren, Donna Karan, Sergio Tacchini. When Terry was growing up he used to wear clothes with other names on too, tags in the back from the previous owner. It's funny, but he's never lusted after money, like some of his friends from those days did. Not having it never made it mystical. Money's a metaphor, that's all, it's standing in for what you need, and so you need *it* to a point, but it's not the be all and end all; it has no intrinsic value. Cuts your fingers when it's new and stinks when it's old, that's what Terry always says about money. Didn't make much of an impact on Zeb, though.

Zebedee carefully transfers an egg, two sausages and two rashers of bacon from a large frying pan to his father's plate; on which a monstrous split, grilled tomato already lounges. He cracks two more eggs for his own breakfast, while Terry sits down, staring at the mountain of food for a moment, feeling slightly queasy, knowing that the grease will help to set him right, though. Or else give him a coronary. It's all right for his son; he's probably off to the gym, calories converted to muscle by lunchtime. He's laid out the usual suspects of condiments on the Formica table, and Terry takes the ketchup, squeezes a splash of colour between the dead pig products. A scab of decrepit sauce has formed around the plastic lid of the bottle. He scrapes it off with a fingernail, and then regrets doing so, when he sees nowhere better to put it. In the end he wipes it on his dressing gown, which needs a wash anyway. Zeb puts a cup of coffee down beside him, and Terry says: 'Ah, thank you,' and picks up his knife and fork, as if he'd just been waiting for this final piece of the puzzle to begin. He dunks a chunk of his tomato into the ketchup, before he realizes the absurdity of the action, and then finds that, in fact, even tomato is improved with ketchup.

After five minutes of hunting, Terry locates his tie, hanging from the key on the back of the wardrobe door, still formed in yesterday's noose. He slips it over his head and tightens it to an approximation of straight. He's got other ties, but they don't have his ID clipped to them. He scratches up a pocketful of coins from the sideboard, as he shouts goodbye, and grabs his wallet and keys. At least it's Friday.

The car skips the first start. It's just messing with him, though; comes in with a roaring over-rev when he hits the accelerator on the second try. He had to pull a lot of strings to get his job transferred up here, to work in another secure unit, alongside being Jack's liaison. Everything's gone like clockwork so far. He doesn't want today to be his first fuck-up. He'd swear Zebedee's trying to turn him into an alcoholic. They've been getting drunk far too frequently since he moved in. But it's been good to spend a bit of quality time with his son. They haven't had that much of it. Though Zeb's always been close to his heart. He laughs to himself, at his little joke, and touches the medallion behind his shirt. It can open up, like a tomato, split into two neat halves; and inside that secret space there's a pair of tiny photos: one of a baby Zeb and one of a young Zeb, taken not long before the divorce. Terry's worn it ever since then. Of course he'd never tell Zebedee about the hidden compartment. Zeb'd think he was a sentimental old fool. No, they don't have that kind of a relationship.

He turns on the radio as he eases out of the side-streets and into the rush-hour traffic. He's just about on schedule. Still feeling rougher than ideal, for a full day of dealing with disturbed kids; but the fry-up and the aspirin are starting to kick in. Two girls are waiting for a bus, next to where his Sierra stops for the red light. College kids, by the looks of it, probably art students – they're wearing flares.

When Terry wore flares they meant something; they were a statement of intent, not just a fashion statement. No one gives a shit any more, that's the way it seems. Where are all the marches? Where are the demonstrators? Has no one noticed the world's worse than ever?

There's a fly in the car. It should have died off by now, or hibernated or whatever flies do. Maybe it had and the heating's woken it up. It's moving tiredly around, banging at the windows, buzzing at the tension in Terry's head. It's a big, blue, loud bugger. He swipes at it with a backhand, and swerves over the white lines, nearly hitting a Cherokee in the inside lane. It veers away, mimicking his movement, heading for the pavement, but seeing the pedestrians there it swings back again, over-compensating. Crunch. Terry jerks forwards in his seatbelt.

Shit. Whose fault's that? He started the swerving, but it was the Cherokee that hit him. They weren't going that fast, maybe it's not too bad. He gets out of the car and the fly plunges out with him. The Jeep looks all right; it's got massive steel side-protectors fitted, thinly disguised as steps. The left-front wing of Terry's trusty Sierra is crumpled like foil on to its wheel. The driver of the Cherokee gets out, and smiles in slightly smug satisfaction at the unblemished state of his vehicle. He's young, tall, balding, chalk-striped. Someone sounds their horn from the midst of the traffic which is rapidly piling up behind them. The man raises a long arm to the sound, with a single finger at the end of it. But concedes to Terry, in a public school accent which doesn't fit in Manchester, that they'd better pull over to swap details.

Terry bends down to try and pull the wing from the tyre it's bitten into. He can't get it out; clumps of rust and road dust crumble away on his hands. He looks up to see where the Cherokee driver has parked. And discovers that the man has simply driven off while his back was turned. Cars are tearing through the empty space next to him, gunning their engines to demonstrate their displeasure at being held up.

'Do you think I did it on purpose?' Terry shouts, to no one in particular.

Eventually, a car heeds Terry's indicator, and lets him pull over the inside lane and on to the pavement. Luckily he's rear-wheel drive. But the front tyre that isn't turning properly leaves a scar of rubber on the road; and his engine sounds like it would burn out under any more strain.

He phones the secure unit, apologizing profusely. Knowing this means some of the boys will have little or no activity today. Then he phones the AA. Maybe it's better him and the Jeep driver didn't get into blame for the prang. They'd probably have had to get the police involved; he might technically still be over the drink-drive limit. Terry can usually see a bright side.

He wonders whether the Sierra's worth repairing, while he waits for the canary yellow cavalry. He can't even remember how long he's had it. From the days when Jack was still in the home, he knows that. And Jack used to ask about the car when Terry visited the prisons.

'How's the motor, Terry?' he'd say, a proper little cockney. He'd sounded like a kid from Byker Grove when Terry first met him. First realized there was something more to him. It was the day his mother died that changed it all. Terry can remember sitting down on the bed and putting his arm around that puny, ugly, despisable child, and discovering that he could love it.

And somehow after that, the boy had become like his ward, his responsibility. None of the other staff in the secure accommodation had much time for him anyway. They weren't cruel at all, just didn't seem to care. Except that second psychiatrist, maybe, Elizabeth something. She was the only one that ever seemed to really try. Him and Jack both had a lot to thank her for: she'd made the recommendations that had led to the ruling allowing them to maintain contact. All of this would be different if it weren't for her. And she'd made the breakthrough with the boy. It had started to seem like he really might not be guilty, he denied it so strongly, until she'd helped him to come to terms with what he'd done.

What had he done? Something horrible, something terrible, but something he'd done as a child. Can you commit murder in innocence? It's too big a thing for the human mind to take in, that's the problem. And it grew with the ever-larger newspaper pictures of a girl who was near enough an angel, even before she died. Only the young die good. And Angela Milton died young enough to be perfect. A martyr to modern society. Evidence that we are fucked. Though records suggest we always have been. Her hair and eyes had clamoured from the front pages of every paper:

'Never mind locking away, let them swing.' One of them did. She was only ten, but had looked twelve, would soon have been sixteen, though nobody said it. 'The Angel that could have been a model', wrote the *Star* and the *Sun*, brave upholders of women's rights.

If Jack had been nine months younger he would have been innocent, simple as that. How can you have definitions and scales about murder? Why was it all right for the CIA to kill Che in cold blood, a man who really might have changed the world? Or the innocent people in Chile, Argentina, East Timor, Congo, Nicaragua, El Salvador, Haiti, Guatemala, Turkey, Brazil, the Philippines. Political mass murders, that are lucky to make the papers at all. Crimes committed by mercenaries, men who kill for money, not seen to be as bad as someone who acts from some nameless sickness, shameless sudden impulse?

Terry's felt the power of that perverse desire. He believes that everyone has. He can still picture himself as a child, sat on a bus, biting his tongue to stop himself shouting out: 'You're all fucking spastics', at a group of happy, helpless, handicapped. Even as an adult, he's had to fight the need to take his wife, by force, when he found out about her affair. Yes, rape. Just to show her that he could, not from desire, just to wipe that bloody smirk away. Does that mean he's evil? Or is it that without those urges he could not be good? If being good is a denial of the bad then those we deem evil are not worse, they are weaker. And if goodness means anything at all, surely it means the strong helping the weak. That's what Terry thinks.

Zebedee's strong. Jesus but he's strong. He looks like he could pull a man in half with those arms. He's dusting the computer when Terry walks in from the AA tow home. He's told Zeb he's not supposed to touch that computer. But he doesn't scold him, because he can't. Zeb looks so funny, dusting away with no shirt on, like Schwarzenegger doing a spot of hoovering. And he's trying so hard at the moment. It really seems like he wants to make good for everything that's gone wrong in the past. Where does it all go though? Where does all that time disappear to?

V is for Vanish. Find the Lady.

Jack spends Saturday morning phoning Shell. There's no reply on her home phone and her mobile's turned off. After he's heard the answerphone message five times the cheerful nonchalance of her voice is beginning to grate on him. The power is low on his own phone, though, so he keeps calling until it cuts out altogether. Chris has told him the emptier you can get it before you recharge, the better it is for the battery.

Out the window the blue of the heavens is untarnished, the colour of *Wish You Were Here* swimming pools. Kelly's baking a friend's birthday cake in the kitchen. Not having much better to do, Jack decides to walk to Shell's place, and make sure she's really not just ill in bed. Though he knows that wouldn't be much reason for her not to be answering the phone. It's colder outside than you'd think from the cloudless skies. The air makes his eyes water. He's still thinking about Shell.

It's out of character, that's what worries him. She's so organized, so dependable, so concrete. She isn't the sort of person who just disappears. If she's not at home, he wonders whether he should phone her mum's. That's most likely where she is; he might be able to find the number in the book. But then he remembers that her mum's remarried;

she's probably called something different to Shell. This is a world where names are erased after use.

The bell still trails empty echoes through the town house. The table is still blank where her bag should be. Jack's disappointment shows him how much he must have been hoping, against all sense, that she was in. A look through the letterbox shows him the morning mail. Two envelopes have their back to him; the third says that if the missing number's found inside, Shell could be entered in the *Reader's Digest* million-pound draw. The letterbox snaps shut with a clack. Jack opens it and lets it go twice more. In case she just can't hear doorbells and phones. The silence is even louder after the letterbox noise. Jack turns around from the house and walks away down the street. He kicks a Tango can from the pavement, and it ejects the remains of someone's drink, as it rattles into the space where a Clio should be.

It's the third time he's done this walk from Shell's back to his. The first two he stuck to the route she takes in the car. This time Jack allows himself to experiment, and finds he can save himself some distance. Even though he has to turn around from a couple of blockages. Not all roads lead to Rome, there are side-streets and switchbacks, circles and cul-de-sacs. But if you have a sense of the direction you want to head, and you're not so bothered about the how and how-long of getting there, Jack finds most roads are right. In this view he differs from Chris, who believes there is only ever one most appropriate route.

Chris phones not long after Jack gets back. 'Steve the mechanic and Jed have gone to the football,' he says. 'They wondered if we wanted to meet them after, for a couple of beers.'

Jack doesn't feel like going. He's stretched out on the sofa, tired from the walk and stressed from worrying about Shell.

'I'm feeling a bit poorly. I think I might be going down with that thing Michelle's got. Next time, heh?'

'How is Michelle?' Chris asks.

'Not really sure. All right, I hope. I think she's at her mum's.'

'Haven't you rung her?'

'Her phone's switched off.'

'Hang on, I'm pretty sure I've got her mum's number. Michelle moved back there for a bit after she split up with that bloke.' There is a sound of drawers opening, Chris rooting through the remains of his recent past. Eventually he comes up with a number, and reads it out.

They leave it there, with Jack having added another carefully folded pair of lies to Chris' pile.

Shell's mum answers in a thick Salford Manc, most of which Shell must have left behind in the short move to the city centre. The mum sounds kind, like Shell described her. The woman that gave her the security and the will to be someone. But as helpful as she tries to be, she can't change the fact that her daughter isn't there, and she hasn't heard from her. Jack tries to make light, but the conversation ends with both of them more concerned than at its start.

Later he calls Terry. It sounds like Terry had a bad day yesterday. He's smashed up his car. Jack feels a momentary sadness for the Ford, which is a tie to a shared past. He used to see it pull in and out the gates of the secure unit. Sometimes Terry would wave when he left, knowing he'd be watched through the wire-reinforced glass of a second-floor window.

Terry's upbeat as ever, though. He reckons the prang could be the excuse he needs to finally get shot of the Sierra. Jack had secretly hoped that one day he'd be able to buy it off him. But not now; he hasn't got anything much saved and can't even drive.

He tells Terry about Michelle. Wanting to be cheered up and told it's nothing. But he picks up an anxious edge when Terry gives him the words he needs to hear.

'Look, let's go out for Sunday lunch tomorrow,' Terry

finally says. 'I'll meet you at the Firkin at one. But ring me if you hear from Michelle before then.'

The gravy's the same Bisto-brown as Terry's car. Jack's not sure if that's a good omen or a bad one. Michelle is missing, and he is missing her. Both facts hang over the roast dinner, souring the flavours.

Jack tells Terry about the man he thought was following them the other week, and how she had said it was her ex-boyfriend. Terry doesn't disguise his worry when Jack adds the doorman's criminal past.

'Why didn't you tell me about this at the time, Jack?'

'She said it was nothing to bother about. She said he'd done it before.'

'And what happens if he's done something to her? You're on licence. If they even suspect you're involved they're going to take you in, and boyfriends are always the first suspects. That means it'll all be over, this life we've built. Your cover could be blown. We'd have to try and start you up again. All of our work gone down the pan.'

'Terry, if he's done something to her, like you're suggesting, then I don't care about all this. I love her.'

'She's the first girl you've ever been with, Jack. Of course you love her. Shit, she's practically the first girl you've ever met. I knew it was too soon. We should have let you adjust slower.'

'I love her, Terry, this is real. She's disappeared off the face of the earth, and I want you to tell me she's all right. Instead you're saying she's been murdered or something. You just assume it, like it's fucking karma coming back, and it's the most logical thing in the world. There are a million things that could have happened. Her ex is probably nothing to do with it. It's only three days. Maybe she just needed a break. Maybe she just needed to think, to get away. You're supposed to be the optimist.' Jack realizes he's shouting at Terry, the man who's never raised his voice in his life, except perhaps to yell: 'Ban the Bomb.' The man who has sacrificed so much for him. 'I'm sorry,' he says, quietly, with eyes flicked down at the unfinished meal.

'No, I'm sorry,' Terry says. 'You're right. It's crazy to assume something bad's happened. It could be anything; and I didn't mean to doubt your feelings for her. Look, I'll get in touch with the police when I get back to the flat, use some of my contacts, make sure the car hasn't been in an accident or anything.'

There *is* a turquoise Clio by the side of a country road, but the police are not aware of it. There's no reason why they should be. It's parked neatly in a lay-by; it's not abandoned. There's no sign of damage on its womanly curves. Its driver is dishevelled, and certainly feels like she's been in an accident, but the car is her comfort not the cause.

She drove in it straight from work, with the excuse of sickness hardly needed, because of the pain and confusion which was written over her features. She's slept in the Clio for two nights now, each time driving until she found herself a place to pull in, that was concealed from all sides. Resting in secret gardens, nesting in forgotten forests, in alien parts of counties she's never been to before. She only leaves the Clio's security to buy fuel and food, and to toilet when she must. The car is a protective carapace, which clothes her and coats her in a hardness that she needs, because she's suddenly scared the world will discover how soft and squashable she is.

She is living like this because she does indeed need to think, because she thinks best when she's driving and because she doesn't know what else she can do. She is used to problem-solving, to helping herself to what she wants from the world, managing the things around her that can be controlled, and disentangling them from the things that must be left. Her life was previously a mental test, to be ordered and corrected. Her dream has always been to be able, one day, to sit back and admire the balance and perfection of the land that she has built for herself. In recent months, when she thought like this, Jack was beside her, they were stretched back together in her imaginings. A perfect partner to make an even number. Avoiding the loneliness that her mother was never quite able to conceal.

On Friday she cracked the last side of the Rubik's Cube that had been puzzling her for sometime: the part of Jack that somehow didn't quite fit in her scheme of how it all should be. The final few squares clicked into place in her mind, and the finishing face became clear on the cube. But the completed picture was horrible, more horrible than she could begin to think how to deal with. And in solving that one side, she discovered she had ruined the other five. The parts of her life which had been complete were fragmented and distorted, and none of it made sense at all.

She starts the Clio up, and sweeps the layer of litter from the dash. The detritus of a Sunday lunch of crisps and chocolate, crumpled like the creases of her worry, tumbles on to the passenger-side floor. Where, underneath three days' failed attempts at comfort-eating, are the lumps of dirt from Jack's boots that first soiled her car. His footprints have stained her world in the same way, but she doesn't hate him. She can't hate him. Because the place in her that Jack inhabits, the space she would need to hate, is already taken up by hate's opposite. Therein lies the problem, this is what makes things harder. If she could work up the loathing and the anger, she would confront him. She's not scared. Michelle's not scared of anything. But she can't confront him with indecision. She needs to know what she's going to do before she can talk to Jack. She needs a plan, she needs order, so she has to keep driving.

The car in front of her is a learner, taking the road painfully slowly. But Michelle's not in a hurry; she won't

even know where she's going till she gets there. Its L-plate is
hanging off, attached only by one corner, reminding her of
an ad-campaign by the Tories: 'You Can't Trust Labour,'
where the L was a swinging plate like that one. It was the
'trust' that did the job though, that's what scared people: it's
all about trust.

She was crying out for it from Jack. That's why she let
him take those photos, why she gave him one. She was
telling him she trusted him, asking why he couldn't trust her
back. Asking what it was that he couldn't tell her. The
invisible obstacle holding them apart, like the six-inch
dancing rule she had always disobeyed at school.

But when he told her what it was, it still didn't count. He
didn't trust her. He was asleep. The first night they'd been
together when they hadn't had sex. Normally he was
insatiable, he couldn't stop touching her. He was the only
man she'd ever met who could consistently wear her out.
But that night he wasn't interested, said he was too tired and
then didn't fall asleep for hours. He kept her awake too,
squirming like there was a snake in the bed. And when he
did eventually fall asleep, he started talking, calling out a
name: 'Angela, Angela.' Michelle was upset to begin with,
thinking Angela was an ex-girlfriend, thinking maybe that
was his big secret, why he didn't like to talk about his past:
that he was still hung up on her. Then she became angry;
she thought that he must still be seeing this Angela, that he
was leading her on. By morning Michelle was convinced
that the mysterious 'Uncle Terry' was nothing more than a
ruse to shag his other woman. She had been livid in the car
on the way in to work, and he hadn't even noticed; hadn't
even asked what was wrong.

She gets angry with the learner, just thinking about it,
slips the Clio down a gear and snarls the engine, to overtake
though a gap which isn't really big enough. She catches the
vinegary smell of her own armpit as she slides the gear lever

back again. She hasn't had a shower in three days. This isn't good. She can't go on for ever sleeping in her car. But she hasn't sorted out her head yet. She's already decided she's not going in to work tomorrow. Dave can fuck himself if he thinks she's even ringing in. Her phone battery's dead anyway.

The first night she spent hours trying to think who she could call, which of her friends she could talk to about this, whether she could burden her mum with it. By the time she'd decided not to rely on any of them, it was academic. Her Motorola didn't have the power left.

She needs to find somewhere to stay, now. A cheap guest-house or a little B&B. It must be as out of season as it gets; she'll be able to find something. She's not going back to that desk.

She was sat at the desk when it clicked. When the true view slid into place. When the missing past, and the innocence and the guilt, all became a single logical whole. Sneaking a look at the paper, a petty revenge because Dave, as usual, had pissed her off. A story about an Angela, the same name she was competing with. Angela Milton, this one. The memory of a girl, about her own age, but who would remain forever ten. Still in the news nearly a decade and a half after her death. Another paper, a less scrupulous paper it seems, had produced an aged picture of the killer. Might yet be prosecuted for breaking some court-enforced code. Her paper, a good paper, showed only the same photo as always. The single allowed shot of a ten-year-old murderer. A picture she must have seen so many times that it had become familiar. Because the face was familiar; there was no doubting that. And then a shudder passed through her. Like an ice-cube down the back. But not a joke. Far from funny. She wanted to scream.

Michelle is not a screamer by nature. As a kid she laughed at girls who squealed at mice and frogs. Even alone in a park, she once calmly showed her finger to a flasher who showed his wares. But as she pulled the photo of Jack from her purse; her portrait of a man who talks in his sleep, and appears from nowhere with no previous life, as she pressed it flat beside the paper, she struggled to choke down a scream.

She told herself she wasn't right, that it was impossible, far-fetched-fantasy. But she knew suddenly and certainly that it was right, she knew who Jack was. And what she'd always known somewhere, secretly: that he wasn't Jack. That he would never be Jack; no matter how many wallets she had the name put on.

She stared in horror at the only officially released photo, of a boy who became a man that she had slept with, that she loved. Most people would never recognize him from it. He had changed as much as it must be possible for a child to change in fifteen years. The teeth were totally different for a start, the oversized bucked over-bite was gone. But she had curled her tongue around Jack's perfect, false, front-teeth. Licked the joining ridges where those two tombstones must once have been rooted. And the eyes were still there, though even now, more of a pair. Eyes as blue as a husky dog's. That stared at you, wanting something.

Her finger traced the cheekbones in the paper, high and podgy. Puppy-fatted younger brothers to those that she had brushed in soft, long, butterfly kisses, trailing mascara down to his lips. Lips that sneered in pure evil in this picture, but that she had known to whisper and to kiss. His hair was darker in the paper, like a boy who hadn't known sunlight. Though surely the opposite should be true. His face was fatter too. But she knew… The boy was Jack. So Jack was once that boy. And that fact changed everything.

She could have forgiven him if he'd told her; she's sure of that. She's done things as a girl of which she's not proud. She was always the strong one, the loud one, the one with the ideas, the ringleader. And when she looks back, she most likely made life hell, at some times, for some kids. Not in the same ball-park as what he did. Not in the same league. But playing the same game. A sport where someone else's pain is fun. She is not who she once was. No one is. That's what adulthood means. So why should Jack be any different?

Perhaps it's not as simple as that. Maybe she couldn't ever really understand. But she could have forgiven. She's sure. If only he'd told her.

Could she have stayed with him, though? Could she have had kids with him one day? Would she have ever dared leave them with him? Could she do all that still? She can't square the thing that he has done with the man she loves. If she still does. If she still can. If that's even hers to choose.

A sign on the road says 'Blackpool 20m', and this seems like a good idea, a place to start, a place to stay. There must be a million beds and baths in Blackpool, just for a few days or a week. Just time to think.

W is for Worm.
The Worm in the Apple.

It was on the tube that the plan started. He was holding on to the overhead pole, which was as usual greasy to his touch: yellow plastic coating slick with the sweat of commuters. Like those all around him, unwelcome communal body-heat making his own palms hot, making them slide along the side bar. He's squeamish about other people's fluids, sweat included, but the lurch of the underground always demanded that he hold on. Worse than the filth was the fear of falling, of losing face. Around him other passengers, luckier passengers with seats and better lives, rocked gently back and forth like drowsy lunatics. 'Another day another dollar,' he thought. His brain forces these tired platitudes upon him, sentences that he would never consciously create, words that make him cringe even as they smirk into his mind. Stuff his father might say: back-burner bollocks from some should-be-forgotten B–movie.

All films are classed as 'B' to him. He doesn't like them. He resents their unrealistic assumption that everything happens for a reason, and everything will turn out all right. The same shit his dad thinks and probably got from films in the first place. He can't understand the world in which his dad lives. Still hooked up to the television most nights, apart from his sacred Tuesdays. Great plastic stacks of videocassettes surrounding the living room in his flat. Videocassettes, not even DVD. If you like films so much, at least buy the equipment to enjoy them properly. 'You can't recreate the feel of the original,' his dad says. To him it's the same as the sad obsessive vinyl junkies he used to see through the windows of the shop down his old London street. It wasn't even an actual shop, just a house with collapsing cardboard boxes loaded on to trestle tables. 'Real Records', said the scabby sign above the door. He views that shop, and all shops that purvey such unnecessary shod, as the downside of the free market. You have to let any old prick sell any old shit, that's the way it works. It's the demand that should die away. He doesn't understand the demand.

On that day, on the tube, still half an hour away from walking past the crap record shop, a young man with a grey mac and a mop of thick, perfectly tousled hair kept bouncing into him. He was six inches taller at least and had a superhero jaw. But wasn't well-built; clearly didn't work out much; would have been easy enough to beat the piss out of. If only it could be that simple. He suspected that the mac was about to become ultra-fashionable. Alex from his office had one. And he found that he hated that man with the same quiet loathing that he felt for Alex. He hated him for not apologizing for knocking him, and for not moving slightly further away after the first occurrence. He hated him for wearing a grey mac, crisp, all corners, so obviously going to be the new style, when he'd just bought a fucking tan one. Most of all he hated him for the confidence that allowed him to stand there, sure-footed, reading the *Guardian*, being a fucking lefty like his dad, without clutching the clammy bar as he had to. He sneaked a slight revenge: looking at the paper through the crook of the man's arm. And in that space, between a stupidly expensive watch and the gloating grey mac, he saw a story about the release of a murderer. A man who killed a child when he was himself a child. He remembered his joy when the other kid was hanged in prison, years back, supposedly a suicide. Then the disappointment when he discovered it was the wrong one. Not the one his dad had all but adopted.

It came like a sudden download of bytes, the realization. This was what it had all been about – his dad's rushed move to Manchester. The sneaky fuck. He was helping the little bastard again. That was what made him forget the birthday. You travel halfway up the country to try and start afresh with the old man, make your own birthday dinner and he doesn't even come home. Leaves you sitting alone after travelling all that way. Leaves his own son playing second fiddle to that sicko. Just like when he was a boy. Only he wasn't a boy anymore, was he? So what was he going to do about it?

The old man was pathetically grateful when Zed asked if he could move in with him for a bit. Acted like his son was doing him the favour. So Zed played along, played 'Zeb' for a while. Terry's the only person who calls him that, always has to be different doesn't he? He's never understood that names matter.

There's great power in names; Zed knows it. Jews never write 'Yahweh' down, because it's too awesome. You can control a demon when you know its true name. Though it may rend you skin from bone if you get it wrong. Ghosts have names: say 'Candyman' in front of the mirror and he comes. Myths have names: say 'Rumpelstiltskin' and he goes away. And if you happen to find out the name of a monster, even one that hides its hideousness inside, well, that might bring you riches untold.

Monster-hunters can need hiding places too. Sometimes when he prowls the streets Zed is called Jed.

He had a good day at the football yesterday with Steve; was sad to say goodbye. But blamed it on the beers when he felt a tear in his eye on the way back to Terry's. He has to tell himself that they were never real mates, that Steve was just a means to an end. Now he's served his purpose the friendship must disappear, be airbrushed out of existence like the inner lips of 80s porn mags. And still Zed can't help feeling like he's lost something.

Not as much as darling Jack, it seems, when Terry comes back from Sunday lunch, full of drink and worry. Zed has made himself a shoulder to cry on, a voice of concern. His dad, believing he doesn't know anything of the big picture, has been filling in the small details very nicely. 'Alcohol preserves everything except secrets,' is one of his favourite phrases, and as usual the old lush ignores his own advice. The facts come out with the Famous Grouse, and Zed always makes sure the drinks cabinet is well stocked. Invest to earn, that's the number one rule of economics.

The earnings should be even higher now the little bastard's lost his bloater sweetheart, though it's going to push the show forward a bit. Arranging this show's been taking up all of Zed's time; but he's getting more and more confident it'll be spectacular. The old man thinks he's always out at the gym, or looking for work; but he's been doing work, groundwork, plenty of it.

He's thinking of setting up a detective agency with all the money he's going to get. Reckons he'll be good at it, believes he has a flair for the job. He's enjoyed wriggling himself into people's lives, the ease with which it can be done. Abusing the ignorant trust that everyone seems to thrust upon strangers. Even people who aren't who they claim to be, assume that everyone else is. He's taken pleasure in the watching, the creeping, the following, even the computing, which he roundly despised when it was a routine part of his office work. He eventually broke the codes on his dad's computer. It was tricky. Alex couldn't have done it, that's for sure, despite how the other staff used to bleat on about his abilities.

Zed had to write a virus-program, in the end, that memorized all of Terry's user-codes. A variant of the W32/Badtrans-B worm-virus. Badtrans-Z he liked to call it. His invention, his child. His own little worm, working its way through the systems of Terry's Apple Mac, mailing out all encrypted keystrokes. It wasn't hard to work out which ones were passwords. One of the passwords was 'Zebedee', and for a moment he thought about stopping it all. But it was too late, he'd gone too far, invested too much energy to let that spec of guilt get in the way. On Friday he fixed the computer so that Jack's panic button wouldn't work, would always register as a test. Wouldn't alert his dad, and wouldn't alert the police. Leaving the 'special pager' that Terry was so proud of, as nothing but a useless lump of plastic. Leaving Jack carrying the world's most expensive paperweight.

But Terry had come back suddenly, when he crashed his crappy car. He was in the flat before Zed could shut the computer down. It would have all been over, if Zed wasn't so damn good. He switched off the monitor and used his shirt to hide the operating lights. Pretended it was a cloth he was dusting the computer with. Quick thinking, and cool under pressure – that's real intelligence. Alex couldn't have come up with that. Perfect little Alex, who had never been to college, but somehow still knew more long words than him. Alex, who had the women squawking around him on cigarette breaks; flapping about like they'd discovered Robbie Williams chugging a Marlboro Light in the lobby. Not some jumped-up little no-muscle grey-macked twat. On the day he quit, Zed bounced Alex's head off his computer screen. Just a shove as he went by, let him off lightly, really.

'That drive hard enough for you, Alex?' he'd said. Now that's wit, that's the kind of thing James Bond would say. You have to admire Bond, even if the films are shit.

Spying is rather like computing. It's a logical sequence stream, each part fed by and reacting to every other.

Snippets of information which like an excerpt of binary code are meaningless on their own, but when placed in a whole can launch missiles.

Zed followed his dad a few times. That was the trickiest bit in some ways. Keeping the dismally out-of-date shit-brown Sierra just within his sights. Three cars back, they reckon on those crappy movies, but Terry would have known right away something was up, if he'd spotted him at all. He didn't, though, and Zed found Jack's house like that. But Jack was too paranoid to follow. He made Zed once for definite, outside some pub. So he shaved his head before becoming Jed.

If he'd known about the Internet reward in those days, it might have ended when he'd located the little git, with only twenty grand. Which would still have been a tidy score. But back then he thought he needed more. Something that might persuade the papers to break their traitorous promises of anonymity. Some evidence of instability perhaps. He had never hoped that a little digging would release the geyser of filth that eventually erupted.

The *Evening News* was the clue, not so difficult to spot when dear dad bought two copies. And in the photo, at which Terry stared overly long, was the lad he went to drink with on his precious Tuesday nights. The double of the little fuck that he carries in his wallet. Zed's seen the wallet, opened it with a stomach-clenching sickness. Rifled through it, sure that there must be a picture of him too, in it somewhere. But no, just the young pretender, sitting in the plastic enclosed space that should be Zed's by birthright. Live by the sword and you die by the sword, you fuck. The picture in the *Evening News* was Prince Jack's undoing. Nicely presented as it was with his first and second names, but also those of his workmate, a friend, a way in, a wormhole.

The phone book led to Chris and Zed followed him to Steve's one night. When the front door was opened by an uncomplicated-looking blond lad in a DV baseball cap, Zed decided straightaway to shift his attention. He hadn't liked the look of Chris. There was something of the Alex about him. Something altogether too bloody knowing. Anyway, if he failed to make friends with Steve, then he still had Chris. A second chance in case he fucked up. Zed was not unaccustomed to fucking things up.

As it turned out, making friends with Steve was easy. Every Thursday he played killer pool on his own, in a contest at his local. Jed didn't win the pool, but the rest was like blunderbussing fish-tanks. Steve couldn't get over how much they had in common, and Jed couldn't get over how smoothly his lies were laid to the simpleton. Old Stevie liked to talk; he was as bad as Terry: a couple of beers and he wanted nothing more than some friendly ears. And to his joy, Jed found that his new friend was also a good friend of Jack's. Though he called him Bruiser sometimes, because of a fight. Jed, of course, said this would go no further. Certainly he wouldn't mention it in front of Jack, if the lad was sensitive about it.

Zed, on the other hand, made contact with a red-top tabloid and began some complex negotiations. Mainly concerned with proof, but corresponding to very large sums of money. He wore a wire the next time he broached Steve. And he could hear his bank balance clicking up like a milometer, with every word Steve said. He got more than he'd dared hope for. After hearing about the Alton Towers escapade, and posing as TV researcher, he got actual footage of a criminal act, courtesy of a security guard who was saving for a holiday. Invest to earn. It was easier than he would have believed. There wasn't even any need to go pouring through hours of tape. The park renta-cops kept all shots of people breaking and entering, in case they caught them at it again. 'Breaking and entering' seemed a bit strong to Zed, looking at the footage; but that and the alleged

GBH were more than enough for the paper's peace of mind. To reassure a litigation-scarred editor that disclosure was in the public interest. Zed threw in the missing stock at DV as a sweetener. There was nothing to link it to Jack, so the hacks could just use it as background fact. Let the public mull it over as coincidence or not.

But the missing Michelle should be a godsend. An extra twist worth another twenty at least. 'Missing Girl, Blond Like Angela Milton', that's how he sees the headlines. He wishes he'd brought in Max Clifford to do the bargaining. Fuck it, he'll be nicely set up from this. And Jack and Terry both get theirs. The little brat that he's sure caused his parents to divorce and started this slide of shit that's been his life, and the father that ditched him. Zed gets paid and they get paid, everyone's a winner. And Terry gets one more good night out of it…

The evening they go to print, tomorrow night, Zed's going to get him hammered; slip him a mickey too, just to be certain. Make sure he'll sleep all day. Then Zed'll unplug all the phones and Jack'll find out what it really means to be alone. To be deserted by Terry in a time of need. Just one more little stage to set, a few more spotlights to direct, and then the show can go on.

X is for Xmas. X Marks the Spot Where God Used to be.

It's only just gone Guy Fawkes, but there are workmen by the side of the road hanging strings of Christmas lights. They loll unlit between the lamp-posts in the city centre, like badly drawn bunting or burned laundry. It's not just Monday morning blues; the world is darker today. Chris has barely spoken, not even trying the radio quizzes. Shell is still missing and she's left a gap in Jack. But today he realizes everyone's got these holes in them. Spaces that they try and plug with work or hobbies or family or booze, none of which ever really fit, because the thing that was meant to fill them has gone.

Dave calls Jack into his office when they get back to base, after the first round of drops. He wants to know where Michelle is. Jack says that he thinks she's still ill, at her mum's, maybe. He doesn't want her to lose her job, and he doesn't want a manhunt. Not now, not while he can still hope she's fine. While there's a chance for a happy ending.

Kelly isn't there when he gets home. She's working double shifts all this week, so she's staying in the accommodation at the hospital. There's no sign of Marble either. A note in Kelly's neat nurse print reminds Jack to feed it, but baby hoops of biscuit that look like congealed sawdust already slouch untouched in its moulded plastic bowl.

Hoping to find some food for himself, Jack inspects his cupboard. There's plenty of pasta and rice in it, but he can't cope with their bland look, and can't be arsed to cook. He decides to get a burger from the end of the road, when his hunger gets on top of him. There's no pleasure in eating for the sake of it. To enjoy your food it's best to wait until you really need it.

The burger is a disappointment. If he wasn't so hungry, he probably wouldn't finish it. All the relish is slid to one side, like the guy who made it really couldn't give a toss. And it's got sweetcorn in it. Jack hates sweetcorn; little lumps like witches' teeth, yellow and sickly. Hacendado used to say that if sweetcorn was any good for you, it wouldn't come out intact in your shit. That's your body's way of telling you not to bother.

Jack hasn't even got the energy for the telly. There's nothing on anyway, but a film on Channel 5, which is topless tripe. Unplotted, unerotic, the beautiful women so feeble and pleading they are unarousing. He keeps seeing Shell anyway. When she isn't servicing an army of Chippendale-like lovers, she is lying naked in a ditch, eels leaving tracks of dirty water as they slither over her wan skin.

In bed he feels feverish. Maybe he really is coming down with something. The top strip of the duvet, where the foam or feathers don't fill out the cloth, feels like a rope across his throat. And he notices for the first time the stain that his head has left on the pillow. Grease from his hair and face has made the centre dirty and shiny. But the murk lurks all around his room. Pockets of shadow holding something dingier within them, which he hopes has not come from him, is not in him too. His nervous tension has risen to such a level that he nearly screams when a shape bursts from one of the patches of gloom and streaks across the floor. But it's only Marble, some animal urge making it desert the pile of dirty clothes in which it's been dozing. It's just a cat.

In films, when someone realizes it's just a cat, they die in the same scene.

The grubby shadows are still around at 6:04 am, when Jack wakes up so wired there is no point in trying to sleep for such a little while longer. He goes downstairs in his boxer shorts and T-shirt, flipping on lights as he moves. Opening blinds and curtains to begin with, until he sees that the darkness outside sucks away the comfort of the electric bulbs. He is shaky when he goes into the kitchen, where even in this whitest, brightest room the harsh glare of the strip-light is not enough. He opens the fridge to get its diminutive beam on as well. The cold blast on his bare legs makes them crumple into goosebumps and stands their hairs on end. He can't figure out his sudden sensitivity to the dark. Something weird is going on. The hairs on his neck prickle too. And he's not sure if this is caused by the eerie fear, or by the worry that he's losing it entirely.

He tries to eat a bowl of cornflakes, but the cereal is too dry. It plasters itself to his gullet. When he leaves it a few minutes to sponge up the milk, it becomes inedible mush. He pours it into Marble's bowl, in the slot where water should go.

He sits in the lounge not watching an Open University programme about soil creep. His legs are irritated by the feel of the sofa's cloth.

At 6:37 the phone rings. The unexpected noise sends a shock through him. Jack looks at it, bewildered. He can't understand who could be calling at this time in the morning. It rings off just as he finally decides he'd better answer it. While he's dialling 1471 he hears his mobile going upstairs. The ring tone is a spooky tick-tick tune, which is suddenly not funny in the silence of a day that is doing his head in. Everything is conspiring to unnerve him, and his belief in such omens makes every one register deeper than the last. He races upstairs, stubbing his bare toe on his bedroom doorframe. The phone's green glowing screen says it's Dave Vernon. Relieved, but still confused, Jack presses the 'yes' button to take the call.

'Dave?' he says.

There is hesitation at the other end before Dave's voice says: 'Jack?'

'Yes.'

'We're not going to need you at work for the moment. Well…' he tails off.

'What do you mean?'

'Don't come in today.'

'What?'

'Don't come in until… unless… if, I ask you to. It's not good for the business.'

'What's this about, Dave?' Jack is aware of the desperation in his voice. 'Is it the stock? It's not me, I haven't taken a thing.'

'You know what it's about. I'm sorry but that's the end of it. I don't wish to continue this discussion.'

'Dave,' Jack says, 'Dave?' But the line is dead.

He puts his work clothes on anyway, not sure why, perhaps because they are lying ready for him over the chair. He can't understand what just happened. He doesn't want to believe the most obvious explanation for Dave's behaviour: that he knows; somehow he knows.

Jack clips the panic button/pager to his belt, and slides it round to his hip, to beneath his right hand. Swallowing saliva as he realizes what he is admitting to himself. That he believes today he might need this machine. He is tempted to press it straightaway. He actually flips up the screen cap, and his finger hovers over the button. But that would be crazy. As freaked out as he is, he has to stay rational. How would Dave know? He'd be the last one to know. He's got his head up his own arse most of the time. It's much more likely that it's to do with the stolen stock. He's bound to be the first suspect; Dave knows he's done time. He'll wait till half seven or eight, and then phone Terry. He sits down on the sprawl of his unmade bed. Maybe he'd better call Chris now, though, tell him not to bother with the pick-up, in case he doesn't know. Find out what Dave's told him, if he does.

Chris is engaged constantly. It's 6:57 when Jack finally makes the connection. He pours out about being told not to come in, before Chris has a chance to open his mouth.

'I know,' Chris says coldly. 'Dave's given me the day off.'

'Is it the stock?' Jack asks.

'It's you, Jack, or whoever you are. It's about you. How could you? I mean why? I mean what the fuck?' Chris' voice is tremulous now, you can almost hear his lip quivering. But then he spews out in total rage: 'Have you hurt her? Just tell me that, have you hurt Michelle?'

'No, never, I couldn't. What's happened, have they found her?'

'Read the fucking paper. Read the *Sun*. I've already had them phone me this morning.' His anger drops a notch, or at least his voice does. 'All the lies. How could you? How could you keep that up? How could you just squirm your way into our world? I'd tell you I'm done with you. But then, I don't know who the fuck you are anyway.' He puts the phone down.

Jack is left standing in the hallway, with the buzz of his handset in his ear. Hearing this from Chris is like being beaten with his birthday present. But it's his old nemesis, the *Sun*, that's dealt the blow. He needs to know what they've written. Peering through the window of Kelly's room, he sees that the streets are still deserted. Grey with grimy pre-dawn light, looking squalid, ominous, but at least devoid of life. He can run down to the paper shop in less than a minute.

Jack gets his DV cap from the drawer, a hat that has

helped him escape detection before, and pulls it down hard with determined hands. He scans the street once more from Kelly's window, and then again from the front room, before he walks stiff-legged to the door. Every muscle is tense as he twists the Yale lock. He realizes he has no money, and lets it click back into the clasp of the frame, while he dashes upstairs to get his wallet. He has to do this while he still has the nerve. He checks the panic button is still to hand and that he has his keys, before he opens the door again. Cautiously, studying the road, he lets it close behind him.

He has just raised his right leg to provide the starting momentum for his run when the first flash catches him. It blinds him, blurring his vision, leaving an imprint on his eyes. He raises his hand to block out the light, as another flash comes from the same spot: behind a wheely-bin in the neighbour's dark alley. It's joined by a second bulb from a similar concealment across the street, then a third. All now firing in rapid succession. He turns and tries to force his key back into the lock. It won't fit. They must have stuffed something into the hole to keep him out here.

'Have you got anything you want to say?' a man shouts. 'Put your side before they all get here.'

Jack crouches down with his face to the door, and presses the panic button on the pager. Three or four times he pushes it, sinking it as hard as he can. Until the end of his finger bends back and the pain shoots him off it. He starts to topple in towards the door, losing his balance. His left hand goes out automatically to hold him off it. Clutched in his white fingers is the wrong key that he's been trying. With both palms he slides himself up the towering pus-green wood. The flashes, which are close around him now, parade how much his hand is shaking. It appears at different points around the lock, illuminated by this hateful personal strobe show. The key bounces off the lock's metal surround, but this one fits. The door opens to let Jack fall into the hallway.

One final explosion from a long-barrelled Cannon hits his face, before he pushes the lens away and forces the threshold shut. They try and lift the letterbox. But he slams his elbow against it to keep it closed. His head collapses into the crook of the same arm. Only his will is holding them back. Jack feels like the little Dutch boy: jamming the hole that threatens to engulf his world.

After a couple of minutes he scrambles away on all fours, into the living room. He checks his mobile, surprised that there has been no response from Terry to the pager. The phone has a signal but there's no message or missed calls. Jack picks through the menus to recall Terry's mobile number. Panting like a grounded fox. Staring blankly at the screen, which says: *calling… calling… calling… no response*. He tries again, to the same effect. Then he tries Terry's landline. An electronic BT lady tells him the number cannot be reached. He presses the panic button once more. But still nothing happens. Terry's office phone at the secure unit switches straight to answer. Jack just asks Terry to phone him as soon as he can. Sure that the fear in his voice is sufficient to convey the urgency.

He refuses to believe he's on his own, until he's tried all of the numbers again from Kelly's house phone. When every other combination has failed, Jack's finger lingers over the 9 on the smudged keypad. Three short presses would bring at least some response. But what? Arrest most likely. A cell. Questioning. Sneering mouths trying to catch him out. The police might be on their way already. Their eventual arrival is inescapable. If he can't bring Terry, there's not much point in getting them here any quicker.

But there is a deeper, all-devouring beast, that is circling the waters of his mind. A leviathan so vast it could suck him through the gaps in its teeth. What if this is all down to Shell? What if she's the one that's brought them here? What if her whole disappearance was engineered to spear him?

Could she have been faking all of that? Was she laughing at him all the time? And suddenly every memory of her is skewed. There are looks in her eyes that weren't there before, or he never registered. Smirks when his back was turned. Phone calls to papers each time he left her house. That's why she wanted to take a photo of him, not for her purse, for the front page. It was her, he's sure. She's worse than dead, she was never there at all. It was only ever an act to catch him. Which means they must know about the fight. And so it's over. His licence will be revoked. He'll be taken back inside, without even the blanket of anonymity. Deprived of which he will have to live on protection wings. With freaks and sex cases. To be beaten at every opportunity and humiliated relentlessly.

Jack knows that he can't take that. Not now. Not when he's known this freedom. Which brings him inevitably back to the choice. The choice his one-time friend made among the fraggles. But which Jack would prefer to make in the comfort of his own home.

He phones Chris' mobile; it's turned off or engaged, which he had hoped for in a way, to ease what he has to say. It cuts straight to answer service.

'Chris,' he says, 'It's Jack. It was always Jack. The person that you knew, that's who he was. I wish I could have told you more, I really do. Once I nearly did. But just because I couldn't, doesn't mean I lied to you. Only the words were ever lies, if you can understand that. Anyway, this, I guess, is goodbye.' And he can't help the tears which are streaking his vision and dropping to his chest, crumbling the resolution with which he had set his jaw. 'Speak to the *Sun*, when they phone you again. Get what you can from the fuckers. There's nothing else you can do… Except that… maybe you could try and tell them some other stuff too. Show I tried. Say I wasn't all bad. How we saved the girl and that, and how, when I hurt that guy, I was trying to help you. They'll twist it all, but maybe you could try… So, sorry Chris, and like I say, goodbye.'

He wipes his nose on the sleeve of his work fleece, and then tries to clean off the snail-trail it leaves, on his trousers, as if somehow this matters. He wonders if he should leave a note for Terry. He takes the pad that in a different world reminded him to feed the cat. But he can't find the words that he's looking for. How can you cram fifteen years of thanks on to a sheet of faint lined note paper. In the end he writes:

Terry,
I can't go back to being that other person. I like Jack. This seems the only way to hang on to him. Thanks for trying, anyway. I'm really sorry about this. I should have told you about all the stuff when it happened. Maybe you could have helped. It's my fault not yours. So anyway, got to go. Keep the car if you can, it's part of you. Thank you.

I love you.
Jack

He goes into the kitchen, where he knows Kelly keeps a stash of cooking wine. The first slug makes him gag. The screw-lid lands with a splash, safe in the sea of the sink. He takes the bottle with him to the bathroom. The cut-throat's sitting there, folded into its handle, but still glinting: winking, in the artificial light. He lifts it and opens it, and then takes another swig. He tries the blade against his cheek, clearing away the negligible stubble of one day, and leaving a strip of sting on the unlubricated skin. Wrists are best done in the bath to avoid too much pain. But you need to put the booster on if you want that much hot water in the morning. It would make such a mess as well; house rules are courtesy and common sense. Maybe he should leave Kelly a note too?

But he's getting tired of saying goodbye, and somehow it would devalue what he wanted Terry to know.

He folds the razor and puts it in his pocket, opens the mirrored cabinet, and runs a finger over the rows of bottles. One, broad and brown as the bouncers at a party he went to once, contains sleeping pills. And this is what Jack wants. He wants more than anything just to sleep. To leave all this. He pours a handful of the pills and knocks them back, in ones and twos, with the harsh slap of the wine. Not sure how many he will need, he pours out another lot – and then some more – necks them all. Gulps as much of the drink as he can take. But still takes the bottle with him. He wanders back to his room, and looks around it, quite satisfied. Runs his fingers over the shelves and walls, as he did the day he arrived. Then he slips his trainers off. Pairs them neatly by the wardrobe, and climbs into bed. It seems to Jack that he probably didn't even need the tablets. Because he's so weary of this world, he's so exhausted by what it does to him, that he feels, when he closes his eyes, like he would never wake again anyway.

Y is for Why?

It was a day like no other. The first of the summer. The start of the holidays, holding significance even for those who hardly went to school. It meant that other kids would be around, but for *A* those old fears had been allayed. Word had shiftily spread that he was not one to be messed with anymore. He was no longer Davy Crockett, no longer a loner; he had a partner. More of a Butch and Sundance affair. And when the *sun* shone, like it did on that day, you couldn't help but *dance*. Inside anyway, lest your friend think you soft. Actually though, *A* considered *B* to be the better Sundance, the surly dangerous one. He should be Butch Cassidy, who was handsome and popular. If you're going to daydream, you might as well go all the way.

They started that Monday in the rec. Once a park, built by some mine-owner in a rare act of public kindness. When it had fallen into disrepair, the gardens were bulldozed and replaced with soccer pitches, swings and slides. When these fell into disrepair, they were left to it. Philanthropy had gone from Stonelee by then.

Football teams no longer trained on the field. The Stonelee side was called The Nomads, because they only played away. The posts were still up, but there was too much broken glass dug into the grass to risk a dive or a slide. Probably even to risk a ball. The swings were high and well built. Hung from the top of tough vandal-proof A-frames.

But generally you had to shin up the steep poles and unwind the gun-metal-grey chains if you wanted a go. The same sort of people who stuffed all the bog paper down the public toilets would swing them until they wrapped tight around the cross bar. Sometimes these people were *A* and *B*, wreaking vengeance for other times, when all they wanted was to shit or to swing.

Mostly though, they went to the rec for the roundabout. It was an old-fashioned, concrete-edged, fast-as-you-like roundabout. It had chipped orange paint on the steel handrails, and had smashed more teeth in than *B*'s brother. In one of its eight segments the floor had given way and been burned, or broken up for dogs to chase. If you looked down there you could see the ground spinning faster than anything you could imagine. Faster than a car could drive, faster than a bird could fly. *A* and *B* would dare each other to hold themselves down there. Pressing their cheeks or their noses so close to the ground that they could feel its breath as they span. With the other one pushing a bar at full pelt, till it ran quicker than them, away from their legs. Leaving them stranded till another pass let them jump on board. Watching the sky and riding the wind and waiting for their turn to push their face into the hole. To take their chance with the stones that would certainly shred them, and might well snap their neck if they went too far. But maybe they didn't really understand the finality of that.

The closest *A* had seen to the end was the finish of Butch and Sundance on the telly. You knew they died. There were too many Spics for them to have killed them all. But they didn't die in the film. They ran out there, into the square, and the volleys of gunfire echoed around them. But they were frozen. Butch and Sundance stopped just before the drop. They stayed in the still photo in his mind. Forever just about to die. But never dead. You were never sure. That's the way to go.

When they tired of the roundabout that day, they threw stones for the ducks. Which were clever enough not to eat them, but not clever enough to give up the hope that the next splash would be a bit of bread. The boys bored before the birds: three bedraggled brown mallards. The only beasts hardy, or unlucky, or just plain dumb enough, to live among the road cones and shopping trolleys of the pond some landowner had once called a lake.

The scant few shopowners in the high street were wise to the pair. Had them logged as a brace of bandits, not even to be allowed in one at a time. Only the newly opened Cut Price Booze and General Store tolerated them. Perhaps through ignorance, not having had time to connect their visits to missing sweets. If they had an understanding of consequence they might have left him alone. It would have been nice to have one shop for the times when they actually had money. But the owner was swiftly to condemn them with the rest.

They had just been ejected when they saw her, *A* smarting with the indignity of being flung out by the collar, *B* still holding a Marathon bar like a runner's baton. She was a girl from *A*'s class: Angela Milton, the undisputed princess of Stonelee JMI. She looked like an advert. Her teeth were as white as Colgate new minty gel. Her hair as blond as the corn in Hovis fields. Her clothes straight off the racks of Etam, Top Girl and Miss Selfridge, places that existed only in Durham City, maybe only Newcastle. Even the girls had crushes on her.

Angela was on her own that Monday, walking with the unknowing self-importance that only cats, and those who've seen the effect of their beauty from birth, can achieve. It was the decision of a second to follow her. Unspoken, a choice of eyes and nodded heads. She was utterly unaware of them behind her. She had always been unaware of *A*, except as something that other children hurt in attempts to impress her.

The newly installed CCTV cameras saw them, though. Observed them with unblinking eyes, as they darted from dingy alley to dirty doorway, along the straight and narrow road of the high street.

Down out of town she walked, shadowed at a distance by Butch and Sundance. She stopped at a bench, on the way to that part of the Byrne that had become the hole in the wall for the two-man Hole In The Wall Gang. They ducked behind a bank. And prone on the grass, among sun-dried dog-turds, they watched while she waited.

A was about to suggest they give it up for something more fun, when the boy came along. They knew his face, and his floppy fine hair, though he was nameless. His dad drove a Volvo, and was connected to the Parliament or the Army. He was too old for the JMI: twelve at least, maybe thirteen, but he wouldn't have gone there anyway. He went to a special school. Not the sort which *B*'s brother had attended, but the one at Barnard Castle, that wore purple blazers, and only came home for holidays.

The boy took Angela's hand, in a possessive way. As if going to school in a castle gave him every right to a princess. And he led her down the slope to the Byrne, out of sight from the road. *A* and *B* crossed over and squatted in the matted shrubbery at the foot of an elm tree, to keep the two in view.

The part of the Byrne to which he'd led her might once have been picturesque. It was still less littered, and steeper, so the water's colour cleared a bit in faster flow. Almost as soon as they sat down on the bank, he leaned across her and pressed his lips to hers. Her arms stuck out at right angles, like a scarecrow's, as he started to kiss her. But after a few minutes wrapped around his body, in echo of what his arms did to her. *A* began to get cramp in his shins from crouching in the bushes, but he didn't want to leave. It was entrancing, seeing them sucking this pleasure from each other. *B,* by his side, was focused, too. As patient as he'd been when they were eel-fishing. As still as the plaster monk in the church.

After maybe a quarter of an hour, the boy eased Angela down on to her back, without breaking the seal of their mouths. In this position his hands became more adventurous. They roamed her bare legs, which A knew to be so delicate that you could see patches of blue on them, where her royal blood showed through beneath the pale skin. His right hand strayed up her top, to feel one of the tiny bumps that you could only barely see when she wore her tightest school blouse. They were not yet even the promise of breasts. And Angela clearly felt they were not promised to this boy, because she sat up a moment or two after his fingers crept there, and forcibly removed his hand. The boy sat up too, and smiled and shook his head; and obviously spoke kindly or cleverly enough to calm her down again. Because soon his arm was around her and they were once more joined at the face.

A couldn't have left if he'd wanted to by then. A part of him was almost poking out the leg of his shorts. It skewered him into the squat, and would have made walking embarrassing if not impossible. He was not accustomed to this feeling, outside of a waking need to wee. But it didn't worry him, only made the watching more necessary somehow.

The boy, better versed in the world's ways, had let his hands stroll to Angela's thighs once again. Brushing the boundaries of her short white-lace skirt. This time though, one hand sank down, between her legs, beneath the cloth. She tried to raise herself from the ground, but his far bulkier chest was on top of her. She shook her mouth free of his, but he just lowered his head to kiss and suck at her neck. His arm showed the continued movement of his buried hand. Only when, eventually, she began to rain blows down on his back, did he remove his urgent fingers. At which he looked with some revulsion. He sat up, and as he did so she slapped him. The boy looked shocked. For a moment he looked as if he might sob, but then he raised a single middle digit at her, and stormed away. Angela stayed sat where she was, but pulled her knees to her chest and shook.

'She's crying,' *A* said.

'Let's go and see if she'll do it to us too,' said his friend.

A knew this was stupid, a plan sure to fail. But it was also the first day of the summer holidays. It was one of those days where you knew that anything could happen. One of those days that could change your life.

'Are you all right?' *A* asked her.

She turned to him with a look of such disgust and loathing that it seemed to stop her tears. She wiped her eyes, even as her mouth twisted in a disdainful: 'What do you want?'

B seemed not to notice these obvious signs. 'We were wondering if you fancied doing that to us. You know, kissing and that.'

Angela stood up; she was taller than either of them. *A* noticed that there were tiny flecks of red on her skirt. Like speckles of something spilled. 'You two are sick little spying shit-bags and you can both piss off.'

A turned to go, shoulders slumped with the inevitability of the attack.

But *B* was taken aback. He looked genuinely shocked by the outburst, offended even. He grabbed her by the arm, and with his face straining in effort, like a dog on the lead, started to pull her along the path, towards the bridge which ran over the Byrne. *A*, remembering that this was not just any old Monday, grabbed her other side and dragged too.

Until five minutes before, Angela had lived in a world where bad things did not happen. She struggled to free herself with girlish shakes of her arms, and her shoes left trails like tram-tracks in the dirt. But she didn't scream. Probably didn't even see how she could need to.

When they got her to the dark of the troll bridge, and stopped, it was clear they had reached the end of any plan.

'Well done. You've got me here, now let me go, or you're really going to pay.' She turned to *A*, who she knew had witnessed her authority, and said: 'You leave off my wrist this second, or you're going to regret it.'

They both dropped her arms and pulled back. But *B* produced the Stanley knife, the Stonelee knife, the knife whose news print picture would sit on coffee tables and trains throughout the country.

Angela Milton looked at the knife, and then from one of the boys to the other in absolute amazement.

'You little freaks,' she spat. 'You've got no idea, have you? I'm going to make sure everyone knows what animals you are! Your lives are going to be hell! You're going to wish you'd never been born!'

A felt a numb horror, because he knew she could do what she said. Because he didn't want to go back to a time of fear and hiding. He liked this new sepia world, in the shadows, under the ring road. Where actions were unreal, jumpy, like old films. Where you could do what you wanted, and no one would stop you. Where you were powerful. Where to ants and eels you were a god. And maybe you could be to girls.

B passed the knife edgily from hand to hand.

Angela tried to push through them, but was knocked to the floor, by one or other, or both. It was hard to say. Everything was indistinct under the bridge, out of the sun.

It was *B* who pushed out the short locking blade, and slashed at her thrashing arm. Of that Jack is pretty sure.

But he also remembers another boy, who watched the drop of Angela's jaw and revelled in the sudden shock that passed her eyes, as she realized she was not in charge.

It was *B* who first drew blood. He must have started the game.

But together they killed an Angel, and made her spell come true.

Z is for Zero.

With his eyes closed, Jack feels himself slipping, dropping. He can hear cars pulling up outside. He wonders if it's the police, but there's no ring at the door. Just more excited press chatter. Sounds he can remember from outside a court in Newcastle. Shouts like the bark of a dog pack. They know he's dug in. They know he's finished. They're just waiting. Unaware that he is escaping from them even while he lies here. But something makes him draw back his lids. And through the open bedroom door, he can see a patch of the sea-green hallway carpet illuminated. A beam of white shines through the skylight, like God showing the promised land. Dust and motes dance within its brilliance, swirling around each other. He can almost believe that this is his pathway to heaven. That this is a divine force showing him the getaway route he will take. Only, would he really be getting away? He can picture a blanket-covered form on an ambulance trolley, snarling faces, flashing cameras. Even when he's dead they will have him.

Suddenly it seems to Jack that the light is telling him something totally different. It is saying that this isn't the day to die. Not in here, not like this, not with the pack all around him. Not without a struggle. He pulls his duvet off, almost robotically, the action is so pronounced, so deliberate. What he has to do is clear.

The Nike Air Escape trainers that Terry bought him, that he has kept meticulously white, are still sat side by side at his wardrobe. He puts them on, not tucking the laces in, like he usually wears them, but pulled taut and tied tight. Their name reinforces the message of the beam of light, confirms his decision.

But first he has to visit the toilet. He kneels down on the rug before it, as if in prayer. Here, too, the window faces east, and it bathes him in the first forgiving rays of the sun. With his fingers he pushes at the back of his throat, until he feels a retch, which brings forth his breakfast of tablets and alcohol. The white pills bob in the Beaujolais waves of the bowl. Thankfully they still look pristine, not even dissolved at the edges. Taking no chances, he makes himself vomit again and again. Until it is the very lining of his stomach he is heaving. He already feels strangely cleansed by being so totally empty. But he washes his hands and face at the sink and cleans his teeth to be more so. Jack returns to the bedroom, to put on his cap – though some of the press have seen it, it may disguise him against the public. Then, with one last look around, he steps out into the bright white beam, as if into a teleporter.

The skylight is stiff to open; the gap it leaves barely large enough for him to fit through. It would be easier with a chair. But somehow there is a solemnity to this moment of exit, which would be spoiled if he went to get one now. With a heave, and legs kicking into nothingness, he gets his head and shoulders out on to the roof. The air is fresh. It smells of victory, not the fear he's leaving in the house. He pulls his whole body out on to the sloping roof. Slowly. Careful not to roll. He is surprised to find that the tiles are not slate, like he imagined, but a kind of coarse plasticky stuff, warm to lie on. Prone like this he can see he is quite invisible to anyone watching the house from below, even if there are any in the back alley. He closes the skylight and begins to move cautiously across the rooftop. Sliding his knees, in the commando crawl that he has seen so many times on TV. Though without a gun to hold, his hands can grip the tiles too. He's still scared, but it's channelled now. He uses it to fuel his progress. There is even a momentary flash of joy as he reaches the barely discernible boundary with the neighbouring house. Thank God for terraces.

It takes the best part of an hour for Jack to make his way up the street like this. The further he gets from number ten, the higher he allows himself to rise. By the end of the road he is moving in a crouched walk, right hand raised to clasp the peak of the roof as he goes. He knows where he is getting down. He's seen it from afar. The second to last house has a small extension, or a brick shed, jutting out from it. Something he could drop on to, and from there to the ground.

It is easier in the imagination; reality shows further to fall. But the house has sturdy iron guttering, which allows Jack to hang by his fingertips before the drop. He lands with a thud, and rolls on to his back to lose the impact, like a parachutist. He's uninjured, scrambles quickly to the end of the flat roof, in case the noise draws the owners out. The gate at the end of the short yard is already ajar. He has his eye on it as he takes the shorter second drop, and maybe this is what makes him twist on the impact. What creates the snap and the surge of hurt in his left knee. Takes it from under him.

He doesn't even allow himself to test the leg as he gets up. The pain tells him it isn't all right, but that's not the point. It has to be all right enough to walk on, and adrenalin ensures it is. Jack limps out of the gate and then out of the alley. On to the road the paper shop is on, where he was headed first of all.

It's not safe here though. It's too open. He feels very vulnerable, less than a street away from where the hordes are surrounding his home. They might even be aware that he's gone by now, if the police have turned up for him. At the end of this road is one of the main arterial routes. A direction he's taken countless times in the comfort of a white van. If he can make it down there, he might be able to hitch right out of the city. He heads towards it, hat pulled down, left knee excruciating. It's almost the peak of rush hour now. Occasionally people push past as they walk much faster up the pavement, hurrying to another inconsequential day at work. There are too many faces around, too many watching eyes, staring at the guy who plods so obviously in pain. The end of the street is an impossibly long way off under such scrutiny, and hitchhiking suddenly seems far too risky a route. Who's going to pick him up? Probably the police. He wouldn't give himself a lift like this: injured, dishevelled, terrified.

When he sees a train rumbling across a grey bridge over the road, Jack's plan changes immediately. He's momentarily alone under the passover's shadow, as he reaches it. And he climbs as fast as he can up the concrete bank towards the track. His leg screams with the strain of the steep ascent, forcing him to rest at the top, concealed by the concrete parapet. He's shaking with the pain and the fear and the cold. He wishes he'd worn a coat, as well as his thin work fleece. Who knows where he's going to sleep tonight?

The ground Jack's sitting on is a narrow dirt trail, pressed flat by kid feet. Probably a short-cut to the back of the houses which run alongside the train-tracks. His knee has ballooned. He can feel its swollen shape through his trousers. But worried that he'll be discovered here, he decides to move on.

He follows the rails away from the city centre. He hadn't counted on how much harder it would be to walk on this uneven surface. The stones give way under his trainers, and with agonizing frequency his knee gives way too. When he tries to walk further from the tracks, in the long grass of the banks, he finds it difficult to judge where to put his feet. Slowing his progress and shaking his confidence. He ends up winding his way, like a wounded snake, between the verge and the grey stones. Where do they get them from, so many identical stones?

When the trains rage past he has to stand well away, for fear that he'll fall under them. But the rush to move quickly when he sees them makes a fall all the more likely. A couple of times he only just steadies himself on shifting shale as the front of an Intercity reaches him. But this threat of death is better than simply giving in and dying. The harder it gets, the more important it is to survive.

His leg has begun to numb a bit by the time he reaches a station. Though he can't see how the walk can have helped it. A limping stagger that has taken close enough to two hours, including the rests when his knee became unbearable. Maybe his brain has just stopped letting as much pain through.

A gap in the fence allows him into the station car park unobserved. So he approaches the building at the normal entrance, by some steps. In spite of everything he feels some satisfaction, as he pulls himself up the blood-red, metal hand-rail. He's pretty sure he's made it this far unspotted. If he can get away he'll come up with something. Maybe out of the country, abroad, where no one will ever recognize him. They're always going on about the numbers of illegal immigrants getting in to Britain. It must be a piece of piss to get out.

First things first. Just get out of Manchester. He stares around the small station building for a map or a timetable, something to tell him where he can flee to from here. There is a news-stand to one side, racks of tabloids facing out in rows. With heart-stopping horror he sees that one, the *Sun*, carries the headline: 'Milton killer in violent attack', and then: 'Bruiser', above an almost full-page photo of him. Not just any photo. The one taken by the *Evening News*. They've cut it off, so that instead of standing shoulder to shoulder with Chris, he's on his own. Alone, and wearing exactly the same clothes as he is now. It could have been taken outside the station.

Jack looks around him, expecting to see a police snatch squad or a baying mob. But no one seems to have noticed, no one is even looking at him. The danger gives him an explosion of energy. He rips off the DV cap and hobbles, faster than his knee could have stood a second before, towards the matchstick man that marks the toilet.

Inside a scrawled stall, Jack sets about changing his appearance. The cap he stuffs into the cistern, once he's prised its lid off. But deciding this might be found, he takes it out again. With the cut-throat from his pocket, he cuts it into strips thin enough to be confident they'll flush. He pulls off the fleece and T-shirt, and hangs them from the lock. And with toilet paper he tries to buff a shine onto the steel roll-holder. He gets it good enough to see his reflection, though it appears stretched and ghoulish, the sickening spirit of a muppet. With the razor, he starts to strip away his hair. He washes the blade after every long stroke, in the still-open cistern. Which burbles away to itself like a baby, unaware of the anguish around it. Halfway through the shaving process, Jack realizes he's probably marking himself more by doing it. The skin of his scalp is as white and crinkled as an arse in the bath, but with angry red blotches where he's cut too close. Only he's gone too far to stop. He has to go forward. So many clumps of blond swim about in the cistern by the end that he can't get the razor clean. He has to scoop out some of the wet chunks of hair, and put them in the bowl with the sliced-up hat.

His top is lined in blue, so he cuts off the washing instructions and size label and puts it on inside out, to change the colour and hide the company logo. With more toilet roll, he cleans up the most obvious bits of scattered hair, and watches to make sure everything flushes away. For a moment it looks like the bowl is going to flood. But the blockage bursts, and hat, hair, labels and paper are sucked into the sewers. He pockets the cut-throat in his trousers, closer to hand in case he needs it.

Examining himself in the mirror by the wash-basins, which are crusted with ancient soap smears, Jack decides that the fleece looks all right, not obviously on wrong way round. His head isn't too bad either. Maybe it was a good idea to shave it. He's managed without any major cuts, even at the back, and it's certainly altered his appearance. He looks like a Romanian Aids orphan: sickly, sad and doomed.

He gets on the first train that's heading out of the city. Not knowing where it's going, not really caring, so long as it is far away. He finds a seat at the end of a carriage, so nobody can sit opposite him. No one on board so far can even see his face. With the weight off his knee, and his leg extended, the pain almost subsides. Exhaustion hits him like a PP-9. He hopes it's not the tablets acting as well. He needs to have his wits about him.

It's a struggle to hold down the panic when the ticket collector comes round. The guy is a kindly-looking, middle-aged West Indian, but Jack has a deeply drilled fear of uniforms. This one is Nazi grey, and a ticket machine hangs Uzi-like from a polished leather shoulder strap. Jack tries to control his breathing, fights the urge to bolt, as the inspector moves down the carriage towards him. But there's nowhere to run to on the train, even if he could run. He has to brazen it out and buy a ticket. Shit, he doesn't even know where the train's going. He strains to hear a destination from another passenger. They've all paid at the station, just hand over slips of card. Which are clipped with a click that goes right through Jack.

'Ticket?' the collector says.

'Haven't got one,' Jack says, keeping his voice monotone. 'Had to run for the train.' His knee twinges at the very idea.

'Where you going, son?'

'All the way.' He forces a smile. It must look false; his face feels contorted.

The inspector seems not to notice. 'Right you are,' he chuckles. 'All the way. Are you coming all the way back as well?'

'Sorry?' Has he been rumbled after all?

'Single or return?' The man's pink-nailed hand hovers over the buttons on his machine.

Jack wants to say return. Single is suspicious, surely, but suddenly the question of payment hits him. He has no idea how much this costs. He's only been on a train once before. On a trip from the home with Terry. The thought of Terry nearly breaks him. He feels a gulp, a gasp for air shuddering through his chest. 'Single,' he says, quickly. While he still can.

The machine makes an electronic clatter, the rapid crunch of tiny printing wheels, ejects a cream and orange credit-card-shaped sheet. 'Ten pound thirty,' the guard says.

For a moment Jack believes he's lost his wallet somewhere on the trail. But tracks it down by panicky patting of the numerous pockets of his trousers. He struggles to get it from his second zippered hip, fumbles it out on to his lap. Then knocks it to the floor like a spider, when he sees the branded letters of his name, burned script like a Western 'Wanted' poster.

'Are you all right, son?' asks the inspector, his eyebrows wrinkled in concern.

'Fine, sorry, I'm fine.' Jack opens the wallet, with his hand over the name on it. To his relief, he has a twenty inside. He knows the police could track his switch card.

The man gives him the change and ticket, watches while he slots them into the wallet, and says: 'You look after yourself now.' And he nods to emphasize the importance of his advice.

Jack watches him through the window into the next carriage. He doesn't talk into a radio or phone, just carries on collecting tickets. It looks like he's got away with it; he's unrecognized.

A fat man in a tweed jacket gets on at the next stop, still in the city outskirts. He sits down across the aisle from Jack; who slumps his head as if asleep, so the man can only see the top of his shaven scalp. Traces of the tablets must be still swimming through Jack's bloodstream, because, before he's even aware he's drifting, the sleep is no longer an act.

He wakes with a shake, dispelling dreams of a vanished lady. It's not him that's shaking though, or rather it is, but someone else is doing it. He comes round to pain, and a brown mouth blocking his vision. For a moment he's back inside, in Feltham, the tooth-spitting beating of his first day. He often wondered whether it might have been better if it ended then. But this mouth is smiling, laughing to itself.

'Come on, son,' it says. 'You're here now. "All the way", end of the line.'

Jack pulls himself upright on the seat.

'I thought you were dead for a second there,' the ticket collector says. 'Never seen such a deep sleeper."

Jack thanks the man, and waves a half wave as he walks off. There's no one else in the carriage, probably not on the whole train. His knee is immovable. It's stiffened completely, like it's splinted itself. It's less agonizing than before, when he puts weight on it. Still not what you'd call fun. But there isn't another option.

The carriage doors are open, the platform empty. The tracks stop abruptly at wood buffers. This is indeed the end of the line. Beyond them, British Rail-blue letters on a white sign read 'Blackpool'.

Things make sense then. Jack can see what's meant to be. And he is finally beside the seaside. Beside the sea.

The station empties on to a road. It's the sort of road that leads inevitably somewhere. So that, even if you have a leg that shrieks with every stride, you can't help but hurry down it. It's the sort of road that smells of salt and sand, and salted chips and sandwiches. And also cooking fat, cheap fags, candy floss. It's the sort of road that only seems to run one way, even though there are two sides for the traffic. Everything heads down on roads like these. Everything must end at the sea.

Jack is emptied out on to a promenade, and across from it is a pier. 'North Pier', a street sign says. And he takes this as another achievement: some bit of northerliness finally reached. The air fills his lungs in a way that makes it seem like all the breaths he's taken before were imitations. This is what air should be like. This is what someone had in mind when they first made it.

To his left Jack can see the Blackpool Tower. No, not *can*; he *has* to see it. It demands it. Huge, dark-girdered, unashamedly phallic. Love me or fuck off, it says. Like all of Blackpool seems to. Fortune tellers, fish and chips, kiss me quicks. But Jack is drawn to the pier. This is what has brought him here.

He walks past an arcade, which advertizes free toilets, and rattles out the sound of tumbling coins so loudly he's sure it must be on speakers. Or is it that everything is magnified in Blackpool? The pier seems to go on for miles. There is even a tram to take you to the end. But, despite his protesting leg, Jack wants to walk along it.

He passes a Punch and Judy stand, abandoned, out of season. He's never seen the show, but he knows the plot: deformity, domestic violence, infanticide. Kids' stuff.

The sea, through the gaps in the planks, jostles itself about. It's calling to Jack, knocking him up, asking him out to play. His mum would tell it he's not in, say it's too rough. But she's not here. There's nobody home but him. And it's true what they say about sea air being good for you. Jack can feel his knee healing with every step. He can feel his soul healing too, his spirit lifting. This isn't about the choice. This is about abdicating choice altogether. Leaving it to the sea to decide. Sometimes you don't want to take any decisions at all. None, nada, nil, nothing, zip, zilch, zero. He realizes it's not the gaps. The gaps are good. The contents cause the problems. It's the filling that makes the holes. For once he wants to be totally unfilled. As empty as the wire Jesus the day they buried his mother. A crucifix which had seemed cruel at the time, but which he now sees was only honest.

There are boats moored to buoys, a way out from the end of the pier. Little white motor launches. He's sure they'll have blankets on board, and probably food. And Jack thinks that if he swims, then he'll swim out to one of them. He knows how to hot-wire. They must be easy enough to drive. It's not like you can crash them; you've got the whole of the ocean to learn in, the whole of the world to reach. He could head round the coast, head for France, across *la mer*. Head for who knows where. It doesn't matter, they'll never catch him if he's got a boat.

And if he sinks, well then it just wasn't meant to be. It's a beautiful day, down beside the sea, and he feels free. Empty of guilt and sadness. He's known love, he's had a job, he's made friends, had sex, saved a life. He's had his day in the sun and it's still shining. There could be no better time or place to end than this. And that's supposed to be the way to go: drowning. If you're going to go, then that's the way to do it. He can picture himself, over-brimmed with salt water, spiralling downwards to a sandy bottom. If the waves taste like they smell, then it won't be so bad. That's the way to do it.

He climbs the railing and swings his bad leg over first. He wants to be quick, before anyone spots him. Doesn't want to be saved or stopped from reaching his boat. He's seen which one he wants. It's not the biggest or the grandest of the craft, but it's the one that looks the best to him. It's the one he can imagine himself curled within.

The trainers would hinder his attempts to swim. He doesn't want to give sinking an unfair advantage. So he kicks them off. One. Two. Watches them plunge into the sea. Then he toes his socks off too. They take longer to sail down. Show him the true distance. But he's confident he'll survive the fall. It's just the drowning that might get him.

He stands on the lower rung of the railings, savouring the moment he needs to get his balance. His launch outwards almost takes him by surprise. No count down. He just jumps.

It's a glorious leap, there's no doubt about it. Framed in the sun. Far away from this last outpost of a country that hates him. Up above the pier. Rising higher than he started.

And, like he suspected, there is a moment, when ascension has stopped but before the drop, where everything pauses. Neither falling nor flying. An instant where time is frozen. It doesn't last as long as in the cartoons. It could be less than a second. But it's long enough to consider, with arms outstretched and bare feet together, if it might be better not to struggle anymore.

A Guide for Reading Groups

Research shows that children who commit murder (of whom there have been around 100 in the UK in recent times) and other violent crimes have themselves suffered abusive, neglected and brutalised childhoods. To what degree, if at all, can suffering ever be a mitigating factor in crime?

Does Jack's own childhood in any way explain his involvement in the crime?

Does Terry's relationship with Zeb affect how he deals with Jack, and vice versa? Is Terry a good father?

How much responsibility for Jack's fate lies with the media? How much is of his own making?

Society struggles with its attitudes towards childhood, and child killers are arguably portrayed as even more 'evil' than adults who commit similar crimes. Why do we struggle to understand these acts?

It can be argued that fiction has a role to play, in allowing us to discuss subjects that are taboo or uncomfortable. How does *Boy A* fit with this argument?

Boy A prompts questions of liberal versus conservative values, particularly when it addresses our preconceptions of child offenders. Is this liberalism as damaging as the mob mentality of the tabloid press?

It can be argued that Jack's release from prison is a rebirth, and his experiences of the world are naïve. How does this device colour our perceptions of Jack?

To what degree is *Boy A* a classic coming of age novel? Through Jack's extreme difference, are we also examining what it means to be a 'normal' young man in Britain today?

We do not gain any insight into the narrative voice or perspective of Angela's family and their loss. If the author had included their point of view for balance, would our feelings towards Jack change?

The end of the novel is often controversial among reading groups for its apparent ambiguities. But there may be clues throughout the novel – particularly in Jack's final body position and in the Butch and Sundance references in the previous chapter – as to what the author intends us to believe about Jack's chances of survival when the freeze-frame continues. What are these clues?

Does Jack learn anything by the end of the book? Is his character 'redeemed' in any way? And what about our redemption as readers? Do we get the ending we want/deserve?